DARK ANGELS RISING

DARK ANGELS RISING

Book Three
of
THE DARK ANGELS

Ian Whates

NewCon Press
England

First published in the UK April 2020 by NewCon Press
41 Wheatsheaf Road, Alconbury Weston, Cambs, PE28 4LF

NCP 233 (limited edition hardback)
NCP 234 (softback)

10 9 8 7 6 5 4 3 2 1

ISBN:

978-1-912950-58-4 (hardback)
978-1-912950-59-1 (softback)

Cover illustration by Jim Burns
Cover layout by Ian Whates

Text layout by Ian Whates and Storm Constantine

ONE

A reputation has to be earned, especially on Callia III, and Clay Arter took pride in his. When he walked into a room people *noticed*, and he loved that – the looks, the whispers, the subtle edging away as he took a seat at the bar. The curiosity in the eyes of some of the women as they glanced his way didn't harm either. They respected him, feared him, maybe wondered what it would be like to bed him, and he sat a little taller for knowing it.

Clay was aware of the things they whispered – that he wasn't a man to be crossed, that he was responsible for the deaths of many and had witnessed the demise of still more – nor were they wrong. In recent times most of these deaths had occurred here in this hot and airless room without windows, or places that were indistinguishable from it. The meat room, they called it, for reasons that shouldn't need explaining.

The latest 'guest' currently hung from chains hammered into the long wall, where he had spent much of the previous evening. Clay didn't know the man's name, he didn't need to.

He wasn't dead yet, but it wouldn't be long now if Clay were any judge. He had offered no hint of resistance as they dragged him out and chained him in place this morning, and now slumped forward, legs sagging and head bowed, upright only because the chains wouldn't permit him to crumple into a sorry heap. His naked torso was a mass of bruises and cuts and caked blood – the aftermath of the previous day's ministrations – while more blood stained the stone floor at his feet. Not necessarily his, or not entirely so at any rate. Many had hung where he now did and the stone beneath was permanently stained. The floor slanted down towards a grated hole, allowing excess blood to drain away – a feature that caused Clay to wonder if the room might have been built with its current purpose in mind.

Vissecz would be along shortly to finish the job. The previous evening had seen no attempt to interrogate, simply the application of pain, so it wasn't about information on this occasion, it was all about punishment – whether a case of simple revenge or a lesson intended for others, Clay couldn't say. Not his business. Unless told otherwise, he and his men were present merely to guard and provide a deterrent should any of the subject's friends consider mounting a rescue. Not that anyone had friends *that* loyal, in his experience.

Everyone reacted differently when brought in here, but generally they could be grouped into three types: some were defiant, challenging the torturer to do his worst – never a wise approach – some were pleading and broken even before they were touched, while others were resigned of their fate.

This latest subject belonged to the latter category, but from the off he had stood out. There was something about him that spoke of more than the usual stoic acceptance, a sense that nothing mattered from here on in, as if whatever he had done to earn the boss' displeasure was worth any punishment that might await him. Even as Clay helped chain him to the wall he knew that while they might break this one's body they'd never crush his spirit.

You had to admire something like that.

Clay had watched Vissecz at work many times but that didn't mean he looked forward to the torturer's arrival. The man's penchant for inflicting pain went beyond anything Clay had seen before. Nothing wrong with a bit of good honest violence, but that wasn't what Vissecz was about. There was something chilling and unwholesome about him and his devotion to the suffering of others.

None of which explained the vague sense of foreboding that Clay couldn't shake that morning.

Even the toughest of men have their weak points, and for

Clay it was his nose.

He had borne witness to beatings, gorings, dismemberment, subtle tortures and brutal murders, participating when appropriate. None of these fazed him in the slightest. A subject's agonised shrieks, their pleading and whimpers, the crunch of bones cracking and the whirring of implements biting into flesh, they all washed over him unheeded… It was smells that did it, or rather one specific smell.

Excrement; faeces, shit, call it what you will.

The rich sweet-metal smell of blood, the ammonia-tinged sourness of urine, he was fine with those, but the foul reek that rolled across the room when a subject voided their bowels turned his stomach. They knew this – the men who worked under him – it was a joke to them, though they soon learned not to show as much in his presence; not twice, at any rate.

The worst times were when the smell manifested without proper cause, such as today. Clay could smell it from the moment he stepped out the front door, just a hint on the breeze, and it pursued him all the way to work, growing stronger with every step. He knew even before he entered the meat room that it would be worst of all here, and so it proved.

The way Gethyn and Myers – one just finishing their shift the other about to begin – jumped to obey his orders and set about cleaning the place with barely a grumble bore testament to that reputation Clay was so proud of.

Yet still the stench lingered, even above the antiseptic. It wasn't the captive, they'd ascertained that much, even though the smell intensified when they dragged his limp form from the dark box cell in which he had spent the night and chained him to the wall once more. The foulness had sunk into the very bricks, it would seem, defying all effort to shift it.

This was set to be a bad day, that was the only explanation he could think of.

"What the hell?"

Gethyn's exclamation drew Clay from his brooding. He

followed the bald man's gaze to where a diminutive figure walked in through the open door. A doll; a pale-skinned, brown eyed mannequin, small enough that it reached only partway up his shin. Blonde hair tied in bunches, the doll wore the type of plastic, unreal face that could only be its owner's choice in these days of hi-tech wonder.

The doll stopped, turning its head to look up at Clay before smiling. "Hello," it said in a jolly little girl's voice. "My name is Jai. What's your name?"

The absurdity of the toy's presence had thrown Clay for a moment, but the sound of her over-twee voice snapped him out of it, and he determined to deal with the two most immediate issues.

"Geth, get rid of that thing," and he gestured towards the doll. "Myers, go check on how it got in here."

"And what will you be doing?" Myers had the temerity to ask.

Clay drew the compact pistol he always carried, its familiar weight in his hand a reassurance. "Guarding the prisoner, of course." The words were accompanied by a glare that ensured no further lip came from the youngster.

As the two men snapped out of their own surprise at the unlikely intrusion and went to obey him, something odd started happening to the doll. Its hands seemed to melt like heated wax, peeling back to reveal sleek tubes beneath. Barrels, Clay realised. Gun barrels.

Before he had fully registered the threat he heard a twin popping sound, two noises so close together they were almost one. Myers dropped as if poleaxed. Geth looked puzzled, reaching to clutch a hand to his side where blood blossomed to outline his fingers in red. He went down in stages, collapsing to his knees and then his haunches before keeling over.

Even as Geth crumpled towards the floor Clay reacted, advancing on the murderous doll before it could swing those barrels towards him. One more stride and he'd be able to stomp down on the thing, crushing it against the cold stone.

He caught movement in the corner of his eye, from a part of the room where no one had a right to be, and swivelled in time to see a black figure lunging towards him. The shape rapidly gained definition and substance as he watched, transforming from the vague suggestion of humanity into a lithe woman who looked all too human... And knives; he registered knives. She was too slight to worry him physically, but the blades were another matter.

Clay used to wear a stibre vest beneath his shirt as a matter of course – a sensible precaution in this line of work, the garment's stiffened fibres designed to deflect precisely this sort of attack – but stibre wasn't the most comfortable of fabrics and it was so hot in this damned room that he'd abandoned the habit a while back. A complacency he might yet live to regret.

He was lighter on his feet than he looked – an attribute that had saved his life more than once. He leapt backwards and sideways, the doll forgotten. As he moved, he brought the gun to bear and fired. She was quick, this one, following his evasion as if she'd anticipated it, the gun's short burst of lethal energy missing her to expend itself harmlessly against the wall beyond. In passing, the woman flicked out her right arm to draw one of the blades across his belly, an action that appeared almost nonchalant.

There was little pain to begin with, just a stinging sensation – adrenalin acting as anaesthetic – but Clay instinctively reached for the wound with his free hand, dismayed to discover how deep it was, and how long; a slash that would have opened up his belly completely if he'd been a fraction slower to react.

He looked around but there was no sign of the woman. *Where's the bitch gone to?* She had disappeared as quickly as she'd materialised, leaving him alone in the meat room with the prisoner, the bodies of his two men, and... the doll!

Almost too late he remembered the harbinger of this whole mess, the treacherous little twin-barrelled mechanoid. His head whipped around to find one of those barrels pointing directly at him. He tried to duck and leap aside but the effort was only half successful, hampered by a shaft of searing agony that coursed through his belly as he started to move, the pain breaking through in earnest at last.

Pain exploded in his right arm too, a little below the shoulder. A detached part of him marvelled at the impact from what had to be a low calibre weapon. Most of him stopped thinking about much at all, as he was spun around to crash against the wall, blood welling with renewed vigour from his belly wound, the gun spinning away from his uncooperative fingers.

Clay fell heavily, half sliding down the wall he'd struck as his legs went from under him. He gazed across the room to where the prisoner still hung from his chains. His right arm was useless, bones shattered, the pain growing with every passing second. He clutched his stomach with his good left hand, trying to hold the flesh together, knowing that he was in danger of bleeding out if help didn't arrive soon.

Taken down by a woman and a toy, and a woman made of smoke at that. It didn't bear thinking about. He struggled to stay conscious; it would be so easy to relax and succumb, but he worried that if he did so he might never wake up again.

Where the hell is Vissecz? The torturer ought to have arrived by now, surely.

The smoke woman appeared again, seeming to emerge from the very wall itself, solidifying into a very feminine figure that seemed to be dressed from head to foot in a coating of crude oil. Someone else entered the room – via the door this time – another woman, a little shorter and stockier than Smoke Woman but in every other regard her antithesis, light to her darkness. The newcomer shone with silver, like an angel.

Why did that ring a bell: a shining woman clad in silver, another in black who stepped from shadows... Angels...? He wasn't thinking clearly enough to make the connection. Maybe later, assuming there *was* a later.

He watched numbly as they freed the prisoner, who stirred at last, showing vague signs of life. The two women took the man's limp form between them, one under each arm, and half-led half-carried him from the room. The doll regarded Clay for one last moment, before turning and following after.

In their wake, stillness enveloped the room. The only thing to disturb it was the sound of Clay's own laboured breathing. As darkness reached out to claim him despite his best efforts, he reflected on how wrong he had been. Evidently some friends *were* that loyal after all.

Two

"Come on, Mosi, move your feet for Elders' sake."

Who said that? Mosi bobbed back to consciousness despite himself. He couldn't understand what was happening. *Where are the chains?*

He seemed to be moving, being carried. Who was holding him up? They looked like... *Jen, Leesa?* He tried to say their names but all that emerged was a groan. *No, it can't be them. I'm hallucinating, conflating the past and the present.* After all, Jen and Leesa had saved him the last time; they couldn't possibly be here to do the same again...

Darkness claimed him, and his thoughts slid backwards into the past.

It took nearly dying to remind Mosi Jalloh what life was all about and that he had some unfinished business to attend to before he could even consider abandoning it.

When he first washed up in the Callia system a little more than a decade ago he had been a lost soul, choosing Callia III purely because he couldn't think of anywhere else to go. His family were all dead – at least everyone he had ever counted as family – and now he had lost his sister. Again.

This time it was final, he knew that. The Dark Angels were never likely to get back together again and without them Najat would be forever beyond his reach. He felt bereft, as if a part of him – the better part at that – had been brutally ripped away and the wound left to bleed unchecked, uncauterised.

This time around, losing Najat hit him even harder than when she had died the first time, and there wasn't even anyone he could talk to about it, because the only friends he had in the universe had just parted company, scattering across the inhabited worlds. The worst part was that he didn't even know why, not really. Cornische had given his reasons for disbanding the crew but none of them rang true to Mosi's ear.

Where else could he head but Callia III, the last place he remembered being truly happy? They'd only been kids then, him and Naj, and inseparable: 'the tandem twins: joined at the hip... peas in a pod... gender swap clones...' They had been called that and more in those days, and took delight in every affectionate epithet.

That was then. Now was proving to be a whole lot harsher. Callia III had changed. Either that or it was a very different place when viewed through the filter of adult eyes. This wasn't the world he had been born on but it was the one where he and Naj had spent their formative years, before their mother's work had seen the family uproot again and move to a different world and a different culture entirely.

Coates World. Not a place he would ever consider returning to. Coates was where Naj had died. His childhood had ended abruptly that night. Now that she'd gone for a second time, he felt that his adulthood would soon follow.

Mosi didn't go back to Callia III to die as such, but nor did he arrive with any plans to live.

The house his family had called home was long gone; in fact the whole street had disappeared. In its place stood an edifice that rose like a sore thumb to tower over the area. He was so flummoxed by this grotesque building – a concoction of smoked glass and plating that would have looked more at home among the cloud scrapers of New Sparta than here – that he had to double check to ensure his memory hadn't played him false. But no. A quick glance through local records confirmed that the Arkel Centre – a 'nexus for creativity and culture' – had been erected some eight years previously. Half a dozen residential streets whose names he recognised, whose corners he had hidden round and surfaces he'd pounded along, had been purchased and knocked down to facilitate it, with an equal number truncated or diverted. His past: compulsory purchased and demolished.

So much for coming home.

It wasn't just the house and the physical landscape, the whole community had changed. The Khdayin – a pale skinned race from the south that he had never knowingly encountered before, had settled here in large numbers. The Walk, an upmarket shopping street he recalled spending long hours in with his dad, was now unrecognisable. Fads changed – real time shops were considered so sophisticated one minute and passé the next. E-shopping was in vogue once more it would seem, the stores of his childhood consigned to history, to be replaced by a strip of VR arcades, drinking dives and the occasional grocery stall selling unfamiliar food stuffs.

Intellectually, Mosi knew it was unreasonable to expect everything to have stayed the same in the decades he'd been away, but he couldn't escape the sense that Callia III had deserted him along with everyone else. If he had come here hoping that the familiar surroundings might somehow bring Naj closer, he was disappointed. Had there been anywhere else to go he might have accepted that and moved on.

Instead he lingered, taking whatever menial jobs he could get, and drinking whatever he earned.

These were dark days, which could only have ended one way if it weren't for Taylor.

Mosi still had no idea what she saw in him, he was just grateful that she had found *something*. They met one evening in a drinking dive just off The Walk, the sort of place he never knew existed during his first period on Callia III; perhaps they hadn't, but they proliferated now. This one was unadorned – no VR booths, no enterstainments, no edrugs, just good old fashioned alcohol and a real barman: human rather than a hologram and a clever algorithm, which was the main reason he favoured the place.

It was a slow night, with few of the tables occupied, and Mosi and Taylor were both propping up the bar – him because he'd just been fired from his latest job after a bust up with the boss, her because she'd just dumped a long-term boyfriend after catching him in the sack with another man.

He was barely aware of her presence, wrapped up in his own cocoon of self-pity – just him and the glass. The last thing he expected was for her to talk to him, but she did. Even more surprisingly, he replied.

She was Khdayin, that much was obvious, and by no means pretty in the conventional sense, but there was strength in her features, intelligence in her eyes, and an energy about her that shone through clearly despite her mood, and to him she was beautiful. She was also way out of his league, though he hungered for her with a desperation that caught him unawares.

Mosi had always been fascinated by how things work, the clever ways mechanisms utilise power, a curiosity that developed into an obsession with gadgets and machinery. Aboard the *Ion Raider*, if Leesa was ship's mechanic, he was her assistant.

Taylor, it turned out, was a falcon racer, and a good one. That was her obsession and she was forever tinkering with her bird in an effort to improve performance. It did their relationship no harm at all when Mosi was able to join in. They quickly fell into step, synchronising skills to become a team, as if they always had been.

"I've been studying the thermals at Southern Breach," she would say, "and I reckon if we strengthen the front struts, just a fraction, and taper the pinions more gently, we could squeeze a bit more lift, which will give me a much better approach coming into Devil's Peak. Look."

She conjured graphics on the flat screen, showing the air flow over a wing's cross-section. She then manipulated the image to show her suggested improvements and the small increase in lift that resulted.

"Okay…" Mosi said, studying the diagram, which was looped on repeat, from current design to projected. "But won't the longer pinions risk fouling up in the corkscrew?"

She shook her head. "Not if we're careful, look…"

He loved these days. Thanks to Taylor the spectre of Najat had receded. She never went away entirely, and Mosi still spoke to her sometimes, when he was alone, keeping her up-to-date on what they'd done that day.

Taylor was showing him how to live again, and he knew that Naj would have approved.

Falcon racing had nothing to do with predatory hawks and everything to do with gliders: single person flying frames, constructed from the lightest, strongest materials available, traditionally built and flown by enthusiasts such as Taylor.

Mosi vividly recalled the first time he took a falcon up. This wasn't Taylor's racing rig, she would never trust him or anyone else with that, but a tired old frame they had picked up for next to nothing and modified so that he could get a taste of what it was like.

"I started with a rig just like this," she told him. "We all do."

Yeah, but I bet you were a lot younger and lighter then than I am now, he thought but didn't say.

Conscious of how far down it was and that they were at the lip of a precipice, he climbed into the harness with Taylor's help, lying prone with head raised, his body sleeved in the protective yet aerodynamic flight suit. He adjusted his position until he was comfortable, hands clutching the twin bars that would enable him to steer – left right, up down. Around him, the hollow pipes of the falcon's chassis seemed ridiculously flimsy. He wondered if there was still time to back out… But he couldn't do that, for Taylor's sake, or rather for the sake of his own esteem in her eyes.

So he gripped the steering bars, wriggled the tail fins a couple of times to ensure they responded, scanned the telemetry displayed by his goggles – the most high tech aspect of the whole set up – checked that both the jointed wings were properly furled, and tried to ignore the gusting wind that buffeted his exposed body as if to emphasise how scant the rig's framework really was. The sense that he was encased within a skeleton rather than anything of substance did little to calm his nerves. *And people do this for fun?*

He even managed a nod and the approximation of a smile when Taylor called out, "Are you okay?"

Then the countdown started. *Surely not yet*, he quailed, but the wink of descending digits in his goggles argued otherwise. Then, before he was ready, he found himself flung outward, a trajectory that quickly became a plummet – the 'stoop' as Taylor called it. Wind whipped past him and he suffered a moment of pure panic – *what if the wings don't open?*

They did, of course, at his command some three seconds after his fall began, and he knew they would have done so two seconds later even had he been too panicked to act – a failsafe that all falcons were equipped with and which he had helped set earlier that morning.

In an instant his fear turned to joy, as the falcon's tapered wings deployed – paper thin in parts but stronger than steel throughout, catching the wind and transforming his fall into a curving glide. Suddenly he was soaring.

This was unlike anything he had ever experienced before.

All the hours spent in VR simulations of flying, which he used to consider so convincing, were shown to be nothing more than shams, pale imitations of glorious reality. The genuine article was thrilling and wonderful beyond his imagining.

The falcons' bodywork had been reduced to a minimum to eliminate weight, the ultimate in pared-back glider design. With no engines, they relied on wind and their pilot's skill to keep them aloft. He had by way of tools his wings, tail fins, and the repellors which ensured the craft and its occupant bounced away from crags and other obstructions rather than ploughing into them. Falcon racing only took place among the mountain peaks, where ridge lift – air currents striking obstructions and being forced upwards, lifting the falcons and their pilots – was plentiful but the winds were strong and treacherous and the opportunities for mishap abounded. In the arena of extreme sports this was the ultimate, the most dangerous challenge around, and Mosi had always considered those who attempted it insane.

Yet here he was, strapped within a rig, staring at the mottled terrain that slipped past, marvelling at the beauty of the world as sunlight glittered off the rocks below, angling his wings to slip between a pair of jutting peaks, delighting in a sense of freedom he had never experienced before... and *laughing* for the pure joy of it.

"You should try the repellors at least once," Taylor had advised. "If only to get a feel of them."

He did as suggested, skimming closer to a jutting formation than was wise – an indication of how much his confidence had grown – feeling the repellors kick in as he approached, to lift the rig up and away. In doing so, he came to understand how a pilot could manipulate the effect to gain a little more height and prolong the flight by precious seconds – he had understood the concept in principle, but now he had *lived* it.

All too soon it was over. Despite the sense that he was King of the Air, in truth this was just a nursery flight over a course that was considered free of any significant hazards. Moments after he had stooped from the cliff edge, Mosi found himself approaching a glacial lake, its surface rippled into crinkled waves by the wind. He was so low by this point that he felt tempted to reach out with a hand as he skirted the lake's shore and run his fingertips through the water.

Disengaging the repellors, he angled the wings to shed momentum as practiced and, as the ground rushed towards him – still too quickly, surely – opened the back of the harness to free his legs. At the last moment the wings retracted, furled and folded, while the tail section of the rig swung up to rest against his back. Then came the jolt of contact as his feet met solid ground. He was running, trying to stay upright and bring himself to a dignified halt, but, as suspected, he'd failed to shed enough momentum. Five rushed steps, with the rig on his back seeming determined to go faster than his legs could carry him, and suddenly he was sprawling forward, to skid to a stop on his stomach.

He took a second to get his breath back before wriggling backwards out of the harness, pushing the rig to one side. His flying suit had protected him from anything worse than a few bruises.

As soon as he was on his feet, Mosi scanned the heavens, spotting Taylor almost at once. She was high up, having retained far more altitude than he'd managed by this point. As he watched, she folded her wings and stooped, plummeting towards the lake, only to bottom out in a long curve as she opened the wings again and came racing across the water towards him.

She landed on her feet directly in front of him, with a precision he could only envy.

"Well," she said, "how was it?"

"Incredible… Everything you said it would be and more. Can we go again?"

She laughed and hugged him and kissed him. He had never been happier.

Mosi tried to focus. He hurt in more ways than he knew a body could hurt. Then, with horror, he remembered the torture, the calm professional way the man who introduced himself as Vissecz had gone about his work, the agony he wrought, which intensified by stages and never seemed to end…

Mosi blinked. He wasn't in the meat room any more, and he was lying down. Where had they brought him? What new torments lay in store? If he could just get a hold of something sharp, find a way to end this, to rob them of their sport…

A ship, this looks like the inside of a ship.

"I'm putting you under again," said a voice he almost recognised, "to facilitate the accelerated healing."

"No, wait…" he tried to say, but already the room was

receding and his thoughts fled back to the comfort of the past.

Mosi had no ambitions to race himself – he was too heavy and had come to the sport too late. He still went up occasionally for pure pleasure, but did his racing vicariously through Taylor, whose reputation grew with each passing season. She steadily worked her way up through the rankings to be placed in several significant races and people started to notice her. Mosi would never forget the day she finally won a major, the Wind Hawk Cup. She came into the competition as second favourite and flew brilliantly, winning by a margin, with pre-race favourite Sonje trailing in a lowly fourth.

The fact that Sonje had made some disparaging comments about Taylor's Khdayin heritage in the build-up to the event made victory all the sweeter.

They were still celebrating – Taylor having successfully negotiated the circus of photo calls and media requests – when an unwelcome visitor turned up at their door.

They both knew Cory Blind, everyone on the circuit knew him: the manager and public face of Team Lanner, who boasted four flyers in the top ten, including the beaten favourite Sonje. There was money to be made in falcon racing these days, an increasing amount. Taylor's success in the past couple of seasons ensured that neither she nor Mosi had gone short, and winning the Wind Hawk Cup meant that they could have taken the rest of the year off and partied the whole while had they wished to. They didn't. There was one more race to plan for, one more race to win.

There would always be those keen to cash in when they smelled a lucrative opportunity, and in recent years several corporations had begun to invest in sponsorship deals, building teams of talented flyers with a view to dominating the sport and claiming the accolades and rewards. Team Lanner were among the most prominent of these and currently the most successful.

They probably should have anticipated Blind's visit. He had

come sniffing around Taylor before, trying to recruit her.

"Congratulations!" he said, all smiles and holding out a bottle of expensive off-world champagne.

"Thank you, Cory. What do you want?"

Mosi always had admired Taylor's directness.

"You. On the team. I've made no secret of that."

"And I've made my answer clear. I already have a team." She glanced towards Mosi.

"I know, I know, and you've done incredibly well." The smile never wavered. "But come on, Taylor. Things are changing, rapidly. The days of the noble amateur tinkering on their rig in a cramped workshop are over. Falcon racing is a professional sport now. Seven of the top ten racers are signed up to pro teams and within the next two years that will be ten out of ten. Don't get left behind. You're too talented for that."

"You've already had your answer, Blind," Mosi interjected.

"Hear me out." Blind raised his hands as if in surrender. "I'm willing to double my previous offer. That'll make you our top paid pilot, our number one. A three-year contract. You'll get the best crew of mechanics, the best rig, the best support network in the business."

"I thought Sonje was your number one."

"She was. Now she'll have to get used to being number two. And Mosi, I'm not undervaluing your contribution. You two come as a package, we know that, and why break up a winning team? Senior mechanic on Taylor's crew, with a senior pay grade to match. Think about it. Look at what the two of you've achieved on your own. Imagine how much more you can do with the resources of Team Lanner behind you. Together, we can rule racing for the next ten years, and we'll make you the biggest star the sport has ever known."

That last was a miscalculation. Doubtless it would have pushed the buttons of many an ambitious flyer, but not Taylor. Fame had never been her motivation. Never the less, the offer was tempting, more than tempting. To Mosi it had sounded like a dream come true: the opportunity to do what they did but on a grander scale, with contracted salaries that would be paid no matter how the race went. But this was Taylor's call. He was the latecomer here and under no illusion as to who the senior partner was in their collaboration. Taylor was already shaking her head.

"Thank you for the offer, Cory, and I really mean that. It's nice to feel wanted, but for me racing is all about the feel of wind in your face and the *freedom*, and that's the one thing we'd never have at Lanner. Working to your timetable, to your beat, being at your beck and call... That's not for us."

Mosi felt his heart drop just a little, but then it swelled with pride. He'd known what her answer would be, even before she had spoken, and now that the decision was made he would back her all the way.

"You've got us all wrong, Taylor. Sure there would be expectations, but you'd be calling the shots. You're the star. We'd work things around you. But..." and here he spread his hands, in a gesture of acceptance. "I can see there's no point in pursuing this right now. Mosi, talk to her, will you?"

Had Blind sensed that he was tempted?

"Think about what we're offering, Taylor. We're not trying to stifle your dreams but to help you realise them. It's not too late to change your mind – you know where I am. I'll leave you to get back to your celebrating. You deserve it – that was a fine race today. But make the most of it, because you won't be winning another, unless it's in our colours."

Mosi felt his blood turn cold and took a step towards their visitor. "Is that a threat?"

"No, no threat. A prediction. It's the King of the Mountains next, the climax of the whole season, and I promise you that Lanner are going to win it, come what may."

With that Blind nodded to each of them, smiled broadly, and left.

After he'd gone they tried to get back to celebrating, but somehow their hearts weren't in it any more.

To his credit, Blind left them in peace after that, doubtless sensing that pestering would never work. He had made his point. The rest was up to them.

Come the day of the race, Taylor was more pumped up than Mosi had ever seen her. Not through overconfidence, he knew her well enough to know this was all excitement with just a little bit of nerves thrown in for good measure.

"This is the big one," she said as they ran through the falcon's final checks.

He stopped and looked at her. "I know. And you'll be wonderful."

She kissed him and spun away, unable to keep still.

Only the top twenty-five ranked flyers qualified to enter the King of the Mountains. In one sense, the season of ten majors prior to this represented a competitive league; in another, those were just the qualifiers. Sonje was still the favourite for the race and would win the overall league whatever this day's outcome but, following her triumph in the Wind Hawk, Taylor was pushing her close in the betting.

The start site was a levelled plateau, which was now a hive of activity, full to bursting with flyers, their support crews, race officials, reporters, and a privileged few fans who had paid a fortune to be here in person. The setting was not exactly conducive to peace and tranquillity, but as the start time drew nearer Taylor calmed down, becoming focussed, channelling her energies as Mosi had seen her do so many times before.

Moments before the flyers were due to be called to their machines, Blind decided to come over. It was a distraction neither of them welcomed, but his approach seemed friendly enough.

"I just wanted to say no hard feelings and to wish you well in the race," he said.

Taylor, deep in her race zone, barely acknowledged him. Mosi was prepared to be civil at least, but then Blind did something unforgiveable. In what appeared to be an unconscious action, performed without malice, he ran his fingers along one of the falcon's support struts.

Nobody but a flyer and their crew were permitted to touch a rig in the build up to a race. It was against both protocol and superstition.

"Fuck off, Blind!" Mosi said, balling his fists and struggling not to punch the man.

"I... I'm sorry." Blind backed away, looking both suitably embarrassed by his action and dismayed by the ferocity of Mosi's response. He hurried back to where the Lanner Team was gathered.

"Relax," Taylor said. "He didn't mean anything by it."

"Maybe." Mosi was already giving the machine another once over, running scanners and diagnostic sensors across the strut Blind had defiled. Everything seemed normal. Perhaps it had been just a thoughtless mistake after all.

Despite this, Mosi couldn't escape a sense of foreboding as he helped Taylor climb into the racing harness.

He always got a rush at the start of a race. There was something magnificent about the way the field took to the air and then plummeted downward – a flock of hurtling raptors – and the huge roar from the crowd as they set off. Then came the magical moment when the falcons opened their wings, all at fractionally different times dictated by each flyer's race strategy.

The plateau provided the perfect vantage point, and viewed from above the sight always brought to mind for Mosi a field of flowers opening in time-lapse rapidity, as each competitor unveiled their rig's liveried wings. Team Lanner, who boasted four birds in the race, had a mobile design which started as dark grey against paler grey scalloping – in imitation of their namesake's wings, but then rippled through a random sequence of colour changes. Set on top of this in unchanging white was a single letter representing the first letter of the pilot's name. Mosi had always found the choice over the top and garish. Taylor's livery, on the other hand, could not have been simpler: the black silhouette of a falcon set against a plain blue wing to represent the open sky.

Of course he looked for her bird first. She came out of the stoop in fifth or sixth place – not that it mattered too much at this early stage. Difficult to judge the varying heights from this perspective, but fortunately the army of flying cameras – nearly three hundred of them in total – were on hand to catch every detail. Some were stationed at crucial parts of the course, others followed the race or focussed on individual falcons. The watching public wouldn't miss a thing.

Already those on the plateau were retreating back to the viewing lounges, where they would settle back in comfort, safely out of the wind, and enjoy their individual 3D feeds, offering a choice of viewing perspectives which they could switch between at will.

Mosi lingered, as was his wont, to watch with naked eye as the field negotiated the first hazard, the Spire Turn. Only as he saw Taylor emerge safely and disappear from direct line of sight among the peaks did he activate his own viewer.

Sonje, who always started quickly, was in the lead, while Taylor came out from the Spire in fourth, having swooped past another independent, Ketta, in the turn. Mosi had seen something that worried him, though, a suspicion that grew once he used his viewer to zoom out and get a broader picture.

Taylor was bracketed by two other Team Lanner flyers, identified by the bold white T and N on their wings as Tammi and Niall respectively.

Neither showed any inclination to catch the flyers ahead of them. Instead they seemed more intent on shepherding Taylor. Lanner were working as the team they claimed to be and had clearly identified Taylor as the principle threat to their prospects.

One flyer could never have done it. Taylor would simply have slipped past them at some point and left them behind, but two working in concert... Sure enough, as Mosi watched, Niall overtook the hampered Taylor, who now had two blockers directly in front of her. To add insult to injury, at the next turn Ketta sailed past all three of them.

Tammi and Niall were sacrificing their own chances in the race to ensure victory for Sonje.

Taylor would be livid – this went against everything she believed falcon racing should be about. Mosi watched as she dipped and soared, trying to get past these mobile obstacles, but one of them always went with her, allowing the other to move a little ahead to be in the way even if she succeeded in giving the first the slip.

No one else caught them, but Sonje continued to pull away at the front.

Disaster struck shortly before the halfway point. There was a particularly tricky turn called the Funnel, where flyers had to negotiate a canyon defined by a long concave-curved rock face with a jutting overhang that played havoc with wind currents. The best approach was to come in hard with wings tilted at around thirty-five degrees, but Taylor must have been desperate by this point, seeing the Funnel as her opportunity to get past both the Lanners. She tilted her wings at closer to forty degrees, taking her in a tighter turn and away from the rock face where winds were more predictable, towards the more irregular far wall.

Niall reacted to the bold move, adjusting his own angle and coming across to block her, but he was a fraction too slow and a bit too aggressive. His manoeuvre put the two birds on a collision course. Mosi could only look on in horror, anticipating what was to come but unable to do a thing about it. The repellors kicked in at the last moment, as they were designed to, flinging the two falcons apart.

Niall's bird started to tumble, dropping like a stone. Mosi lost sight of him immediately because he was concentrating on the other bird. Taylor was thrown towards the inner rock face... and she struck it.

That should never happen. *Where are the repellors?*

Mosi watched in horror as the falcon he had worked on with

such devotion for years came apart, and the woman he loved plummeted towards the rocks that waited below.

"She died doing what she loved best," might have been true but it didn't help, no matter how often he heard the phrase in the days that followed.

Team Lanner sent a big bunch of white flowers. Many people sent flowers. The whole place was swamped with fucking flowers. They didn't help either.

Niall perished in the same incident that claimed Taylor, giving Team Lanner their own reason to mourn. The race went on despite the tragedy and Sonje was crowned King of the Mountains. Mosi heard these facts without caring. Of course the race hadn't been stopped – falcon racing was a dangerous sport; two riders had died in separate incidents earlier in the season. Tragic, but the ever-present sense of risk was one of the factors that made the sport so popular.

Four riders perished this season. It had been five the previous year.

The woman who gave him reason to breathe had just become a statistic.

He fell apart.

Thanks to Taylor's success he wasn't short of credit to fuel his binges, and he set about running through money with abandon: alcohol, stims, VR trips – the more extreme the better – anything to put a buffer between him and the real world.

There were times when he believed that the only reason he hadn't taken his own life was because he lacked the courage to do so. At others he wondered if somewhere deep down a spark of hope still lingered that, despite everything, things might somehow get better.

It took an assassination attempt to make him face the fact that neither was entirely true. He hadn't ended his own life for the simple reason there was still one thing he needed to do before he died.

He could still see the consternation on Leesa and Jen's faces. They had popped up out of nowhere to pull him from a jury-rigged VR death trap over at Pedre's arcade – a favourite haunt in those dark days – identified an organisation called 'Saflik' as being responsible, and then seen him refuse to join their cause. They couldn't believe it, but he couldn't join them; not yet and maybe not ever. He had some unfinished business to attend to.

The official enquiry ruled that Taylor's death had been an accident, while acknowledging that Team Lanner's tactics were a contributory factor. Mosi didn't believe it for a minute.

Blind's words kept coming back to him: *you won't be winning another*, and then there was that inappropriate touching of the falcon's strut immediately before the race. What if it hadn't been so innocent? Team Lanner had resources that Mosi could only dream of, was it so implausible that they might have developed a means of neutralising the repellors that was beyond his ability to spot, ensuring that they malfunctioned during the race? The repellors were newly fitted and Mosi had checked them a dozen times prior to the start. They had been working earlier in the race yet failed at the vital moment.

Whether through deliberate sabotage or callous tactics, there was only one person responsible for Taylor's death: Mr Team Lanner himself, Cory Blind.

Leesa and Jen left him reluctantly after the incident at Pedre's. It was obvious they didn't believe his promises to join them when he could and they were right not to. He had drunk away the best part of half a year. Nearly dying had sobered him up enough to start noticing the outside world again. The first thing he noticed was that falcon racing had returned, the new season already under way.

The world moved on, without him, without Taylor.

The Sun Peaks Trophy was always the second big event on the race calendar. Mosi was a familiar face and no one questioned him when he turned up at the start plateau. There was an unusual tension in the air, though that had nothing to do with his presence. There was talk of postponing the race — the winds were uncharacteristically subdued — but Mosi knew they would have to be all but absent before an expensive decision like that was taken. Everyone would prefer an exciting race, but even a dull one was preferable to no race at all.

Echoes of Taylor surrounded him at every turn — only a year ago they had been here together. Her laughter, her smile, her scent pursued him as he made his way across to where Team Lanner had established themselves. As usual, they weren't hard to spot.

He didn't go there with any intention beyond confronting Blind and getting the truth out of him, an admission of guilt. They were so wrapped up in prepping for the race, *as if nothing had ever happened*, that no one spotted him until the last minute. Once they had, Blind stepped forward.

"Mosi, it's good to see you around the circuit again. I understand…"

"You bastard! You rigged it, didn't you. You *murdered* her to claim the crown!"

"Now, Mosi, you're still grieving…"

Mosi hit him, cutting off the parade of platitudes. The blow wasn't premeditated, though perhaps that wasn't entirely true; certainly he'd pictured himself punching Blind a hundred times, he just hadn't realised he was going to do so there and then.

What happened next was a little hazy. Blind had pushed him away, forcefully, and he'd staggered back, half falling against something. Was that when he'd grabbed the solder blade? He couldn't remember, but when he punched Blind a second time it wasn't just his knuckles that sank into the corporate man's belly.

Then they were on him — a whole mass of Lanner crew, punching, kicking, forcing him down. The last thing he recalled was his cheek pressed against the ground as something struck the back of his head.

He came to in a dark cubbyhole, barely large enough to contain him. He didn't cry out, didn't hammer against the walls, he simply sat there and replayed events in his mind. He didn't even know whether Blind was alive or dead.

They came for him soon after. Not the police as he might have expected, but a squad of muscle-bound goons. They wrenched him out into fading daylight – the race clearly over long ago, the plateau empty apart from one black flyer. He was bundled inside and flown to the Elders only knew where, after which they fetched him to the meat room. To Vissecz.

Mosi thought he knew all there was to know about pain, but Vissecz introduced him to whole new meanings of the word. He was taken to the brink of passing out, revived, and then taken back again.

Finally, mercifully, he was allowed to tip over that brink and into temporary oblivion. *This is just the beginning,* Vissecz murmured as consciousness fled. *Gather your strength. Tomorrow we'll get properly acquainted.*

Plans, however, had evidently changed, because now as he swam back to a degree of awareness, he was clearly somewhere else. Had he dreamed half waking before, was he really... *on a ship?*

Mosi blinked, determined to focus properly. He tried to lift his hand, just to confirm that he really wasn't chained to anything, not any more. The limb responded listlessly. Finally he managed a semblance of clarity. Only then did he realise that he wasn't alone; a figure stood at his shoulder.

"You're mostly healed, so we've had Raider bring you round," said a voice he had never expected to hear again.

He forced his head to lift up off the pillow and squinted, his mind struggling to process what he thought he was seeing. "*Captain,*" he managed at last, "is that really you?"

THREE

Drake still felt like an imposter. Over the past year he had struggled to maintain his assumed identity as an unflappable and resourceful field operative for First Solar Bank, sensing that he had outgrown that persona but unable to see a way of moving on. Now, when he had been gifted the opportunity to leave Drake behind for good, he was finding it hard to think of himself as anyone else. The irony didn't escape him.

A decade had passed since he disbanded the Dark Angels and mothballed the *Ion Raider*. More than once in the intervening years he had found himself questioning his reasons for doing so, but he knew deep down that it had been the right decision taken at the right time.

Their notoriety had grown to the point where even the vastness of space felt too restrictive. Life took on a constant ambient level of stress, as an increasing number of worlds were closed to them and, more often than not, disguise became their only recourse. The crew had grown individually wealthy thanks to their exploits but they were getting precious little time to enjoy that wealth, plus the strain of being 'the Dark Angels' was beginning to tell. He never had liked the name much, but after a young girl whose life Leesa had saved called them that and the media picked up on it, there was no escape.

No, he had no regrets; even Raider had backed his decision to draw a line under the Angels when he did. The Elder aspect that came to inhabit the ship's computer when the Dark Angels were born had been so much a part of everything they did back then; it had been his confidante as he wrestled with the issue, supporting his decision, encouraging it even. Drake had been left with a sense that Raider believed the Dark Angels' story had reached a natural conclusion for the time being, but not necessarily for ever.

In the years that followed, he slowly came to terms with the thought that this nebulous sense of 'business unfinished' had been nothing more than his own imagining, a placebo to make the disbanding of his crew more acceptable.

Now, he wasn't so sure.

Whatever the truth of that, he had always thought that his return, if and when it ever happened, would be more... memorable: a joyous homecoming, a triumphant restoration of how things ought to be. Instead he felt only numb, detached, an outsider looking in.

Here he was, back where he belonged: aboard the *Ion Raider* with members of his old crew around him – people who knew him as Cornische rather than Drake – so why did *he* find it so hard to resume the mantle of the man they expected him to be?

Perhaps while inhabiting the role of a dapper banking agent he had outgrown Cornische as well, without ever realising it. Or maybe it was just that events had been moving at such breakneck pace that he was finding it hard to keep up.

He had thought he was dead. That was the truth of it.

His jump from the cache chamber on Enduril II had been blind, motivated by the need to escape and with no notion of where the Elder relic he had activated would deposit him. When he emerged on a barren world with too thin an atmosphere to support human life he had genuinely believed that was it, his time was up. His last desperate gamble had been no more than a delaying tactic in face of the inevitable.

He would never forget the mercifully few moments spent on that world, the realisation of his impotence: fully aware of what was happening to him and powerless to affect the outcome; the headache, the nausea, the growing pressure on his chest as breathing became more difficult, the sucking in of great lungfuls in a futile attempt to scour precious oxygen from the sparse atmosphere, the sense of impending suffocation that he could liken only to claustrophobia, for all that he was in a wide open space. In the end his legs were no longer able to hold him upright. The overwhelming despair, the realisation of defeat that swept over him as he collapsed to the ground, remained vivid, seared into his memory, haunting his dreams whenever sleep claimed him...

There would be no escape this time, no last minute rescue. This was his end and no one would even know what had become of him. In many ways, that seemed fitting.

Then, the sight of feet striding towards him; the impossible, inconceivable promise of rescue that they represented.

Hel N... He dismissed her appearance as mirage, the last desperate sparking of a dying brain starved of oxygen and stubbornly refusing to accept the universe's judgement. *Of all the people in all the universe, why her?*

Even when he felt himself lifted up he could only interpret it as another step closer to the end, this sense of floating...

Despite Leesa's timely intervention it had been touch and go. If not for Raider's ministrations, his story would have ended there on that unnamed world teetering on the very edge of the galaxy. What made it worse was that in a very real sense the rescue represented the beginning of his problems rather than the end of them, and this time his problems were everyone's.

As life started to re-colonise his abused body and he got used to the idea that he wasn't going to die after all, one thing troubled him more than any other.

"Raider," he asked, "how much did you know about all this – about Mudball and the threat he represented?"

Mudball: his constant companion for more than half a decade, and Drake had to admit that he missed the little alien's sardonic presence in his mind, for all that the little shit turned out to be a duplicitous power-seeking monstrosity.

"Considerably less than I would have liked to and not as

much as I do now," the ship's entity responded, "but a little more than I felt able to confide."

"Well I'm not going anywhere in a hurry, so now seems as good a time as any to change that."

Perhaps the biggest shock to confront him as he recovered health and strength was the physical change to Saavi. He owed his life to the strange savant. If she hadn't foreseen the need to take the *Ion Raider* to an unlikely far-flung corner of the galaxy, persuading the others to journey to a world so far towards the galactic rim that its star system's only name was a designated sequence of letters and numbers, he would have died an anonymous death.

Saavi had always been a little odd, cocooned within her own perception of the universe and its workings, but somehow the aging process had run in reverse for her since the crew disbanded, and at an accelerated rate, until she now bore the physical form of a young girl. Her mind seemed as sharp and well-developed as ever, but her body...

"I have halted the regression," Raider reported when Drake raised the matter, "but I can do nothing to reverse it."

"What happens next?" Drake asked. "Will Saavi age normally from here on in, or will the process of getting younger start up again if she's denied regular access to the cloud chamber?"

"Unknown. The cloud chamber environment was never intended for human use. The effects of exposure on your race's physiology have proved unpredictable."

No one was about to argue with that.

Saavi demonstrated her worth again when she guided them to Callia III, even if she remained frustratingly vague as to the reason.

"The potentials are shifting all the time," she explained. "I've never seen it like this. Any sort of clear prediction is next to impossible. I can only do my best to steer us to key points that promise the most beneficial outcomes."

"Callia III is where we left Mosi," Jen noted.

"No prizes for guessing why we're back here then," Leesa said.

Nor was she wrong. Mosi, it turned out, was in trouble. Drake had recovered significantly by this point but not fully, so he and Saavi stayed aboard the *Raider* while the two women went to extricate Mosi, accompanied by Jai, Saavi's deceptively innocent-looking T'kai engineered bodyguard, currently configured as a doll.

Drake quickly discovered that it wasn't in his make-up to wait around while others did the dirty work. He hated having to sit this one out and resolved that it would be the last time he did so, irrespective of Raider's medical advice.

He paced the ship's compact ops room like a caged tiger, while Saavi darted between ops and the cloud chamber. She seemed unable to stay away from the place for a protracted period of time, causing Drake to wonder how she ever managed to sleep. It was like an addiction.

Finally Raider reported that the party was approaching the ship.

"Is he alive?" Saavi asked as they summoned up a visual.

The figure that slumped between Leesa and Jen looked to be anything but. Behind the group, Drake could make out the diminutive form of Jai, shadowing them as a good bodyguard should.

"I don't see why they'd go to all the trouble of lugging him back here if he weren't," Drake said.

"I am detecting life signs," Raider assured them. That was something, at least.

Drake had seen enough. "Saavi, get the gurney and meet us at the airlock," he instructed as he hurried out of ops.

"Captain," Raider said, "I would advise against strenuous physical activity given your condition."

"Noted."

He kept going, out the airlock and down the smoothly

deployed ramp, hurrying to intercept the burdened women. He took Jen's place, sliding in under Mosi's arm and draping the limp limb across his shoulders. Jen looked just about spent – how far had they been forced to carry Mosi anyway? Jen was tough as wire and deadly as a snake, but lugging around what amounted to a grown man's dead weight for any distance would have taxed anybody. Even Leesa with her auganic enhancements was showing the strain.

For his part, Drake immediately realised how unfit he'd become.

"Heavier than he looks, isn't he," he said.

"Yeah, and growing heavier with every step," Leesa confirmed.

As they negotiated the short distance to the ship, Drake gained a better appreciation of the state Mosi was in. Small cuts, bruises, and dried blood covered his naked upper torso.

"What the hell have they been doing to him?" he said.

"Torture," Leesa supplied in clipped voice, evidently saving her breath.

"I hope you got the bastards who did this."

"Some of them. Probably not the right ones."

Saavi waited at the bottom of the ramp with the gurney, which hovered just above the ground. They poured and pushed their unresisting burden into its embrace and Drake could draw proper breath again.

"For pity's sake, Cloud," Leesa said by way of greeting, "can't you bring us to these places a little bit earlier? Mosi's half dead, and if we'd been any later he'd be the other half as well. Are we meant to tear around the stars collecting a ship full of the comatose and wounded to go save the universe with? Is that the plan?"

"Lighten up, Lees," Jen said.

Both women had to be exhausted, and it was obvious that Leesa was just letting off steam with Saavi the most convenient target.

Obvious to everyone except Saavi. "I give you as much notice as I can!" the girl/woman said. "The possible futures are so turbulent right now that it's a miracle I'm able to pick a path at all. Just be grateful I can see *anything*."

"Without Saavi we would never have found the captain or Mosi," Jen said. "They'd both be dead by now."

"I know, I know... Sorry, Saavi. Ignore me."

The girl gave a brief nod, acknowledging the apology without necessarily accepting it.

"It's just that... It would be nice if we could get there for once before all the bad shit happens, you know? To find an old crewmate who's still fighting fit for a change rather than half dead."

"I'm getting there," Drake said.

He saw the corner of Jen's mouth twitch at that.

"I know, Captain, sorry," Leesa said. "I didn't mean... Oh hell, I need a beer."

With that, she stomped up the ramp to disappear into the ship's interior, leaving the rest of them to tend to Mosi.

Leesa felt embarrassed by her outburst at Cloud, and did her best to stay out of the other woman's way for the next couple of days – no mean feat bearing in mind the close confines of the ship. The amount of time Saavi spent closeted away in her precious cloud chamber helped in that regard.

They had lifted off from Callia III as soon as Mosi was on board and put the *Raider* into orbit around Callia V, a gas giant towards the edge of the system, while Saavi attempted to determine their next destination.

Leesa had been pleased to see the captain leave the ship to help them with Mosi. It showed how far his recovery had progressed. He was walking far more comfortably now and seemed almost back to his old self. Given the state he'd been in when they found him, she considered this a minor miracle. He still carried his cane, but she knew that to be far more than a mere walking stick. She wondered, too, whether it was an indication that he wasn't yet ready to let go of the Drake persona.

That was fine by her; whatever it took. Maybe things were starting to look up after all.

When the *Ion Raider* had emerged from a gruelling series of jumps through RzSpace, it seemed their only reward was a barren world with little atmosphere circling an insipid sun that clung to the furthest rim of the galaxy. That had been a low point for all of them, their spirits already dampened by the long exposure to Rz. Even her faith in Cloud's prescience had been tested.

Then they spotted a single life sign and suddenly all was good with the universe again. They *knew* this had to be the reason they were here. Despite that, they were almost too late.

Having landed the *Ion Raider* with reckless haste, Leesa leapt from the ship almost before it had settled, her auganic enhancements enabling her to work in the deficient atmosphere without an oxygen reserve for the short period of time necessary. While Jen was still donning her suit, Leesa dashed across to the fallen figure. It was obviously a man. She had no idea how he came to be here and knew there was a story to be told; all she had to do was ensure he survived long enough to tell it.

Only when she reached the fallen figure and picked him up did she realise who it was. The very man they'd been hunting.

Cornische was more dead than alive. Leesa was shaken to the core. Not so much by the captain's condition, no, that she could deal with. She was horrified by how close they had been to not venturing here at all. It was a long trip and even longer odds that anything worthwhile would be waiting at the end of it. More than once during the course of the journey she had teetered on the verge of suggesting they abandon the quest and turn back. Only stubbornness had prevented her. At outset she had argued against Jen that they should trust Saavi's instincts instead of continuing to Enduril II. When doubt set in, she refused to admit she'd been wrong and had determined to see things through. To her credit, Jen never once said 'I told you so', even when their spirits were at the lowest ebb.

Thank the Elders for stubbornness. If she had failed to side with Saavi in that initial argument, or been a little less resolute in the face of the will-sapping effects of Rz, the captain would have been lost to them without their even realising it.

One thing was for certain: she would never question Saavi's predictions again; which made snapping at her like that all the more unforgiveable. There was only one thing for it. Leesa would have to apologise, something that had never been her strong suit.

Jen came into the ops room, joining her.

"How's Mosi doing?" she asked.

"Raider?"

"Geminum's injuries are extensive but superficial." The response came in the rich, reassuring tones they knew so well.

The voice was female, something Leesa had asked Cornische about once upon a time. He'd shrugged, saying, "The computer was modified for audio coms when I bought the ship and that was the voice she came with. I've grown used to it, so kept the same one even after she became Raider." Leesa had to admit that hearing Raider speak in any other tone would have seemed odd – the voice, neither young nor old, was reassuring, implying a level of wisdom that could be trusted. She guessed *she'd* grown used to it as well.

"There are no broken bones or significant internal injuries," Raider continued, "but the cumulative effect of the pain inflicted on him is alarming. Whoever was responsible for his torture is an individual of sadistic competence but also measured restraint.

"For his own comfort, I have kept him sedated whilst accelerated healing proceeds. Going forward, that may no longer be necessary."

"Thanks, Raider." Jen smiled at Leesa. "Looks like we're *all* getting there."

Leesa couldn't help but grin in response. "Okay, I know, I've been an ass."

"Don't worry, I'm getting used to that by now."

"Don't push it, farmer girl."

Saavi chose that moment to burst into the room – she had a habit of doing that, dashing around like... well, a child, which only helped reinforce that impression, even though they knew her small frame held an adult intellect.

"I've found it," she said breathlessly, "our next destination."

She beamed at Leesa, who remembered that they were supposed to be making up. "Well done!" she said. *Careful, don't overdo it.* The last thing she needed was for Saavi to think she was being patronising.

Leesa glanced across at Jen, who was still grinning. Maybe things really were looking up.

Then Saavi added, "The Enduril System."

"What, again?"

FOUR

As they exited RzSpace the ship bucked and juddered violently around them. Drake was seated in one of the twin pilot chairs, otherwise he would have been sent sprawling by the unexpected upheaval.

"What the hell?" Leesa exclaimed. "Have we hit something?"

The old spacers' dread, that their ship would come out of Rz into a volume of space already occupied by something else. In theory, that was impossible, but since when had that ever stood in the way of a good bar room horror story?

"Other way around." Jen's voice sounded tight, strained. "We're under attack!"

"Raider?" Drake could have pored over instruments and read outs to get an idea of what was going on, but Raider could do so far more efficiently.

"We appear to have emerged from RzSpace in the midst of an ongoing skirmish," the computer's unflappable voice reported.

"No kidding," Leesa muttered.

The ship bucked again, but this time under Jen's direction as she took evasive manoeuvres.

"Hang onto something," she advised, "I'm not holding back on the gs."

Drake felt himself pressed back into the chair's upholstery. "Can we go back into Rz?" he said.

"Regrettably not at present," Raider replied. "The ship has sustained some damage."

"Crap!" Leesa exclaimed. "It would have to be the engines. It's *always* the engines. I'm on it. Jen, ease up for just a moment, would you?"

She didn't wait for a reply, sprinting out of ops and presumably taking Jen's compliance for granted.

41

"Do we have any idea who's shooting at who?"

"Just checking that out..." Jen replied. "Shit!"

"What?"

"One of them – the one doing the shooting – is showing as *Darkness Mourning*."

"The Night Hammer ship?" Drake stared at her. "Are you sure?"

"Yes." Her clipped tone brooked no further query.

Things just kept getting better. *Darkness Mourning* was infamous. The ship had a string of atrocities attributed to it. As for the Night Hammers, they were an outlawed military group with a reputation for being both formidable and ruthless. They were also supposed to be defunct, their last remaining ships destroyed.

"Who are they shooting at?"

"No idea. I can't even see another ship."

"Raider?"

"There is something there..." the computer sounded oddly hesitant. "Very effectively camouflaged, and elusive."

"The Night Hammers must have some shit-hot tech to even suspect the presence of another ship," Jen said. "I *know* they're out there, and I'm still struggling to get a handle on their position. Just a rough idea based on minutely delayed info rather than anything else – it's a step up from guesswork but not by much. Without the foreknowledge to look for something, I'd never spot them."

"Unless the other vessel did something to give itself away before we arrived," Drake suggested.

"Maybe." Jen didn't sound convinced. "Whoa... Whoever this is, they're boxing clever. There are now a score of 'ghost' readings, all of them as difficult to spot as the next. They're dispersing quickly and randomly. As decoys go, these are as good as any I've ever seen."

"Are the Night Hammers showing any interest in us at all?"

"Not that you'd notice. They're concentrating on the other

ship. I think we just got in the way."

That was something, at least. It would almost certainly change though, once *Darkness Mourning* had nailed its primary target. With the Rz drive out, they were a sitting duck, and in time honoured tradition the Night Hammers wouldn't want to leave any witnesses behind.

"We're pretty close to one of the smaller moons," Jen continued. "Enduril's a greedy gas giant, she lays claim to sixty-five of them in all. I'm aiming to put this one between us and the shooting,"

That made sense, but it was no more than a temporary respite. The Night Hammers weren't likely to forget about them.

"Raider, what colours are we flying?"

"We're still showing as the *Blue Angel*," Raider replied, naming the false hull ident they'd adopted in order to slip into the Callia system unnoticed.

"So as far as the Night Hammers are concerned, we're just a standard Comet class trader that's blundered into the wrong part of space at the wrong time."

"That would seem likely, yes."

"Okay, let's make that work for us." He turned to Jen. "Tell me when we're about to slip behind that moon."

"Will do."

"The Rz drive is well and truly fried," Leesa said, her voice relayed by Raider. "I can't make repairs or even jury-rig anything with what we've got on board. I'm coming back up to ops."

Drake acknowledged her report but his attention was focussed elsewhere.

"How long, Jen?"

"Nearly there. Two minutes, for whatever difference it's likely to make."

They both knew that if Leesa couldn't repair the engines, hiding only delayed the inevitable. Despite the gs Jen had poured on to get them away from the action, they were still no real distance from the Night Hammer ship.

"Is she showing any response to our retreat yet?"

"No, she's still picking off the decoy ghosts."

"Good. This ought to get her attention, then. Raider, hit *Darkness Mourning* with both beams."

"Understood. Complying."

Comets were not generally armed. The *Ion Raider* was; not as heavily as Drake might have liked at a time like this, but she punched above her weight and carried a surprise or two.

In addition to a range of missiles with different payloads for different purposes, her arsenal included two energy weapons; one particularly tight-beamed and lethal, which any warship might be proud of, the other considerably more unusual. Gleaned from the same Elder source that had given birth to the Dark Angels, the alien weapon had been christened by the crew 'Dead Leg'. Essentially, it piggy-backed on the conventional weapon's discharge and took advantage of any hole the tight beam made in a target ship's armour to slip in and wreak havoc, disabling every system it encountered.

Immediately the weapons were fired, the *Ion Raider* slipped behind the dead moon, using it as a shield against potential retaliation. Drake braced himself again as Jen used the engines to shed momentum. The moon's mass wouldn't be much help if *Darkness Mourning* responded with hunter missiles, but it would shield them from any energy weapons the Night Hammers might bring to bear. Of course, the hope was that they'd be in no fit state to mount any sort of response.

The distances involved were small, the wait correspondingly brief.

"Nailed her!" Jen declared. "No sign of a reply. In fact their weapons have cut out entirely. They're not even taking pot shots at the ghost ship and its decoys any more."

All of which might be a ruse, but past experience had shown how effective 'Dead Leg' could be, and, besides, Drake wasn't prepared to hang around hiding forever.

"Okay," he said, "let's take a closer look."

As they moved out of the moon's shadow and headed back towards *Darkness Mourning*, Leesa returned.

"You might have warned me you were going to shed gs," she grumbled, rubbing her left shoulder dramatically.

"Sorry," Jen replied without glancing up. "I was busy. She looks dead, skipper," she continued. "Minimal energy readings, no activity from engines or weapons. Her shielding is still sufficiently intact to prevent me from knowing crew complement or their current status, but we've definitely hurt her."

"Thanks, Jen." Drake turned to Leesa. "No hope for the Rz drive?"

She shook her head. "We're stuck at sub-light until we can get replacement parts."

"I hate to state the obvious," Jen said, "but if we need to go looking for parts the only settled world within reach is Enduril II."

"Not an option," Drake said quickly, recalling his recent visit to Enduril. "That's Saflik's home territory."

"I didn't really think it would be. Mind you, who said we had to ask them nicely?"

Drake chose to ignore the comment. "Any reaction from our ghost ship?"

"Not yet," Jen said. "They seem to be sitting tight to see what develops."

"Why go to all that trouble, not to mention waste so much time limping over to Enduril II for parts, when there's another source closer to hand?" Leesa asked.

"You mean… *Darkness Mourning*?"

"Exactly. We can strip whatever we need from her and let the Night Hammers do the limping back to Enduril, licking their wounds."

"Would that work?"

Leesa nodded. "Should do. At a bare minimum, I need an inversion tube and a pulse governor, and they're pretty generic – one size fits all, sort of thing."

"Okay." Drake took a heartbeat to think that through. "If we're going to go calling, we need Geminum."

"Mosi's not up to it," Jen said.

"He'll have to be. We're talking about boarding a disabled Night Hammer ship and cannibalising its drive. Goodness only knows how many are on board or what surprises the crew will have cooked up for us by the time we put on EVA suits, get across there and force our way in. We need to catch them now, before they're ready for us, and make sure they're out of action before we pay them a visit. Geminum's the only one who can do that."

"Captain, you do remember that slab of meat we dragged back to the *Raider* a couple of days ago, don't you?"

"I do, but Mosi's our only play. Besides, that was then. His wounds were extensive but superficial, right, Raider?"

"Indeed."

"We reached him before any real damage was done, and he's been recuperating since."

"Don't forget the ghost ship's still lurking out there," Jen said. "What if whoever they are decides to take advantage of the situation and blow their tormentor to bits while Mosi's still on board?"

"Or I am," Leesa added.

"We'll talk it down, establish communication before we commit," Drake said. "Raider, is Mosi still in the sickbay?"

"No. He recently entered the artefact room."

Drake and Jen stared at each other. Both knew there was only one reason for Mosi to go there.

"Well," Leesa said, "I guess that settles it."

From the moment he awoke and realised where he was — *accepted* that he really was back on the *Ion Raider* — Mosi had been itching to go to the artefact room. It drew him like a siren's call, demanding his attention and precluding all other thought.

He knew they were in RzSpace — he could sense that from the

moment the captain roused him – but the lure of the artefact room transcended even Rz's deadening influence. Nor could he blame his injuries for his reluctance to head straight down there; he was pretty much healed. It was nothing physical that stopped him. It was as if, in some perverse way, he savoured the anguish caused by holding back, as if he felt at a deep-rooted level that he deserved to suffer. For abandoning Naj. For Taylor's death. For surviving them both.

Then came the emergence from Rz and the world juddering violently around him, almost flinging him to the floor.

"The ship has emerged in the midst of a conflict, nature unknown," Raider explained in answer to his query.

Mosi knew then that he had delayed too long. Hours had passed since he woke to find the captain waiting for him, and he had yet to get up. He had just lain there, resisting the urge to reclaim his past. Now he was forced to wait a little longer still, as acceleration pushed him back into his sickbed. Presumably the *Ion Raider* was getting the hell away from the shooting.

As soon as the pressure eased he acted, hauling himself to his feet, glad at how reassuringly steady his legs felt. He left the compact sickbay, heading along a walkway and down the steps to the cargo deck, part of which had been sectioned off to form the artefact room.

He didn't hesitate at the threshold but plunged straight in. Now that he was actually here he couldn't wait to reclaim the torque, to become Geminum again, and wondered why he had procrastinated in the first place.

He barely registered the presence of the mannequin that confronted him as the door slid open, despite it mimicking Cornische so effectively. Instead he turned smartly to his left, following the antiseptically white wall to where a short, stubby plinth stood unobtrusively in the corner.

He stopped before the plinth, holding out his right hand to hover with fingers splayed just above the plain surface. It was all he could do to keep the hand steady as his excitement mounted.

Almost immediately, the top of the plinth began to change, seeming to melt as the surface flowed to either side. Something solid and metallic rose from the plinth's interior, rising up on a pseudopod platform to meet Mosi's flat hand.

A crescent of silvered metal, flat on the inside of the curve, embossed with elegant and indecipherable designs on the outer. The metal was warm to the touch, and the moment his fingers closed around it Mosi imagined he could sense her. The torque, which formed a sort of too-broad half collar, had always felt alive like this, from the very first time he had picked it up.

Without hesitation he reached back behind his head and pressed the crescent to the nape of his neck. It fitted snugly, as it always had, despite not appearing to be the right shape to do so. Mosi held his breath, waiting for the gentle sting that signalled the torque melding to him.

He felt it like a kiss and she was there, filling his mind, his awareness.

"Hi, bro', what kept you?" said Najat, the voice that had haunted his dreams for a decade.

"A thousand things, none of them reason enough."

"Does this mean we're back in business?"

"So it would seem. Are you ready?"

"Hell, yeah. You know me."

He sensed her smile, her joy at being woken. The years that had passed since they were last joined melted away. She didn't ask to be updated and he didn't offer. He was whole again. That was all that mattered.

There was a suit, too, a costume that went with the Geminum identity, but unlike Hel N's silvered skin this wasn't integral to his abilities. It was nothing more than camouflage, a prop to maintain the wearer's anonymity. He grabbed it on the way out, but only as an afterthought.

"Welcome back, Geminum. The others are waiting for you in ops," said Raider as he left the artefact room.

His was no smartsuit like Leesa's, it wouldn't flow up or

down his body at his whim but had to be pulled on the old fashioned way. He stopped to do so before continuing, leaving his head bare for comfort's sake. Then he continued to ops.

They were all there – Cornische, Hel N, Shadow, and a dark-skinned girl he didn't recognise at first. She had some sort of robotic dog by her side, which watched her intently.

"I made a mistake, and I don't know how," the girl was saying.

"We don't know that for sure, yet," Jen replied.

"Oh, I think we have a few clues," Leesa said. "Being shot at, for example. Don't beat yourself up over it, though, Saavi, we're all human. Well, mostly."

Saavi? That young girl was Cloud? He could see it now, in her eyes, her posture. Someone would have to explain to him later how the woman he remembered had become the child who now stood in her stead. These were the Dark Angels, after all: weird came with the territory.

Cornische spotted him hovering in the doorway, grinned and nodded as if it were the most natural thing in the world. "Glad you could join us, Geminum. Your timing is impeccable."

Jen gave him a quick hug, Saavi too. Leesa didn't but smiled and said something reassuring – she never had been the touchy feely sort.

Despite the welcome camaraderie, the implication of the captain's greeting hadn't escaped him. "How can I help?"

"There's a crippled ship out there, which we need to raid, cannibalising its Rz drive for parts to get *Raider's* back on line," the captain explained. "It'll be easier to do so if we know the crew are out of action before we board."

"I can do that!" Najat said. Mosi had to smile at her eagerness, though he knew he was the only one who could hear her. "We're good to go," he said aloud.

"One thing," the captain added. "It's a Night Hammer ship."

"Ooh... This should be fun," Naj said in his head.

Mosi nodded. "Thanks for the heads-up."

"We'll get suited and ready," Jen said, heading out of ops with Leesa close behind. "Give us five minutes, Mosi, and then do your thing."

Mosi used the time to get as much information as he could from Raider regarding the target, which proved to be precious little. Current distance to the Night Hammer ship and its outer dimensions, that was about it. *Darkness Mourning* was too heavily shielded for Raider to tell how many were on board or even confirm the ship's internal layout. They called up schematics dating from when she was built but that didn't take into account any subsequent modifications – anyone basing expectations of the *Ion Raider* on the original layout would be in for a shock once they stepped aboard.

"Hel N and Shadow are ready," the captain told him.

Mosi nodded, and sat down in a vacant chair. He then pulled the mask up over his head – a purely symbolic action, but it did help him to feel that he really was Geminum again.

"Over to you, little sis," he said in his thoughts.

"Gotcha!" and she was gone.

He had tried to explain to the other Angels what it felt like. The closest he could manage was, "There's no sense of loss; it's not a severance as such, more a stretching. The link is still there, but it's as if I'm watching her race away from me down a long tunnel of light that goes on forever, receding with every heartbeat. Then she arrives and I snap back to her in an instant, as if tugged by elastic."

For the split second he felt his sister leave him, Mosi was reminded of that attempt at an explanation. As descriptions went it was woefully inadequate, but he had yet to come up with anything better. He just about had time to revel in the return of this familiar and much-missed experience before Najat reached her goal and his consciousness was pulled towards her. Quick as thought, he sped through a tunnel limned with silver lightnings, the merest suggestion of energies that danced past without ever touching, left behind before he could fully register their presence. Then he arrived, drawing breath and marvelling, as he always did.

Freed of their shared form and having reached her destination, Naj took on a body of her own, or so it always seemed to Mosi when he joined her. He knew that was largely illusion and the truth was far more complex, but he *felt* as if he occupied a physical form much like his own but proportioned in unfamiliar ways and... *different*; a woman's form rather than a man's.

Whereas in his own body he was the dominant partner and Naj's persona a constant but subordinate presence, effectively a passenger, here the roles were reversed. Naj held the upper hand and he was the subsidiary, on hand to observe and advise but not much else.

Mosi had no idea how the Elder collar did it, what arcane tech it utilised to bring his sister back – an adult version of her at that – presumably by plumbing the recesses of his own memory and extrapolating from there, but it always felt a great deal more than that. This really was Naj, he felt it in every fibre: how she would have been if she had survived to reach adulthood rather than dying as an adolescent on Coates World. She possessed much the same phobias and anxieties his sister had harboured, but progressed and matured, and also the quick wit and the joie de vivre that he had never quite been able to find in himself after she had gone.

He asked Raider once, about how real she was, afraid that he was deluding himself, but the computer had assured him this wasn't the case. The torque operated on quantum levels that humanity had yet to grasp, drawing on more than one reality to breathe life into Naj's aspect. In every sense that counted, this genuinely was Naj reborn. Mosi was content with that. To him, she was utterly real, and that was all that mattered.

"Are you with me, bro'?"

"All the way," he assured her.

FIVE

There was no disguising the moment Mosi departed. His face went blank, features slack, while his body became a rigid statue as consciousness fled, tugged irresistibly in his sister's wake. The rigidity was why he generally chose to sit down – returning to a body that had toppled over and broken a limb wasn't something he relished, apparently.

Of all the talents gifted to them by scavenged Elder tech, Mosi's was by far the most remarkable in Drake's opinion. He'd heard explanations of quantum dabbling but essentially had no idea how the Geminum torque resurrected a credible semblance of Najat, or enabled Mosi to project her over such distances irrespective of physical obstacles. More than once, however, circumstances had given him cause to be grateful that it did.

"Captain," Raider interrupted his reveries, "the ghost ship has shut down its decoys."

"Thank you, Raider."

"Maybe they've decided to trust us now that we've kicked the Night Hammers' collective ass," Saavi said.

"Maybe," Drake said; or perhaps it was just that generating the decoys sapped too much energy and they couldn't maintain them for long. Still, the disappearance of the ghost's ghosts could only be interpreted as a good sign. "Let's find out, shall we? Raider, open a channel, audio only.

"This is the independent trader the *Blue Angel* calling cloaked vessel. Please show yourself. The danger has passed, the Night Hammer ship has been disabled and is no longer a threat." *And you're making me nervous.*

No response.

He tried again. "*Blue Angel* to unknown vessel: we are not your enemy. Please do not give us cause to believe that you may be ours."

As veiled threats went, Drake reckoned that was fair enough. They didn't have time for niceties. Despite the need to get their engines back online, he wasn't about to commit Leesa and Jen to an EVA crossing without assurances that the ghost ship wouldn't try to finish off *Mourning Glory* while they did so. Caught in the open like that, they wouldn't stand a chance.

Whoever was in command of that ship *had* to be considering their options. If, as Drake suspected, maintaining the decoys had been a drain on their energy reserves, surely whatever they were using to generate an instrument-foxing cloak must be another, especially if it was related to the Ptarmigan device Pelquin had employed on their jaunt into Xter space.

As if on cue, the 'ghost' materialised. Smaller than he would have anticipated, and of a type Drake – who knew a fair bit about ships – had never seen before. The matt hull seemed designed to absorb light, and, even without the cloaking system, the ship would be difficult enough to spot in the vastness of space if its engines were cold and you didn't know where to look.

"Trading vessel?" said a man's voice – deep toned with a nasal accent that Drake struggled to place. "Since when did any Comet class trader carry enough firepower to disable a warship, let alone a Night Hammer ship? Who the hell are you really?"

"I was about to ask you the same thing. That's some cloaking mechanism you have there."

This was followed by a pause, beyond anything attributable to comms lag. Drake could imagine the debate, internal or otherwise, that must be taking place on the other vessel. So far, this confusing Comet class ship hadn't shown any aggression towards them, but it had shown itself to be dangerous. Could the old 'enemy of my enemy' adage be relied on here? Did it justify a leap of faith?

Evidently, someone decided it might.

"I am Commander Deepak Thapa of the stealth ship *Sabre 1*, out of New Sparta, and if you're the *Blue Angel* then I'm a trainee gen pet groomer."

"New Sparta?" That couldn't be a coincidence. "Who sent you here, Commander?"

"That, I'm not at liberty to discuss. Besides, shouldn't it be your turn to share?"

"New Sparta," Drake repeated, refusing to be deflected. "It wouldn't be one of the banks by any chance, would it, Commander?"

There had been rumours: black ops units operating at the highest levels of secrecy, on call as a last resort to ensure the banks' interests were protected should anything go spectacularly wrong. He had always dismissed the notion as fanciful, a way for banking agents to pander to their egos, deluding themselves that their job was more glamorous and dangerous than it generally proved to be, but a part of him had always wondered: might there be a grain of truth somewhere in the tales?

"First Solar, perhaps?" Drake continued out loud.

"Who are you?" the commander asked again, more sharply this time.

"I will tell you," he promised, "but first I need your assurance that you're not intending to take any pot-shots at *Darkness Mourning* now she's vulnerable. We've settled that score for you. I'm about to send an away team across there and I want to make sure my people won't be at risk."

The shock in Thapa's voice was obvious. "You're sending an *away team* to a Night Hammer ship?"

"That's what I said. We have our reasons."

"I'm sure you do. You took some damage, then, when you were caught in the crossfire." Not stupid, this one.

"A little. Nothing major, but we'd rather sort it out here and now."

"If you say so. Very well, you have my word that we won't open fire on *Darkness Mourning* while your people are exposed."

"Until they're safely back with us," Drake said, to avoid any possible ambiguity.

"Agreed."

Could he trust this Commander Thapa? The concession had come too easily for his liking, which suggested either Thapa had never intended to renew hostilities in the first place or he was lying. Drake only had his gut to go on, and made a decision. "Thank you." He turned his head to the right, a signal for Raider to hold communications. "Give the away team the green light, and when you put me back in touch with Thapa, transmit visual as well as audio, keeping the focus tight; show him only me." He didn't want anyone to see Saavi, a child, hovering at the margins of the image, nor the zombie-like Mosi for that matter – no point in raising questions that didn't need to be asked.

"Okay, Commander Thapa, here I am: Corbin Thadeus Drake, registered agent for First Solar Bank, New Sparta, at your service."

After the briefest of hesitations a reciprocal image appeared in front of Drake, showing what had to be ops of *Sabre 1*. He noted with approval that the commander remained cautious, the image was as tightly focussed as Drake's own must appear to him, showing little beyond the man's face and shoulders and offering only limited opportunity to pore over the recordings later to glean information about this unconventional ship. As for Thapa himself, he looked to be a little younger than Drake – perhaps early thirties – and a little darker skinned, with strong features and eyes that held a steely quality suggesting an abundance of self-belief.

"A banking agent captaining a trading vessel, that's a new one on me," Thapa said.

"Needs must," Drake replied. "As I'm sure you're aware, we're granted a considerable degree of discretion in pursuit of our assignments."

"That much I do know." Thapa studied him for a moment then said: "Tell me something, Mr Drake. A short while ago we were stationed off Enduril II..." Were they now? That was interesting. "...when a Comet class trader dropped out of Rz close to our position and then dived straight back in again, much faster than any ship ought to. Before she disappeared, we managed to ping her ident, which registered as the *Ion Raider*. You wouldn't happen to know anything about that, would you?"

Drake did his best to keep his expression neutral, and slowly shook his head. "Sorry, not got a clue."

"Of course you haven't."

Thapa seemed to reach a decision of his own. "Mr Drake, we were sent to the Enduril system in response to concerns for both your safety and the legitimacy of your assignment."

"I'm flattered."

"There were credible grounds to believe that you may have been sent into a situation you were ill prepared for." They'd got that much right.

"You have failed to maintain the regular contact stipulated at the outset of the mission and that's made your superiors anxious," Thapa continued. "Now that we've located you, I must insist that you accompany us back to New Sparta for debriefing."

Seriously? The narrow focus of priorities this demonstrated almost made Drake laugh. He had to remind himself that Thapa and the higher-ups back on New Sparta were oblivious to what was going on here; they had no idea of the threat that Mudball and Saflik represented. Perhaps it was time to change that.

"I'm afraid I can't do that, Commander," he said, his voice firm. "My assignment is still ongoing, though the parameters have expanded considerably. I was prevented from reporting by circumstances beyond my control." Which was true enough initially, at any rate. "It's imperative that I now remain in the field to see the mission through. You recall that discretion we spoke about earlier? Well, I'm exercising it right now. Unless I'm much mistaken, we work for the same employer, and there's a reason they've always granted me such extensive autonomy. It's because they know that situations can develop rapidly in unexpected ways, often requiring swift and decisive action, *unconventional* action from the person on the spot, and they trust me to make the right call when it matters."

Thapa went to say something but Drake spoke over him. "Believe me, Commander Thapa, it has *never* mattered more than now."

"So you're maintaining that you continue to act in your employers' best interests."

"Absolutely, yes I do." Not a lie; after all, he was acting for the benefit of *all* humanity.

The commander stared back, lips pursed, doubtless debating whether to challenge him on this. Drake didn't point out that *Sabre 1* was outgunned if push came to shove, he didn't need to. Thapa wasn't to know that the Dead Leg was a one shot wonder which would need extensive recharging before it could be deployed again. All he had to go on was the fact that this unassuming little vessel had just disabled a Night Hammer warship, and Drake saw no reason to disabuse him.

"At this juncture, I *do* need to report back to First Solar, and thanks to your intervention, I'm finally in a position to do so. I'm relying on you to bring a recording of our conversation to the highest authorities you can reach, Commander Thapa." Drake had been rehearsing what he was about to say in his head while they spoke. He didn't wait for the commander to acknowledge but ploughed straight on.

"This is Corbin Thadeus Drake, reporting to Terry Reese and the senior officers of First Solar Bank. As we suspected, the situation at Enduril II has proved to be far more complex than it appeared. The petition that led to my assignment there was false, and is in fact just one small element in a far wider plot. Matters have escalated rapidly and continue to do so, developments that represent a state of utmost peril." A trigger phrase, specific wording that Reese would recognise. "One of the key players here is a well-established far-reaching criminal organisation that styles itself 'Saflik'. They are making a power play, attempting to undermine the current structure of our entire civilisation and reshape it to their will."

What he'd said so far was enough to test anybody's credibility, but what came next sounded close to ridiculous, even to him. "Saflik are fanatics, motivated by a twisted faith in the sanctity of the Elders and the conviction that we have systematically desecrated their legacy by misusing the artefacts they left behind."

He paused, determined to get this final part right. "By drawing on and combining the essence of a number of guardian entities collected from several Elder caches, Saflik have succeeded in resurrecting a composite being that approximates to a member of the long dead Elder race. They now follow this being zealously. Unfortunately, the entity in question seems quite insane by our standards. The threat this poses cannot be overstated, especially as the entity in question possesses knowledge relating to the whereabouts of Lenbya, the fabled 'Ultimate Cache of the Elders'.

"More than a decade ago, Lenbya's tech gave birth to the group of freebooters known as the Dark Angels and equipped their ship, the *Ion Raider*, but in doing so the Dark Angels barely scratched the surface of what is held there. Under the entity's guidance, Saflik have determined to breach Lenbya and utilise its vast resources of exotic technology to their own ends, starting with the subjugation of human space.

"It is vital that this threat should be met and countered at the earliest opportunity, contained before it can gather momentum. To that end, I urge First Solar to mobilise whatever resources it can muster and to use every scrap of influence it can bring to bear. We need to assemble a fleet, the like of which hasn't been seen since the final stages of the Auganics Wars, and send it to the co-ordinates I'll provide at the end of this message. There is no time to lose in endless debate on the matter. First Solar itself has been compromised, and I regret to report that one of my fellow agents, Representative Cillian Archer, has been working for Saflik. I have no idea how long this association has been established or if it's an isolated case. I *do* know, however, that any delay in responding, any indecision regarding whether or not to take this report seriously, could prove disastrous. Decisive action is our only recourse. I am currently occupied in gathering resources of my own, and will head for those same co-ordinates as soon as I've finished doing so. I hope to meet you there. End of message."

Thapa stared at him in evident shock. "Are you for real?"

Drake met his gaze without flinching. "Totally."

The Night Hammer ship was damaged, that much was obvious. Grav and life support still functioned but Naj had arrived in pitch darkness. Even so, it took little more than a heartbeat for her to orientate herself.

"Ops ought to be this way." What Mosi knew, she knew, including all that he had learned from studying the ship's schematics.

Naj moved with preternatural speed, seeming to flow along the darkened corridor far more swiftly than his physical form could ever have managed.

They encountered the first signs of life almost immediately: bobbing torch beams coming towards them. The light proved to emanate from helmets worn by two men. The Night Hammers didn't see them coming; literally.

Raider had explained it this way: Naj's aspect, which Mosi now resided in as a passenger, existed in a different quantum state, fractionally out of phase with the rest of reality, only able to move fully into it for brief moments. Until she did so, people were unable to see her, to sense her.

The two men ghosted past.

"I could take them from behind!" she said, turning to prowl after the oblivious pair.

"No! These are Night Hammers, trained soldiers, and we're unarmed. You might catch one of them by surprise but then the other one..."

"I'd phase out before he could touch me."

"And then he'd alert everyone aboard to our presence. No, it's too risky."

"Killjoy."

She must have known he was right, though, or she would have done it anyway. For a brief moment Naj lingered, torn between the urge to commit violence and the dictates of common sense. They watched as the two torch-limned figures disappeared along the corridor, and the moment was gone. Naj shrugged and then they carried on towards ops.

"That's the longest I've ever heard you speak in one go."

Drake grunted, momentarily turning his attention away from the monitor fields to regard Saavi, who had spoken. "I've had to learn new skills in the decade since we mothballed the *Raider*."

"So I noticed. I think I even caught you smiling at one point."

Drake couldn't help but grin.

"Make that twice."

He nodded in acknowledgement before resuming his study of the monitors. Drake was keenly aware that his message to Terry Reese had been economical with the truth in certain aspects. He had avoided, for example, any mention of Mudball, or of his own unwitting role in helping the diminutive alien gather so many cache guardian aspects over the years. Nor had he mentioned that the whereabouts of Lenbya had been dredged from his own memory by the treacherous alien. He felt embarrassed enough by his unintended complicity in all this without broadcasting it.

"Do you really think New Sparta will respond?" Saavi asked.

"Honestly? I've no idea, but at least now we've given them the opportunity to do so." And he liked to think that Terry Reese for one would give credence to his warning. Whether she carried enough weight to make others listen was a different matter entirely. "Besides, every financial institution on New Sparta has been obsessed with finding Lenbya since they were founded, even while they persist in denying the possibility of its existence, and we've just told them precisely where Lenbya is."

That, if nothing else, ought to stir things up and guarantee some sort of a response from the banks. He just hoped it would prove both swift enough and forceful enough.

He watched as Jen and Leesa, anonymous in their suits, floated away from *Raider* and towards the stricken Night Hammer ship, the flare of their manoeuvring rockets blinking on and off sporadically. This time his staying behind wasn't so hard to accept. He had a purpose beyond simply waiting around and fretting. *Sabre 1* seemed to be preparing to leave the system as agreed, and Drake could see no reason for them to do otherwise, but he'd still breathe a sigh of relief when they were gone and no longer posed a threat to the Night Hammer ship that had come close to destroying them.

The two women appeared to move in slow motion, the weightlessness of the environment lending their actions a deceptive sense of languid grace. Despite this, they covered the distance in surprisingly short order, almost catching Drake by surprise as they reached the hull of *Darkness Mourning* and declared, "Okay, we're at the airlock. About to go in."

At almost the same moment, Mosi spoke, the voice emanating eerily from the still-slack face, his mouth working in isolation from the rest of his features. Apart from that, his frame remained frozen in place; this wasn't Mosi returning, it was Naj communicating through his physical anchor. Drake had seen this a couple of times before and it never failed to unsettle him. The voice emerged in a flat monotone, devoid of inflection, which only made the words it uttered all the more chilling.

"Captain, help. We're trapped."

Six

Captain, help! We're trapped. Mosi had no way of telling whether the message got through. He thought it did, but by then things were starting to fall apart.

Matters seemed to go well enough to start with. They found ops where it ought to be according to the ship's blueprints – maybe Night Hammers lacked the imagination to make modifications, or, more likely, they weren't permitted to.

One thing that did come as a surprise was how few people there seemed to be on board. True, the crew might have been confined to quarters during what was clearly an emergency, but apart from the two torchbearers in the corridor they had encountered no one until they arrived at ops, and here they found just the captain and three other officers. Unlike the *Ion Raider*, where ops was an afterthought appended to the cramped cockpit/bridge, this was a warship with a custom built ops room that could have accommodated three times this number with ease. Besides, when the ship came under attack, shouldn't all personnel have hurried to their stations, including those assigned to ops?

It was clear immediately that the *Raider*'s attack had been more effective than they could possibly have hoped. Almost none of the systems were up and the room was bathed in a wan light that could only be fuelled by emergency power.

The captain wasn't backward in venting his frustration. "For gods' sake get me some information!" he stormed. "Visuals, readings, some-bloody-thing. That tin crate could be up to anything out there."

"Yes, sir!" The sharp reply came from a broad-shouldered woman occupying the command chair while the captain paced behind her.

"Taken out by a puny little trader without us even firing a shot!" the captain continued. "Correct me if I'm wrong, but we are supposed to be a warship, aren't we? A Night Hammer ship."

"Yes, sir!"

"Then how about we show them that, Number One? How about we *retaliate*!" He visibly took a grip of himself and said, far more calmly, "How long before we have eyes, any sort of eyes?"

"I'm working on it, sir. Whatever they hit us with... I've never seen anything like it, sir. It wreaked havoc with systems I didn't even know we had – external comms, sensors, weapons, they're all down. I'm trying to rig..."

"Number One, what is the one thing I detest most in this whole gods-forsaken universe?"

"Excuses, sir."

"Excuses. *So stop giving them to me and deliver results.*"

"Sir!"

Mosi felt a small swell of pride. In taking down a warship the size of *Darkness Mourning*, *Raider* had been a minnow standing up to a shark, albeit a minnow with an oversized bite.

The woman, Number One, hunched a little further forward – as defensive a posture as Mosi had ever seen – her hands were a blur as she summoned up screens and data fields which were instantly dismissed to be replaced by more. Whether or not any of this would help her fulfil the captain's orders seemed debatable to Mosi, but she was making a point of trying to do so. Her deft machine-rapid movements along with the crescent-shaped silver implant visible on the left side of her head – not quite hidden by the sweep of her hair – suggested a level of augmentation illegal since the Auganics Wars.

"Mr Pine?" The captain paused in his pacing to hover over the room's other occupant, a wire-framed man hunched over a jury-rigged work station

"Still nothing, Captain. As Number One says, whatever they hit us with has burned out systems and sub-routines all over the place. I'm trying to build a new command pathway by determining what's left and rerouting. It should be possible to cobble something together, but I'm working blind."

"Again, spare me the excuses, Mr Pine."

"Sir."

The desperate nature of what Mosi saw here meant that they could relax. Blinded as they clearly were, the Night Hammers would never see Leesa and Jen coming.

"True, but that's not the point," Naj said in response to the thought. "Our job is to make sure the Night Hammers are in no position to interfere, remember?"

She was right, of course.

"Okay," he acknowledged. "Let's do this."

His instinct would have been to take out the captain first, but Naj was in charge and she evidently had other ideas. She closed on the officer the captain had addressed as Pine.

"Don't you think the senior officer should be our priority?" Mosi said.

"No. Pine is the one working directly on getting their systems back up, which makes him the biggest threat to Hel N and Shadow. We take him out first and then move on to the others."

She made it sound so simple.

"It will be," she whispered to him.

She phased into physical form immediately behind her target, gripping the back of his head and slamming it into the instrument boards in front of him: once, twice, in rapid succession, all her strength and weight behind the actions. Naj had no enhanced strength like Hel N, nor did she have Shadow's agility and combat skills, but Mosi had been trained extensively by Jen, and what he knew Naj knew, so she was far from helpless.

Before anyone else in the room could react she was gone, phasing back into her natural state and leaving the Night Hammer, Pine, to slide to the floor, unconscious or worse.

There was shouting: the captain barking orders and hurrying across to his stricken officer.

Naj took advantage, emerging into solid form to trip and

push, using the captain's own momentum to topple him over, but he landed and rolled and found his feet again in one movement.

She had already disappeared, but Mosi could sense that it had surprised her. "They're good," she noted.

"Told you."

"Change of plan. Let's concentrate on taking out whatever equipment the woman in the command seat has. We don't need to fight them directly to blind them."

Mosi couldn't have agreed more.

The woman hadn't moved, as if whatever she was doing in that chair was too important to interrupt, no matter the incentive. All the more reason they *should* interrupt, by Mosi's way of thinking.

It was as Naj phased back into the physical beside the woman that the world skewed impossibly around them. Suddenly shapes elongated, seeming to stretch upwards for eternity, and colours fractured into rainbow hues that swirled and bled towards the heavens. Most alarming of all, they couldn't move.

"Naj!" he screamed. "Phase out."

"I... I can't." He could hear the panic in her voice. "I can't phase back *or* manifest fully in the physical. We're trapped."

How was that even possible?

"Captain, help!" Naj called through him.

Jen had spent the weightless crossing between ships working hard to convince herself that this was just another mission. So far, it wasn't working. Firstly, because she had always hated EVA work; secondly, because this was a Night Hammer ship.

"Are you okay?" Leesa asked as they approached the warship's airlock. Leesa was fully aware of the first reason she might not be, though not necessarily the second.

"Yes, I'm fine," Jen lied.

They reached *Darkness Mourning*'s hull, their suits' pulsed manoeuvrings softening the impact as they arrived beside the airlock, the touch-tech in their gloves anchoring them in place.

"Okay, we're at the airlock," Leesa reported to Raider. "About to go in."

They'd already ruled out any help from Raider. The AI wasn't able to access the other ship's systems, which had either crashed spectacularly or were shielded too well; quite possibly both.

Leesa attached a hand-sized bulbous disc to the airlock door. It was something Jen had seen her use before, a device designed by Raider which enabled the augmented side of her friend to reach out into other mechanisms – designed by an Elder aspect but built by humans; did that mean it qualified as Elder tech or not? Jen quashed the pointless semantics, recognising it as an avoidance mechanism, a means of distracting herself from what came next.

The outer airlock door slid open and they dragged themselves inside. Just as it was closing, a further message came through from Cornische: "Lees, Jen, Geminum is in trouble."

"What sort of trouble?"

"Unclear, but she's in ops and would seem to be trapped in some way."

Leesa cursed.

"Told you Mosi wasn't ready for this," Jen said before she could stop herself.

"Recriminations later, okay?" Cornische replied.

He was right; their priorities now were to help Naj and complete the mission. In that order.

It seemed to take an age for the inner door to open, though in truth it was only a matter of seconds. Their EVA suits were comparatively light and flexible, so not much of an encumbrance, but they shucked them anyway, not wanting to risk their being damaged in what was essentially hostile territory despite whatever Geminum might have achieved. Leesa then led the way at a run, Jen at her heels.

The corridor was dark, power evidently down, so Jen activated her suit's torch, low illumination – just enough to stop her from cannoning into a bulkhead or tripping over some low-level obstruction. Leesa, she knew, would have no such worries.

Leesa stopped abruptly. "Kill the light," she whispered. "There's someone coming."

Jen did so without hesitation, knowing Leesa's augmented senses were far keener than hers. She felt a familiar excitement welling up inside her. "Show me the way," she whispered in turn. "I'm in the mood."

They continued, a little more cautiously in the pitch dark, and soon Jen could make out the glow of a torch, wavering in intensity as if it were a hand-held or suit-mounted device in motion.

Ahead, dimly outlined in the erratic glow, she could make out a bulkhead, where the corridor they were travelling ended, intersecting another. The light seemed to emanate from around the corner to their right. Voices, too, so more than one and, whoever they were – presumably Night Hammers – they felt secure; and why wouldn't they? This was their ship, after all. If the systems were as crippled as they seemed to be, there would be nothing to warn the crew that they'd been boarded.

Close now. The intersection was almost upon them, and the voices were distinct enough to make out individual words – an ongoing moan about some officer or other. Jen gripped Leesa's shoulder and pointed insistently towards the left hand corridor, then tapped her own chest and indicated the right.

Leesa nodded her understanding: she would continue to ops to help Naj and Mosi, leaving Jen to catch up once she'd dealt with things here.

Jen stepped into shadow. Normally when she crossed, the world became a few shades duller, her senses blunted by the shift, but under these circumstances, crossing in darkness, sight at least was enhanced: she could see.

Hugging the nearest wall, she slipped around the corner, aware of Leesa starting out in the opposite direction. There were two of them, both men, ambling along the corridor without a care in the world.

"Hey!" one of them called out, clearly alarmed, having caught sight of Leesa in his torchlight. "Who the hell are y...?"

Jen was upon him before he could finish the final word.

She came off the wall, crossing back into physical reality with knives drawn. The thrill of combat coursed through her veins, powering her muscles as she plunged both point-first into the man who had spoken, giving him no chance to react.

Night Hammer uniform, she had time to note with satisfaction as she drew the uniquely constituted blades across and out, ripping flesh and material alike, leaving her first target to collapse to the deck.

No slouch, this second one. He had leapt back, buying himself precious seconds to assess and react. His own knife was out, held with practised confidence in his right hand.

A fixed blade – longer than hers, so giving him greater reach – with smart handle to accommodate the user's grip, a quillon to protect the hand holding it, and, she knew from experience, a wickedly sharp edge. A combat knife, standard Night Hammer issue; a professional's weapon but a toy when compared to the two she wielded.

She wasn't about to underestimate him, though, and closed warily. As she did so, a small 3D image appeared, to hover over his right arm. He'd activated his tattoogram, summoning the image of Mjölnir – ancient Thor's mallet – the badge of the Night Hammers, which was implanted subdermally in the arm of every successful recruit when they joined the regiment. A tried and trusted tactic, meant to distract and spread fear due to the Hammers' reputation. Big mistake. She laughed, tightening the flexor muscle in her own right forearm, causing an identical projection to rise and hover above it.

"Snap!" she said. And struck.

To his credit, he recovered swiftly from what must have been a shock, parrying her thrust, blade on blade, and leaping backwards. A sudden memory distracted her for an instant – another one-to-one knife fight with an assassin who had just blown up the cosy farmhouse she'd called home back when this all started. Had he been Night Hammer too?

The slight pause gave her opponent a fraction of a second to reassess, and he must have realised that his helmet light made him a target. So he switched it off.

Jen could appreciate the logic; they were both in the dark now, which ought to make for a level playing field. Not his fault that in this instance the opposite was true. She felt a moment of pity tinged with a vague sense of disappointment, having relished the prospect of a proper contest. It seemed a shame. Almost.

She slipped into shadow, immediately seeing the Night Hammer in stark relief. He remained in a fighter's crouch, facing where she had just been, right hand holding his knife before him, left arm raised in defence; presumably he was straining to hear the faintest noise that might give her away.

She didn't make one, instead stepping out of shadow at the last possible instant, her knives already in motion. She struck with both blades simultaneously. Night Hammer uniforms were designed to provide a degree of protection to the throat and neck region, particularly at the base of the skull. Whilst her blades were more than capable of breaching that, she opted to play the percentages, aware that once she reverted to physical form she'd be blind. Her initial aim, therefore, had to be true. A slight movement of his head could have caused a neck shot to miss by a fraction, skidding off the protective collar or merely inflicting a shallow flesh wound. The kidneys were more vulnerable and offered a more certain target.

Jen didn't miss. One blade sliced into the man's wrist, killing nerves and severing tendons, sending his own weapon clattering to the deck, whilst the other plunged into his side, sliding between ribs to puncture a kidney. She felt him stiffen, and then sag.

There was nothing kind in the way she pulled the knife out — this was a Night Hammer, who doubtless deserved all he was getting. She left him dying in a pool of his own blood, diving back into shadow and racing in pursuit of Leesa. Geminum needed them.

Leesa hurried towards ops, ignoring the call of "Hey!" from behind her. After sparing a glance to confirm there were only two in the party she dismissed them from her thoughts, confident that Shadow could handle them.

If anyone else lay in wait between here and ops, well... more fool them. As she went, Hel N's suit flowed upwards to cover her.

Leesa's aug enabled her to move swiftly, picking up on tiny amounts of illumination from winking alarms, dulled warning lights and digital displays wherever they were to be found.

The sounds of combat from behind dogged her progress at first, but otherwise she might have been moving through a ghost ship. No other sounds, no signs of life.

That changed as she drew closer to what could only be ops.

Voices. Echoing down the deserted corridor, the individual words were impossible to distinguish, even for her, but the tone made it apparent that someone was barking out orders, and Leesa could well imagine who they related to. She quickened her pace, as a low glow of illumination appeared ahead, drawing her on.

She burst into ops – there was no time for subtlety – her sudden appearance clearly taking those present by surprise. *Slack; I thought these people were supposed to be professionals...* Three Night Hammers, a fourth crumpled on the deck unmoving.

To her left, close by the command chair occupied by a woman of indeterminate age – presumably the ship's captain or a senior officer – stood a column of amber light, stretching from deck to ceiling. Not incandescent, not even bright, but clearly defined all the same. Trapped within its glow was a figure: Naj.

Somehow they must have caught her in the middle of a phase shift, leaving her stranded neither here nor there, frozen in place like a specimen pinned to a board.

All of this Leesa noted in an instant, while momentum carried her into the room. The man nearest her— who might have been security – reacted first, attempting to draw a weapon. *What type of gun would they risk here, in ops,* she wondered. Not that it mattered. She changed direction slightly and was on him before he could bring the gun to bear.

One hand clutched his arm, making sure the weapon stayed out of play, while with the other she punched him in the throat. There was protection here, but not enough. She felt the shielding buckle and her fist continued, crushing his windpipe. The gun she snatched from his hand, tossing it away even as she flung him against the nearest bulkhead.

Shadow must have arrived during the scuffle. "I've got the captain," she heard Jen call. "You take care of the woman."

Leesa looked up to see Jen confronting the older man who stood behind the command chair. So that was the captain rather than the woman; not that it mattered. He held one arm a little awkwardly, and Leesa guessed that Shadow had already marked him with her blades. He wasn't backing down, though, brandishing a knife in his good hand as he squared up to Jen, who was grinning in a way Leesa knew all too well.

She switched her attention to the female officer, who had risen from the chair and was stepping towards her. She clutched something in her left hand, an object that resembled an elaborate knuckle duster – shaped to fit across each of four fingers but with a flat matt top.

She levelled the device, pointing it at Leesa. An unseen fist slammed into Leesa's chest, hurling her backwards to crash into the bulkhead. She slid down to the deck and sat there for a moment, winded. It was like being hit by Ramrod. *A repellor field,* she realised, similar to the one housed in Drake's cane, and it kicked like a mule.

The Night Hammer hit her with the repellor again, crushing her against the bulkhead, and it *hurt*. Even with the resilience of her auganic nature and the protection afforded by being Hel N, she could feel the aching pressure of the blow bruising her chest, compressing her organs. A stark reminder if any were needed that she wasn't invulnerable. Hard to kill, yes, but not impossible.

Bracing her back against the bulkhead, Leesa struggled to her feet, glaring at the Night Hammer. At the same time, she felt something, an irritation at the back of her mind, an itch that wasn't physical but which stirred memories she never expected to revisit.

Then she saw it – the silvery crescent of an implant behind the Night Hammer's left ear. *She's augmented*, Leesa realised. She reached out through her own aug, seeing surprise on the woman's face as she sensed the contact. Leesa had her measure at once; not auganic, this was far cruder and more basic – an attempt to emulate auganic enhancement without sufficient skill or knowledge to duplicate the procedure.

It was enough, though, to provide a way in.

Leesa tightened her mental grip, and twisted.

The woman screamed. She staggered backwards, both hands rising to clutch her own skull as Leesa continued to exert pressure. She collapsed onto her knees, her eyes screwed shut.

Leesa strode forward to stand in front of the stricken woman, and promptly punched her in the face.

"Thank goodness for that," Jen said as the woman toppled over. "Her screaming was really starting to piss me off."

Jen still had both blades out. She stood over the fallen figure of the Night Hammer captain, who wasn't breathing as far as Leesa could tell. At the same moment, the column of amber light winked out, allowing the slight form of Geminum to collapse to the deck.

Leesa stared, fascinated. Even when the Angels were together the first time around she had rarely seen Naj in person – twice, by her recollection, and no more than fleeting glimpses on either occasion – it was always Mosi.

Jen was across almost before Naj hit the floor, crouching down to tend to her. The contrast between the blood lust that came over Jen in combat and the tenderness, the compassion, that was her natural default the rest of the time never ceased to amaze Leesa.

"I didn't know she could stay physical for this long."

"I don't think she can, normally," Jen replied. "And please don't ask me what that means or even whether it means anything at all, because I've no idea. Good work switching off that column of light, by the way."

"I didn't. Not directly, in any case. I think it must have been linked in some way to the woman officer's aug. When I knocked her out, it shut down as well."

Naj moaned, and moved her head.

"Geminum," Jen said. "It's over. You're free."

Her eyes flickered open and she stared up, frowning. "Jen?"

"Yes, I'm here with Hel N. Can you sit up?"

"If you help, maybe. I've never experienced anything like that before…" she added, as Jen supported her in sitting upright. "I feel sick. Hell, and now I'm slipping out of phase…"

"Geminum, get back home to Raider," Leesa said quickly.

"But we can help you scavenge the parts you need," Naj/Mosi said.

Ever the mechanic. "I know you can," she said out loud, "but I'm also capable of doing it without you, so get lost. You've done your bit, leave the rest to us."

Naj nodded and then blinked out, leaving Jen crouching and empty handed. She looked up to meet Leesa's gaze, turning her empty hands over and back. "Now that was weird." She stood up. "Are you ready to head down to engineering? The sooner we can get back to *Raider* the better."

"No argument from me on that score," Leesa said. "Can you get through to Raider?" It would have been reassuring to know that Geminum had returned safely to Mosi's body, but Jen shook her head.

"Nor can I," Leesa admitted; she had asked more in hope than expectation. "The shielding must be too heavy. Let's go look at those engines so we can get the hell out of here."

"Count me in," Jen said. Her role would be to ride shotgun, watching Leesa's back in case any more Night Hammers showed up, while she scavenged the engine parts they needed.

"We can check on Mosi and Naj from the airlock once we're done," Leesa said as they left ops. "We *know* Raider can hear us from there."

Drake started as Mosi screamed, his arms thrashing and body convulsing. True, it was a sign of life, but they might have hoped for something a little less dramatic.

Saavi reached him first. "Mosi, it's okay, you're back on *Raider*."

The screaming and the thrashing stopped, to be replaced by heaving chest and gasping breaths.

"Saavi...?" The relief that simple word of recognition brought surprised Drake. He'd only just started to reunite the Angels, and couldn't face the prospect of losing any of them so soon.

"Sorry," Mosi said, calming down. "I thought something had gone wrong and we were back there."

"What happened?" Drake asked.

"The Night Hammers trapped us, somehow, I don't *know* how, but we couldn't move, couldn't phase either out or in."

"Hel N and Shadow?"

"They got us out. We left them to complete the mission and came back here, but the crossing felt different. Sorry for the screaming, but for an awful moment I thought we were there again, trapped." He shuddered.

"Go get some rest," Drake said, knowing how much projecting over distance took out of Geminum.

Mosi shook his head. "Later, maybe, but not until I know Jen and Leesa are safe."

They all waited, which was enough to convince Drake that next time he was going on the mission, whatever it might be. He simply wasn't cut out to wait around while others took the risks.

Eventually, the call came through. "Captain?"

"Leesa! Is everything okay?"

"Yes, all good. We got what we came for and are heading back now. Is Geminum with you?

"Yes, a little shaken but he's fine."

Before long the away team were back on board. While Raider took the ship away from *Darkness Mourning*, everyone headed to the galley for some well-deserved relaxation with a side order of alcohol, apart from Mosi, who was excused for a lie down. Both Leesa and Jen were in high spirits – and why shouldn't they be?

Drake remained keen to hear details of the recent mission.

"So this trap that snared Geminum," he said, "was it designed specifically for that, do you think? Or was it just something they had handy which they tried and it worked?"

"Not sure," Jen replied.

"If you want my best guess," Leesa said, "it was specifically designed with Geminum in mind. What Mosi does is so unusual I don't see how it could be otherwise. I mean, what else would you be looking to trap with it but someone shifting between states?"

Drake had been thinking much the same, which, if true, was a worrying development.

"We know they've been working closely with Donal," Jen said, "so presumably he could have provided some inside knowledge on who we are and how we operate."

Drake nodded. "And they've had plenty of time to prepare for us. We know Saflik have been hunting down Dark Angels for years, so it probably shouldn't come as a surprise that they've developed countermeasures for some of us."

"Yeah, but that specific and that effective?"

"Do you think the same trap would have caught you?" he asked.

"I'm not sure," Jen admitted. "And I don't intend going back to find out."

"Your abilities are very different from Geminum's..." Drake said.

"But they both involve switching between physical states,"

Leesa finished for him. "A snare that could immobilise both of you... Now there's a sobering thought." And she took another slug of beer.

"And you're sure there were just the six Night Hammers aboard?

Jen nodded. "Yeah, while Leesa scavenged what she needed from the engines, I went into shadow and scoured the whole ship. There were no others."

"Skeleton crew," Drakes murmured. It didn't take a genius to work out where the rest would be. *Lenbya*. It brought home the urgency of their endeavours all over again.

Saavi was with them but stayed at the fringes of the conversation. She didn't indulge in alcohol, which might have been part of the reason, but Drake sensed it was more than that. She had seemed more like her old self during the mission, when it was just the two of them in ops, but judging by her current expression the weight of recent events had started to prey on her thoughts again. She listened intently as they talked, her hand resting on the head of Jai, currently configured as a metallic dog, as if to seek reassurance, but contributed little.

After a while, she excused herself and went to leave.

"Saavi, are you okay?" Drake said.

"Yes, Captain, fine. Just a few things I want to check up on in the cloud chamber."

"Maybe share that bit about being fine with your face," Leesa suggested. "Only it doesn't seem to have got the message."

Cloud shot her a sullen glare.

The last thing Drake wanted was for Saavi to lose faith in her own abilities, to start second guessing herself to such a degree that she stopped passing her insights on to the rest of them. They needed her unfiltered guidance or it was inevitable they'd miss something. "You were right to bring us here, Saavi," he said quietly.

"You think?" she said, showing a rare flash of passion. "To get Raider disabled and Mosi almost killed... How can that possibly be *right?*"

"Nobody said any of this was going to be simple, Saavi," Jen said. "With the way things are going, we aren't likely to face many straight forward options and there'll be fewer and fewer pain-free choices to be made, but we know you'll always pick the best from a bad bunch. The rest of us can't do that, just you."

"Yeah, and look on the bright side," Leesa added. "At least no one got killed."

Saavi snorted. "So is that how we judge success these days: 'no one got killed'?"

"Sometimes, yes."

"There are worse criteria," Drake said quickly, not wishing to see the exchange between Cloud and Leesa escalate. "Because we were here and *Sabre 1* was here, others are now alerted to what's going on. It's not just us against the universe any more."

"Assuming anyone believes you," Leesa said.

"Oh, they'll believe me all right," *at least some of them will*. "It's whether or not they can agree on what to do about it that concerns me." He turned back to Saavi. "But if you hadn't brought us here, we would still be alone in this, with no allies, no hope of help."

"We still are, if you ask me," Leesa said. "So stop blaming yourself for things that aren't your fault, will you?" She grinned, softening the words. The tension between them had evaporated as swiftly as it flared up. "And get your arse back into that room of mists of yours. We need to know where we're headed next."

Saavi seemed reassured and almost smiled. "All right then," she said. "Remember, though, you asked for it, so don't blame me…"

"We don't!" said more than one voice in chorus.

"Okay, okay. I'm on my way."

Seven

"This is Sullivan Control calling Comet class transport on approach vector four delta seven. Please confirm your identity."

Drake and Leesa had the helm. They exchanged uneasy glances. Whatever this might be, it wasn't normal. They were still showing the false hull ident configured by Raider to get them into the Callia system, which mimicked the code of one of the scrapped Comet class vessels abandoned at the yard where the ship had lain hidden for a decade. In theory, they were an unremarkable if aging ship which any port authority should just wave through without a second glance. So why the challenge? Had they been unlucky, adopting the identity of a ship that was remembered at this port for some historical misdeed?

Drake bit his lip. Only one way to find out, and to delay replying any longer would just invite further suspicion.

"Sullivan Control, this is the *Blue Angel*, on route from Callia III. Is there a problem of some kind?"

The time lag as they waited for a response seemed interminable. Eventually the reply came back. "We hope not, *Blue Angel*. It's just that according to our records your ship was decommissioned years ago."

"Somebody keeps their ship registration list up to date," Leesa muttered sub-voce.

"I don't know about that," Drake replied to Sullivan. "I haven't had her long. Bought her from a dealer in the New Sparta system. It all seemed perfectly legit."

"No doubt there's a simple explanation, *Blue Angel*, but it is an issue we'll need to clear up. Please remain aboard your ship once you've docked and be ready for inspection."

"Is that strictly necessary, Sullivan Control? We're on a tight schedule and not intending to stay long. We'll be out of your hair before you even know we've landed."

"That's as maybe, *Blue Angel*, but there are protocols that have to be observed in a situation like this. We'll process everything as swiftly as possible."

"Thank you, Sullivan, that would be appreciated."

Drake broke the connection.

"For Elder's sake!" Leesa exclaimed. "Now what do we do?"

Good question. They'd have a hard time explaining either the artefact room or the cloud chamber to an inspection team. "Think quickly," was all he said aloud; then, "Raider, how long until we dock?"

"Not long enough," Leesa said before Raider could reply.

They touched down at the allotted berth and waited. Drake had been busy during their approach, as had Raider, though to what effect remained to be seen. Together they had pulled apart financial histories and chased down connections that were never meant to be found easily, then they had made a flurry of calls. Some went unanswered, some were rebuffed with contempt or even anger. Drake seemed to take it all in his stride and just moved onto the next on the list. They were past the point of worrying about whose feathers they ruffled. One or two of those calls, however, showed some promise. Whether or not that promise bore fruit they would discover in the next few moments.

Leesa could do nothing during all this other than stand by and watch, feeling like a spare part and wishing there was some way in which she could help, but knowing that she'd only get in the way.

Drake let her take the ship in, perhaps sensing her need to contribute. They were all there in ops as the ship made port, the whole crew. As far as she knew, there was no Plan B. If this didn't work they were royally screwed.

"I hate this waiting," Jen murmured into the silence that gathered weight following their arrival.

"Yeah, whoever said 'patience is a virtue' must have been trying to convince themselves first and foremost," Leesa said.

"At least no one's tried to board us."

"Yet," Leesa couldn't resist adding.

As an afterthought, she looked across at Saavi and gave what she hoped was a reassuring smile. The kid's confidence had been shaken by the Night Hammer incident. Saavi's gaze was fixed firmly forward, however, and she didn't seem to notice.

"Incoming call," Raider reported, just as Leesa wondered how much more of this she could take.

"Sullivan Control to *Blue Angel*, I've been instructed to inform you that you have one day's grace in which to conclude whatever business you have here – that's one day local time. If you're still in port a minute after that, an inspection team will board you without further notice."

A collective sigh greeted the words.

"Thank you, Sullivan Control, your terms have been duly noted," Drake replied.

"You have some powerful friends, *Blue Angel*, that's all I can say. You're free to disembark. Don't overstay your welcome."

"Understood."

"Thank fuck for that," Leesa allowed herself once the connection was broken.

Almost immediately, another call came in, visual on this occasion.

They were confronted by a pale woman whose face bore the alabaster perfection of rejuve, her hair pulled back in a tight bun, while her dark eyes looked fit to burn someone to cinders.

"Well, Mister Drake, I've ensured the hounds remain leashed for now, at any rate. Don't make me regret doing so."

"I won't, Councillor, and thank you. First Solar is grateful for your assistance."

Assistance which had only been secured by Drake leaning heavily on the fact that her campaign was largely reliant on First Solar's funding. Leesa was coming to appreciate just how far the tendrils of New Sparta's influence, and the banking system it represented, spread. They didn't need an official presence on a world in order to exert their will. She found the implications... disturbing.

"They'd better be," the councillor said. "And let this be an end to it. If you cause trouble or fall foul of any local laws, don't reach out to me again. I won't respond. This is an election year and I have no intention of being embroiled in a scandal, so after this you're on your own. Do I make myself clear?"

"Perfectly."

Her image winked out.

"Nice lady," Jen remarked. "She's got my vote."

"You can't really judge her on that," Drake said. "An election year means she'll be under pressure, and we've just turned that up a few notches, but I know what you mean."

"At least she took your call," Mosi pointed out, "and did what you asked of her, however reluctantly."

"True," Drake said. "So let's not waste the time she's bought us." He turned to Saavi. "Cloud, you're confident of where we need to go?"

"Yes, for once the reading is mercifully unambiguous."

"A bar," Leesa said, "now there's a surprise."

"Ten minutes' walk from the port," Saavi confirmed. "A place called the Spacer's Lament."

"I like the sound of it already."

"And it's definitely a man we're meant to find there," Drake said, going over everything one final time with a thoroughness Leesa found reassuring. *The captain's well and truly back with us.*

"Yes," Saavi said, "but I can't see his face, no matter how hard I try to focus."

"Not to worry, "said Jen. "I'm sure we'll recognise him – it'll be another former Angel, presumably."

"Has to be."

"And, Raider, you can direct us?" Drake said.

"Indeed."

"We're set then." Drake nodded towards her. "Lees, Jen, you're with me. Mosi, stay here with Saavi. Jen, you're to be our back up, so hang back and keep out of sight."

"My speciality."

"Mosi, Saavi, stay alert. This all sounds straight forward enough but let's not take anything for granted."

"One thing," Saavi said at the last moment. "Can you keep any eye open for anything relating to a narwhal – a sign, an emblem, a drawing, graffiti… whatever."

Leesa had no idea what she was on about, nor, she suspected, did anyone else.. "What's a narwhal?" she said.

"It's a mythical beast from Old Earth; think huge fish with a unicorn's horn for a nose."

"Sounds bizarre, but will do."

"Is this important, Saavi?" the captain asked.

"I don't know," she admitted. "The narwhal keeps cropping up in the timelines but I can't figure out the significance, except that it seems to be a blockage of some kind – things go haywire around it and I can't get a handle on what lies beyond. I can't even say for sure if it's on this world or not, but it's somewhere, and yes, I think it *is* important."

Drake nodded. "Okay, we'll let you know."

As the captain and Jen left ops, Leesa lingered for a moment, seeing a sour smile on Mosi's face.

"You all right, Mosi?"

"Fine, it's just Naj moaning about being sidelined."

"You took point last time out, remember? Now it's someone else's turn."

"That's what I told her."

"Besides, the captain's been itching to take the lead in something now that he's recovered. Who are we to deny him?"

"I told her that, too, but she's still moaning."

"Same old Naj. I've missed her."

"So have I, Lees, so have I."

Things had not been going well for Nate Almont. Ever since he returned from Xter space with Pelquin and the rest of the *Comet*'s crew, matters seemed to have slipped away from him somehow. It was funny: you spent much of your life chasing a dream, only to discover when you finally caught up with it that the chase had been the fun part. The dream itself fell way short of expectations.

Pelquin and Bren: who could have seen that one coming? Certainly not Nate, and he'd thought he knew them better than anyone. It seemed fitting that they'd been brought together by imminent death at the hands of zombie alien spacesuits, but he would have preferred them never to have got together at all.

As a consequence, he was reduced to this: sitting in a nondescript bar in a nondescript town on a nondescript world nursing a glass of deep amber spirit with a kick only marginally less lethal than that of the zombie spacesuits.

Oh, everything had seemed fine to begin with. Wealth wasn't about to change them, no sir – they were still the same tightly bound bunch of devil-may-care adventurers they'd always been.

Like hell.

Even after paying the heavy fines levied against them for the ship's precipitous departure from New Spartan airspace, there was still plenty of profit from the Elder cache to share around. They might not have been flush enough to rub shoulders with the upper echelons of New Spartan society, but they each had plenty by anyone's standards. Looking back, it was naïve to think that prosperity wouldn't change the dynamic, to expect everything to continue as it had before with their appetite for new adventures undiminished, but somehow he had.

Leesa, their latest recruit, had been the first to bail out. Nate still wasn't entirely sure of her reasons, except that she had grown increasingly pre-occupied, even as Pelquin and Bren became ever more lost within their burgeoning relationship.

Monkey was the next to go. He had always had a thing for Bren, beneath all their banter and teasing, and seeing her so wrapped up in someone else must have proven too much for him to take. Nate was only too aware of how that felt.

New crew were taken on, but it wasn't the same; this wasn't

his crew any more. Then it had been Nate's turn to quit. There was nothing special about the world – just the latest port of call at which they were collecting goods to move on elsewhere and sell at a small profit – he simply couldn't bear it any more. His anger and frustration were proving increasingly difficult to master, while he couldn't honestly have pointed at a single cause. It was either leave or start hitting things – his old friend Pelquin, most likely, while screaming in his face *don't you remember what happened with Julia?*

So this time, when *Pelquin's Comet* moved on, Nate stayed behind. Pel hadn't even tried to stop him, not really. Perhaps he too sensed that this was the right time for them to go their separate ways.

"No more being dragged off to shady restaurants to sample the local 'delicacies' for me, then," Pel had said, and for a moment Nate sensed their old connection, but it was little more than a fading echo.

"Guess not," he said. "Just a steady diet of pre-programmed authochef meals to look forward to from here on in."

"Sounds like a win win to me."

"Why are you still doing this, Pel?" Couldn't he see that since the cache find they were just going through the motions, that his heart was no longer really in it?

"Because I don't know how to do anything else," which was the most honest thing Nate had heard from him in a long while. The moment evaporated. "Take care of yourself, Nate."

"You too."

Out of all of them, Bren had seemed the most upset, as if she sensed the finality of his going; a line had been drawn, which there was no stepping back from.

"Are you sure about this, Nate?" she said.

He was sure.

"You'll always have a home here… Don't forget us."

He never would, but the *Comet* didn't feel like home to him, not any more. So here he was, sitting in the aptly named Spacer's

Lament bar, facing the imminent prospect of alcoholic oblivion because it postponed the need to wonder what the hell he should do next.

He still had enough credit to ensure that oblivion could last a good long while if he wanted, but that wasn't his style – it never had been. Having said that, there was no rush; it wasn't as if he had anywhere to be…

Nate paid little attention when somebody sat down on the stool to his left, but when a second figure claimed the seat immediately to his right a split second later, defensive instincts kicked in. He didn't look up, not immediately. It might be perfectly innocent but his gut said otherwise. A shakedown, or something more violent?

Male to his left, female to his right, he could sense that much. Lifting his glass with steady hand, he glanced to the right as casually as he could manage… and froze, the drink poised partway to his lips.

"*Leesa*? What in Elders' name are you doing here?"

"Hello, Nate, fancy bumping into you in a place like this. Is that whisky as rough as it smells?"

"Rougher."

"Sounds right up your street then, Lees," said the man to his left. He knew that voice too, and his heart sank at sound of it.

"Drake." Someone up there must really have it in for him.

"Small universe," said the banker.

"Not that small. What the hell is going on here?"

"We have a proposition for you."

Nate wasn't interested. He couldn't have cared less if he never set eyes on Drake again, but he was intrigued. So while Leesa waved the barman over and ordered a round of the tragic excuse for a whisky, he allowed the banker to lead him to a vacant table. There were plenty of those – it was still early and business at the Spacer's Lament was sluggish. Drake looked thinner than he remembered, a little frailer, as if he might actually need that ridiculous walking cane which he still carried.

Had these two really gone to all the trouble of tracing him to this tired bar on an unremarkable little world? It was hard to credit – and Nate had no idea how they could even have achieved such a thing – but it beat the alternative, namely that they had bumped into him purely by chance.

"When did you and Leesa hook up again?" he asked, to fill the silence until Leesa could join them.

"Only recently," Drake replied, which told him nothing. "She found me in the middle of nowhere," which tantalised more than it informed; Nate refused to be drawn in.

"Okay..." he started to say as Leesa plonked three tumblers of sloshing spirit in the middle of the table and claimed an empty seat between the two men. His attention focussed on the glasses for a moment. "Doubles?" he said, with less enthusiasm than he might.

"Of course."

"So tell me," he began again, "how did you track me down and why the hell did you bother?"

"Ah, therein lies the fun part," Leesa said, grinning. "We didn't *know* it was you we were tracking down."

"What the hell is that supposed to mean."

"Almont," Drake cut in. "What are you doing with your life right now?"

The question caught him off guard, and he replied, almost by defensive reflex, "Drinking."

"Alone," Drake pressed, "with, unless I miss my guess, the *Comet* not in port. Have you and the good captain had a falling out again?"

"Fuck off, Drake. I enjoy my own company, that's all, which is what I was busy doing until you two barged in."

"Boys, boys," Leesa said. "Play nicely. Nate, we came to this bar knowing there was somebody important we had to meet here. Then we saw you and realised why. How would you like to join us in bringing down an interstellar conspiracy and whipping the ass of a would-be alien overlord? How would you like to be a hero?"

Nate stared at her. "You *what?*"

They went outside. Nate wasn't entirely sure why he agreed to do so, except that he still wanted some answers and reckoned that playing along offered his best chance of getting them. Leesa led the way, taking them along the side of the building to a dingy alley that ran behind the bar.

Were they planning on attacking him after all, these two former shipmates – well, one shipmate and another who'd been forced upon them? Here, in a dank and dirty alley that reeked of piss? There was no one else in sight, no witnesses, and Nate tensed, half expecting the worst.

"We'd like you to meet a friend of ours," said Leesa.

"What friend? There's nobody…"

The words died on his lips as a shadow on the wall behind Leesa shifted disconcertingly. Nate's head whipped around to look behind him, but there was nothing there, nothing to cause that odd movement. He focussed on the shadow again. It seemed to be moving forward, away from the wall – which defied reason – and as it came it gathered substance and form, transforming into the figure of a woman: slender and incredibly feminine, moving with a grace that was almost mesmerising. She came to stand beside Leesa; a woman carved from black marble and then dipped in oil to judge by the way light rippled across her 'skin'.

"This is Shadow," Drake said.

"*Shadow?*" Nate blurted. "As in the Dark Angels?"

"Got it in one," Leesa said.

As he watched, still trying to process what he'd just seen, a film of silver rose from the ground, hugging Leesa's form as it flowed past her ankles and upwards, to cover her body rapidly from toe to head. The two women stood there and might almost have been twins in negative – yin and yang – one burnished silver, the other gleaming black, though Leesa was a little stockier, more solidly built.

"Hel N," Nate murmured.

"Oh you're *so* good at this," Leesa said, her voice emanating from the silver figure.

Nate's gaze shifted to Drake, who stood off to one side, a look of amusement on his face. *You're enjoying this, you bastard*, Nate realised. All he actually said was, "And that would make you...?"

Drake executed a deep bow with a flourish of extended arm. "Francis Hilary Cornische, Captain of the *Ion Raider*, at your service."

"No fucking way."

EIGHT

Leesa could not have been more surprised on seeing Nate when they entered the Spacer's Lament. There was no mistaking her former shipmate, who sat at the bar, hunched over a drink. He hadn't seen them as yet, apparently lost in his own thoughts.

The captain was a fraction behind her in the recognition stakes. "Is that...?"

"Yeah," she said. "Looks like it's not one of the old team we're here to make contact with after all, but a potential new recruit."

"So it would seem," the captain acknowledged. "Why does it have to be him, though? Bren I could understand – she used to be a soldier, and even Pelquin I could get used to in time, but *Almont?*"

"I know, the proverbial pain in the ass, but he does have his good points."

"You'll have to fill me in on those when we get a moment. I don't imagine you'll need longer than that." Drake drew a deep breath. "Okay, let's do this. You take the stool to his right, I'll go for the one on the left."

The meeting went much as anticipated, though Nate seemed in a particularly lary mood – enough to make her wonder how many of the crude local whiskies he had knocked back before they appeared. Despite this, they succeeded in coaxing him out to an alleyway, which wasn't obviously overlooked, to make the big reveal. The look on Nate's face as she summoned her suit from where it had gathered on the soles of her feet was priceless.

"So if the danger to humankind is as great as you say it is, why aren't the Dark Angels high-tailing it over to confront this threat rather than skittling around different worlds picking up flotsam like me?" Nate asked.

They were in ops, curiosity bringing everyone together to meet the new arrival, and Nate was clearly relishing being the centre of attention.

"Because we're not strong enough as yet," the captain said. "The Dark Angels scattered after I broke up the crew, and not all of them are proving easy to track down again, even with Cloud's input."

"And in the meantime, the bad guys have a free crack at breaking into this Lenbya place."

"Lenbya isn't without its defences, and Saflik haven't yet been able to make any real progress on that front."

"How can you be so sure?"

"Because Raider would know if they had."

"I *am* Lenbya," Raider chipped in, "or an aspect of it, and I can assure you that, for the moment, defences hold."

Cornische was doing his best to appear relaxed, but Leesa could sense that his patience was being tested, while Nate, for his part, seemed to be enjoying himself immensely, taking perverse pleasure in the captain having to court him.

"And you want *me* to join the Dark Angels," he said. "Stepping into a dead man's shoes, as it were."

"No one's forcing you, Nate," Leesa said quickly. "We're offering you the opportunity, that's all. If you don't want to accept, just say so and we'll be gone, leaving you to head straight back to the bar and whatever that excuse for a drink was."

"Of course," Jen joined in, "if you have somewhere else to be, we wouldn't dream of trying to keep you."

Nate stared at her for a moment. "As it happens, I am at a bit of a loose end right now. What were my choices again?"

"Don't push it, Nate," Leesa said. He really was milking this. "We're not that desperate for your company."

"Gabriel," Jen said with deliberation, "Siren – but both their skills are complex enough that they'd take a while to master, so neither would be ideal right now – Spirit, Helix, and Quill."

"Quill, he's the one who could shoot high velocity needles, right?"

"Yeah, they can punch through just about anything."

"Even so, it just sounds a little bit... lame to me," Nate said.

"That pretty much sums up Quill's personality, too," Mosi quipped – the pair had never got on. No one disagreed with him.

"There's always Ramrod," Leesa blurted out, the words escaping before she had the opportunity to back away from saying them. The comment drew a quizzical look from the captain. "Trust me, he definitely won't be coming back to us," she said in response, the words harder to voice than she would have liked.

She caught Jen's sympathetic expression and flashed her a quick smile by way of reassurance.

"Ramrod?" Nate's demeanour brightened visibly. "Now we're talking. He was always one of my favourite Dark Angels."

Leesa looked back at the captain to check that he was okay with the idea of replacing an Angel who was still alive. "That's... a possibility," he said, which was enough to set her mind at ease on that score. "We've got the harness, after all, which is where the power lies. It's just a question of whether you're the right man to wear it. Does this mean you're ready to accept our invitation?"

"Do I get a bit of time to mull this over?"

"No," Drake said. "We might have a little breathing space before Lenbya's walls come tumbling down, but not enough to fritter away. This is a one-time-only offer. Take it, or take your leave."

"Oh, what the hell? You've convinced me. I'm in," said Nate, with a grin that told Leesa he'd been intending to say yes all along.

The captain gave a curt nod. "In that case, Jen, please take our latest recruit to the artefact room."

Leesa felt relieved to be spared that particular task. As it was, seeing someone else in Kyle's gear was going to take some getting used to; she wasn't sure how she would have reacted to witnessing someone else encounter it for the first time.

She kept a tight rein on her emotions as she watched Jen lead Nate out of ops, glad when he disappeared from sight. There was another matter she needed to consider; something she had been trying to avoid ever since returning from the raid on *Darkness Mourning*, but which had been brought to the fore by the prospect of a new Ramrod. When she and Jen had gone to Babylon in a futile attempt to recruit Kyle, the original Ramrod, to their cause, he had triggered a device he referred to as a nullifier, which had suppressed her auganic side.

She had been reminded of it by the trap the Night Hammers had used to capture Geminum, and it seemed to her that parallels could be drawn between the two. Was there a link, or was she just being paranoid?

They knew that one former angel, Donal, had aligned himself with Saflik, might Kyle have done the same? It would certainly explain why he had been so blasé about the threat Saflik posed when Leesa and Jen had explained it to him, and why he refused to join them.

She baulked, though, at even considering the possibility: not *Kyle*, not the man she had shared so much of her life with. Unfortunately, she could imagine all too readily how Saflik – an interstellar criminal organisation – might have come into contact with Kyle, a local crime kingpin in la Gossa. Would he really have betrayed his former friends and shipmates? Much as she hated the idea, she couldn't completely dismiss it, and that fact saddened her.

Leesa decided to keep her suspicions to herself for now. She needed to ponder the matter further before sharing with the captain.

The first thing to confront Nate as the doors to the artefact room slid open was Captain Cornische.

He jerked backwards instinctively. "What the f…" before realising that what he saw wasn't a living thing at all, but a statue, a mannequin, so artfully rendered and posed that it looked as if the figure before him stood ready to leap into action at the door's opening.

"Yes, I know," Jen said as she brushed past him. "The captain hasn't reclaimed his coat, hat and boots as yet, but he will, he will. Come on, this way."

She led him to the left. The walls and floor, the very air, glowed white and bright to the point of making him squint a little, otherworldly in its impact. He noted a number of stands supporting items, and truncated stocky pillars which supported nothing at all, but he found it difficult to concentrate on details.

As they approached the nearest empty pillar, words appeared to hover above its top in gold letters: RAMROD.

"No chance of getting lost, at any rate," Nate said, mounting excitement making him loquacious – certainly not something he could usually be accused of.

Jen ignored him and simply passed her spread hand, palm downwards, over the top of the stand, just beneath the lettering, which promptly dissolved in a shower of glittering sparks. At her gesture, an alabaster bust rose from within the plinth, bearing Ramrod's unmistakeable helmet – no, not just a bust, because it continued to rise, revealing a pale and muscular torso. A mannequin: a figure which ended just below the waist and now appeared to be a seamless extension of the stand.

The torso was naked apart from a rigid-framed harness. Ramrod's paraphernalia could not have been simpler, consisting of a belt that circled the waist from which rose two flattened bars. They travelled up to curve over the shoulders and back down to join the belt once more. *Part harness, part cage*, Nate thought.

"Is this all of it?"

"Yes," Jen confirmed. "The rest – the bodysuit you're used to seeing – is generated by the harness."

He hesitated, still doubting any of this could possibly be real.

"Go on," Jen said.

Encouraged by her prompt, he reached out to grasp the

helmet.

"Lift from the back," Jen advised. "You'll find it comes off more easily that way."

She was right. The mask, the front part of what had seemed a single solid piece, retracted upwards rapidly, like a silk curtain being drawn, and the helmet lifted without resistance.

Nate hefted it in his hand: lighter than he'd expected.

He took a deep breath and donned it in one swift movement. It fitted perfectly, and suddenly he was looking at the world through a golden veil, as the mask flowed down to cover his face.

"It'll take a little getting used to," Jen said, her voice muffled by the helmet. "But once you do, you'll actually be able to see and hear better than with your naked senses."

That was reassuring. Nate just wished the adjustment would hurry up, because for now it felt as if he were interacting with the world through a filter.

He reached with deliberate care to take the harness, his movements uncertain due to the sense of remove. He wanted to make a good first impression on his new teammates, not spoil the moment by clumsily knocking over the alabaster figure.

In every rendering he'd seen – in the corny holodrama and elsewhere – Ramrod's harness had been rigid, cast from what appeared to be polished gold, and that was precisely how it looked now. Until Nate actually touched it. When he did, he found the material to be warm and pliable, a texture more akin to leather than anything metallic.

"What the…?" he said as he took proper hold of the surprisingly light strap, which wilted in his hands as he lifted the harness off the mannequin.

"I know," Jen said. "Weird, isn't it? Totally counterintuitive."

"You might have warned me."

"You reckon? How do you prepare someone for *that*?"

Which was a fair point.

"I hadn't yet joined the crew when your predecessor first took on the guise of Ramrod," Jen said, "but I understand the harness was huge when they first discovered it. As soon as Kyle – the original Ramrod – picked it up, it wilted and, in the process, somehow shrunk to human proportions."

Nate stared at the deceptively limp strip of cloth in his hand. "You mean… this was once worn by an Elder?"

"Probably – a long *long* time ago. What do you think we're dealing with here? Things the Elders knocked up just for our benefit? Stuff they left hanging around purely so we could discover and use it aeons after they were dead?"

"No, of course not." He'd just never thought of any artefact in those terms before.

"Good. So put it on."

He did so, his excitement and – yes – awe tempered a little by the thought that this same material might once have rested on alien flesh, but that didn't really give him pause. Hell, this was a dream come true, and maybe one day he would get the chance to track Pelquin down and gloat, just a little.

The moment the harness settled on his shoulders it all kicked in: the enhanced senses Jen had promised – colours leapt out at him, he could suddenly see dust motes floating in the air and hear every intake and exhalation of Jen's gentle breathing – but it was so much more than that. He felt energised, powerful, his whole body as ramped as his senses. He felt as if he could run headlong through solid walls and punch his way through armour shielding; which, given Ramrod's reputation, he probably could.

"This beats any drug I've ever heard of," he said.

"Just don't get carried away. Until we get you trained up, you genuinely don't know your own strength."

He didn't doubt Jen for a moment. He could easily imagine himself accidently crushing something vital to somebody. He reached up to grasp the back of the helmet and lifted it forwards and off, as Jen had taught him. Instantly, everything turned down a notch. The sense of energy in his limbs remained but the world grew a few shades duller.

As they left the artefact room, Raider's voice spoke from the air. "Welcome to the Dark Angels, Ramrod," it said.

Nine

Terry Reese couldn't help thinking things were getting out of control. This wasn't a feeling she was used to and certainly not one she enjoyed.

She had left her office that afternoon in full knowledge that her days here might be numbered. Her fate would be decided behind the imposing doors of the boardroom. There had always been a risk in offering Cornische a position at First Solar and helping him to establish the persona of Corbin Thaddeus Drake, but it was a calculated one and not a decision she regretted at any stage. Drake proved to be the best banking agent she had ever encountered, with a higher success rate at cache hunts than anyone else in the industry. She found herself having to defend the decision now, though, but she did so bullishly, without any intention of apologising.

In Valter Åkesson, senior partner at First Solar, she felt she had an ally, or at least a sympathetic ear, but his might well prove an isolated voice and it seemed unlikely he would be blatant in his support. To do so would risk diminishing his influence, should his fellows consider him to be biased at outset.

All five senior partners had gathered – a rarity in itself – though Reese suspected that only Åkesson and Son were physically present, the rest attending via projection.

Sara Minier seemed to have adopted the role of chief interrogator for now – whether by default or design, Terry couldn't be sure. She was on nodding acquaintance with Minier, but wouldn't claim to know her well. Their interactions had always been civil, though rare – Minier's responsibilities covered other areas of First Solar's interests. Presumably, this qualified her to take the lead now; as did her reputation for cold hard decision making.

Outwardly, she was all smiles, though the expression never reached as far as her eyes.

"And you didn't think to refer the decision to a superior?" she said.

"I'm fully authorised to vet and recruit my own staff," Terry said, attempting to match Minier's calm tone, "without troubling anyone at board level."

"Under normal circumstances, yes, but this could hardly be construed as 'normal', could it? You were offering the most notorious freebooter in known space a job with a premier financial institution, in the process providing him with a degree of legitimacy beyond anything he could have hoped to find elsewhere. You didn't think that worth referring?"

"I've never troubled any of the partners with administrative matters such as recruitment," Terry said, aware that her smile might be slipping, just a bit. "My understanding has always been that partners have more important matters to deal with than the vetting of new staff, and that they trusted such matters within my department to me. It would be a failure on my part should they ever be consulted on such things."

"I see." That smile again. "So you were seeking to spare us additional work."

"I was taking responsibility for a decision, which is one of the things you pay me for, in the full knowledge that any decision I make may be held to account." No one would miss *that* oblique reference; everyone present knew that Drake had been directly responsible for earning First Solar a significant amount over the course of many years. When it came to 'accounting', Terry was on safe ground; as for the rest...

"It wasn't perhaps because you knew that no partner would condone your actions, but you had already decided to push ahead in any case?"

There was that. Deniability too; Terry suspected that Åkesson knew precisely who Drake was from the get go, but there was no way she could ever prove as much, nor would she wish to.

"As I say, the employment of staff falls under my remit, and I'm experienced enough to make such decisions without the need of validation."

"Yes... as you say. Let's move on. Having decided to offer this notorious vagabond a job, you then conspired to hide his identity, helping him to create a false persona which he then hid behind for the best part of ten years."

"A *new* persona, yes. Without that, he could never have worked for us as a representative in the field."

"And you did so, as far as I can see, on First Solar's time and utilising First Solar's resources."

Really? Was that the best she could come up with: misuse of company time?

"Indeed," Terry confirmed. "And First Solar have benefitted handsomely as a result. The resources invested in creating the legend of Corbin Drake have been repaid many thousands of times over, from the proceeds of the successful cache hunts Drake has conducted on First Solar's behalf."

"What prompted you to take such a risk in the first place?" interjected Son, the oldest and reputedly most conservative of the partners.

"It seemed to me a unique opportunity," Terry said without hesitation. "In establishing and leading the Dark Angels, Cornische had proven himself to be a resourceful and highly effective individual. Qualities which, to my mind, made him ideally suited to the task of rooting out Elder caches and securing their contents. I felt his potential as an agent for First Solar more than justified the comparatively minor investment required to recruit him and establish the Drake identity. I believe the results of doing so have borne out that conviction."

"Why have you now chosen to come clean and admit the deception?" Minier said, clearly determined to regain control of proceedings.

Bitch! "Omission, rather than deception," Terry corrected, calmly. "Because developing events have convinced me that now is the right time to do so." *And because I'd rather you heard it from me than from anyone else.*

"You're referring to the recent assignment to the Enduril system, I presume."

"Yes."

"To which you persuaded Mr Åkesson to commit one of our Sabre units."

"There was little persuasion required," Åkesson assured her. "I trust Ms Reese's judgement implicitly."

Bless you, Valter.

"I'm sure, and with good cause," Minier conceded. "Your record speaks for itself, Ms. Reese. The best loan assessor in the business, would you go along with that?

Terry shook her head, dismissing the very notion. "Not my concern. That's for others to judge. I just do my job to the best of my ability."

"Excuse me one moment," Åkesson said, evidently taking a call of some sort. It had to be important. Terry felt certain that DO NOT DISTURB would have been the edict for the duration of this session. Glances were exchanged between a few of the partners, and Minier made no attempt to hide her annoyance at the interruption.

"I apologise," Åkesson said, "but I hope you'll forgive such rudeness when I tell you that we've just received a message from the commander of *Sabre 1*. His report impacts directly on our current discussion. If no one objects, I'd like to share it with you now."

No one did.

Thapa's image appeared, hovering in the air at the centre of the group, configured so that he seemed to be looking directly at each of them.

"This is Commander Deepak Thapa, of the stealth ship *Sabre 1*, with report summary. A more detailed report will follow on my return to New Sparta."

There were protocols regarding message length, even for

stealth ship commanders, given the exorbitant cost of faster than light communication via RzSpace.

"The presence of *Sabre 1* was detected by the Night Hammer ship *Darkness Mourning…*"

Night Hammers? Nobody else reacted, which led Terry to conclude this wasn't Thapa's first report. She wondered what else the partners might know about the developing situation that she wasn't privy to.

"They engaged us towards the edge of the Enduril system, Thapa continued. "Being outgunned, we were forced to resort to stealth mode. A Comet class trading vessel identifying as *Blue Angel* exited from Rz in the midst of the conflict. The newcomer fired upon *Darkness Mourning* and successfully disabled her."

That caused a few murmurs.

"Subsequently, it emerged that the trader was captained by Corbin Drake, registered agent for this bank and the man we had been assigned to support. Mr Drake asked me to forward as a matter of urgency a record of what he then went on to say, for the attention of the senior officers of First Solar. Given recent experiences and my limited interaction with Mr Drake, I recommend that what follows should be viewed as credible but unproven."

Thapa's features faded, to be replaced by a face Terry knew only too well.

"This is Corbin Thadeus Drake, reporting to Terry Reese and the senior officers of First Solar Bank…"

Drake's entire message lasted less than three minutes – she timed it – yet its impact was profound. A second of stunned silence followed its conclusion and then somebody – Sara Minier – laughed.

"No one's suggesting we should take this seriously, are they?" Minier said.

Åkesson ignored her. "Terry," he said. *First names now, that has to be a good sign.* "You know Drake better than any of us. Is he prone to melodrama, would you say?"

"No, quite the opposite."

Clever Valter. She didn't doubt the question was designed to emphasise that very point rather than obtain information. Any of them could summon up Drake's psych profile with the blink of an eye.

"So you think we should take what he says seriously?"

"Absolutely."

"Has anyone ever heard of this 'Saflik'?" Son asked.

Shakes of the head all round.

"What about Archer, is he one of yours Ms Reese?"

"Not directly. The same department, though."

"Archer is one of Mawson's," Åkesson supplied. In theory, all senior loan advisors could assign any representative to a given mission, but in practice they tended to rely on a handful of favourites, often those they had played some part in recruiting. "Archer was our follow-up representative sent to Enduril II when concerns over Drake's welfare first surfaced."

"Why him?" Minier wanted to know.

"He was between assignments at the time and so available immediately and…" Åkesson was clearly checking a detail, "…he requested the job."

"Hmm."

"If Drake's message is to be deemed credible, this is all very disturbing," said Barnes, the partner Terry knew least.

"It certainly gives us plenty to think about."

"That it does," Åkesson agreed. "Though, unless I've failed to grasp the significance, we've just been told the location of Lenbya and warned that it's at risk of falling into the hands of an inimical organisation, so I suggest we do our thinking quickly."

Terry left the meeting with no clear idea of what was likely to happen next, but at least it seemed she still had a job; for the present, at any rate.

Ten

"For Elders' sake, exercise some control!" Jen roared at him.

"I'm doing my best!" Nate snarled back.

"Well do *better*. You nearly brought that whole bloody building down on top of us."

Nate yanked his helmet off with a frustrated bellow, half tempted to kick it across the street. This was harder than he'd expected. He was good with gadgets, always had been, and the harness was just another overblown gadget, so why was he finding it so difficult to adjust to? Because he wasn't used to so much raw power, he supposed.

Jen had to visibly force down her anger, though in truth she was proving to be a lot more patient than he might have been in similar circumstances, which didn't help his self-esteem either.

"Look, I know this is all new to you and, in all honesty, you're doing okay," she admitted. "But okay isn't good enough. In a matter of days it's the big one – we're going to war – and 'okay' will get you killed. Or, worse still, get *us* killed. We can't afford for you to fuck up, so you need to hit the ground running and pick this up real quick, for all our sakes. You understand?"

He nodded. *I'm not an idiot.*

"Good. So are you ready to go again?"

Is there a choice? Nate jammed his helmet back on. "Yeah, let's do this."

He had a temper, he knew that, and had been fighting to keep it in check for much of his life. It had landed him in trouble more than once, especially in his youth. He grew up in Lower Denrach, a city that had been devastated by war and then left to its own devices once the conflict moved on. With civil infrastructure shattered and officialdom either killed or fled, others had moved in to fill the vacuum, opportunists for whom social welfare was an alien concept. A hierarchy of necessity had taken shape, where strength and self-interest ruled. Being big bad and angry in a place like that was guaranteed to get you noticed, with the likelihood that you would end up either dead or successful as a result.

Nate had been among the lucky ones. He had fallen in with the right crowd, becoming part of the problem rather than a victim of it.

Escaping Lower Denrach's toxic environment and limiting horizons had been the single most important step of his life. He never forgot how fortunate he'd been, getting a berth on a ship which carried him away from the misery, and every day he determined to make the most of the opportunity an impassive universe had seen fit to present him with.

Nate had known friends over the years, many friends, but he was never one to form deep attachments and had always found it easy to move on. Until he crossed paths with Pelquin. He and Pel had a real connection – kindred spirits even though they were different in so many ways. Leaving the *Comet* the first time, following their spat over Julia, had been hard. This second time, not so much, not really.

Maybe there was a nugget of truth in the old adage about never going back… So why, from the moment the Dark Angels had revealed themselves, had his first thought been to share what was going on with his old pal?

If only Pel could see me now had flashed through his mind constantly as they left the Spacer's Lament and made the short journey to the port. For as long as Nate had known him, Pelquin had been obsessed with Cornische and the whole story of the Dark Angels – even had an image of the *Ion Raider* leaping out the wall as you approached the bridge of the *Comet*. It was ironic, looking back; if only Pel had realised how close he had been to his idol, but none of them suspected that First Solar's agent – the unwelcome guest the bank had foisted on them – was none other than Francis Hilary Cornische, nor that Monkey's replacement – the new ship's engineer who had ended up saving all their lives –

was in fact Hel N, Cornische's lieutenant – and, according to some rumours, his lover... The truth was that Pelquin would likely go to his grave never knowing, and that was a genuine shame.

Nate could feel his own excitement mounting as the *Ion Raider* had first come into view. He studied the craft as they drew closer. There was nothing obvious to indicate this was the notorious ship of legend. An additional airlock had been installed just behind where the bridge must be, allowing access to the ship without the need to open the large cargo doors at the back – a modification Nate approved of – but other than that there was little to distinguish this old crate from any other Comet class, including *Pelquin's Comet*, which had been his home for so long. Here was just another well-travelled trader which had seen better days, with dulled metallic hull and no insignia, no adornments of any kind – ident being integral to a ship's hull and, in theory, inviolate unless realigned by official registration systems.

Quite why the ship's very ordinariness should come as such a disappointment, he wasn't sure; after all, how else could the Dark Angels roam around human space incognito? But somehow it did.

"Look sharp!" Jen's voice cut through his reveries, just as a saw-toothed disc spat from a nearby wall, slicing across his upper arm to inflict a stinging wound. "Concentrate!" she yelled.

He couldn't blame her for yelling this time – it was hardly the right place for daydreaming. He'd seen where the disc came from and reacted at once, slamming his fist into the wall on his right. A second disc raced to meet him at the same instant, but it bounced away harmlessly, his aggressive movement triggering the kinetic protection of the harness. He was beginning to get the hang of when that worked and when it was dormant – a lesson learned the hard way via a dozen nicks and bruises. His fist punctured what appeared to be brickwork without any resistance, reaching through to smash into the disc launcher behind it. He sensed a crackle of energy, rendered harmless by the harness, and that section of the wall shimmered and winked out, revealing itself to be no more than a projection, albeit a convincing one.

Two more discs flew from the wall on the opposite side of the empty street, heading directly towards Jen. Had she seen them? He couldn't take the chance, stepping forward to protect her, his arms swinging to intercept first one and then the other, sending both spinning away to clatter to the ground. Jen still hadn't moved. She'd known the discs were there. *A test*, he realised.

Without hesitating, Nate turned to grasp the wrecked disc thrower, wrenching the mechanism from its mounting and hurling it across the street. It disappeared, swallowed by the false wall there. A loud crack punctured the silence and that section of wall vanished. In its stead lay a tangle of wrecked machinery.

"Better," Jen said, "much better. I think that'll do for today. Raider, end simulation."

The light level increased and the world abruptly became less threatening; several more sections of wall disappeared to reveal hidden launchers and devices of various sort. The remaining walls commenced to concertina and collapse back into storage, leaving the two humans in the deceptively small confines of the gym.

"This is one hell of a workout room," Nate observed.

"I normally stick with traditional gym equipment," Jen said. "This sort of mock up is more Leesa's bag, but it comes in handy for training purposes. You okay?" she nodded towards his latest wound, just below the shoulder, which was still weeping blood.

He grunted. "Nothing a patch of nuskin won't sort out. I've had worse."

"That much I can believe."

They took dry showers and dressed in fresh overalls, before heading in the direction of the galley.

He couldn't get a handle on Jen. As yet he was getting no vibe of either friendship or hostility from her, just a neutral pragmatism, as if he was a job she'd been assigned which she had every intention of seeing through to the best of her ability.

It was an attitude Nate would normally have accepted, admired even, since it aligned with his own general outlook, but these were the Dark Angels for Elders' sake, and *he* had just been accepted into their ranks; surely, this once, he could be forgiven a bit of enthusiasm.

"You know they made a holodrama series about the Dark Angels?" he said, breaking the silence. *Hell!* Of all the questions bubbling away in his head, why had he opted to go with this one?

"So I heard," Jen replied.

"In it, you were portrayed as a kind of ninja warrior woman, leaping from the shadows and taking out villains in a blur of martial arts. Is that really you?"

"No idea, I never saw it."

"But the way you fight... It's not all down to the shadowtech, is it?"

"No," she confirmed.

Hardly the icebreaker he'd hoped for, but he was committed now, so ploughed on. "My guess would be that you learned to fight before you became Shadow." She made no effort to either confirm or deny. "So, were you in the military?"

She stopped walking and stared at him coldly, before saying, "Of sorts; it's not something I care to talk about."

Nate clammed up. Even in his current state of excited enthusiasm, he could tell when he was pushing his luck.

Part of Jen resented Leesa for saddling her with this. Oh, she knew the reasons: Kyle had been such a big part of Leesa's life, and the Ramrod outfit was synonymous with Kyle. Jen could appreciate how painful that might make things, but Leesa was still the one who understood Ramrod's abilities better than any of them. On the other hand, Leesa was a mechanic, primarily – despite having fought in the Auganics Wars – while everyone knew that Jen had received formal military training at some point, so from that perspective it made sense that she should be the one to take the new recruit under her wing.

There was just something about Nate, though, that got to her. He tested her patience as few others had, and she found herself wanting to snap at him over the most trivial of things, when in truth he was doing pretty well, all things considered.

"Must be love," Leesa quipped when she shared her frustration over a beer.

"Sod off."

Inevitably Leesa's comment sparked thoughts of Robin and their life together on the farm. A rural idyll that now seemed a lifetime ago, as it increasingly took on the trappings of a dream.

"I'll take tomorrow's session, if you like."

That snapped her attention back to the present. She stared at her friend. "Really?"

Leesa shrugged. "It's only a suit, after all. About time I got over myself, don't you think?"

"Well, I wasn't going to say anything..." She started to grin but abruptly felt guilty. "I don't want you to think I was angling for you to offer."

"Don't be daft."

"Well, if you're sure..."

"I'm sure. Besides, it'll do him good to have a teacher blessed with a little more patience."

Jen snorted. "Right, because that's a quality you're so well known for – your patience."

Leesa's offer was as welcome as it was unexpected; so why did Jen also feel a little bit... disappointed?

Evidently, she wasn't the only one, at least to judge by Nate's reaction when she bumped into him shortly afterwards and told him about the new arrangement.

"Okay, but why?" he wanted to know. "Did I do something wrong?"

"No, of course not."

"Have I upset you in some way?"

"Nothing like that, no. It's just that we felt you'd benefit from being trained by different Angels, and Leesa knows Ramrod's capabilities better than anyone else on board, so she'll be able to offer you invaluable insight from a different perspective."

The explanation seemed to mollify him. "Oh. Yeah, I guess that makes sense. Just didn't want to think I'd messed up without even knowing how."

"If you had, I would tell you, don't worry."

"Good. I'll keep you to that."

The exchange amused Jen considerably. It also pleased her far more than she felt it ought to.

ELEVEN

"Barbary, are you serious?"

The captain seemed to have taken Cloud's revelation of their next destination in his stride, Leesa, less so.

Mosi wasn't sure how he felt.

"Oh come on, bro'," Naj said in his head, "Barbary's never boring."

"The place is a shithole," he responded.

"Yeah, but it's our kind of shithole."

Back in the external world, the captain replied to Leesa with: "We've been made welcome there in the past, Lees."

"Doesn't mean I'm in any great hurry to rush back," she said. "The place is a shithole."

"Told you!" said Mosi to his sister.

"Stop gloating," she responded. "You're better than that."

"Just making the most of a rare opportunity."

"It does make sense, though," the captain said, "that a former Dark Angel might end up there. Raider, how long to reach Barbary from our current position?" he then asked.

"Sixty-four hours, standard time."

"No point in hanging around, then. Set course accordingly. Get ready for the jump into Rz, everyone."

There was a lot of hokum spoken about the transition into RzSpace; it wasn't unpleasant, not really, at least not in Mosi's experience. It could be a little disorientating, certainly, which was why some folk insisted on sitting down or fastening themselves to walls with cling patches, but he found that simply holding onto something solid worked for him, and even that was only by way of a precaution.

The moment came and went: a fleeting transition in which he felt at one with the universe, his consciousness expanding to touch every distant corner, quickly followed by the emotional dampening of Rz.

With the ship safely side-stepping the restraints of light speed via the non-place that was Rz, the crew made for the galley.

"Are you joining us, Saavi?" Mosi asked, knowing that more often than not she would demur and head for the cloud chamber instead, on the pretext of double checking some detail or other. He suspected that crowds made her uncomfortable, which was not a reaction he recalled from when she'd been a physical adult. "We're underway, after all," he added, "so there's not much more you can do for now."

"You're putting her on the spot," Naj said in his head.

"No I'm not. I just want her to feel included."

"Okay, I'll come for a while," Saavi said.

It was evening, by ship's reckoning. 'Day' and 'night' had no real relevance in transit, but the human body still required downtime, so the convention was still observed on most vessels, including the *Ion Raider*: twenty-four standard hours, with nine allocated for darkness. Of course, lights could be activated at any time, either individually or collectively, but the convention provided a useful framework, especially in the soporific environs of RzSpace.

The galley was equipped with comfy chairs and low tables – more in keeping with a bar than a dining area, but no one spoke of a 'bar' on a ship unless it was a private yacht or passenger vessel.

"Sixty-four hours," Nate said as they sat down.

"At least that'll give us a few more days to train you up," Jen said.

"Why, are you expecting trouble at Barbary?"

"You never can tell, not where Barbary's concerned," Leesa assured him.

"It's a safe haven for every lowlife and miscreant to ever travel the spaceways," Jen said.

"I've heard of the place, of course," said Nate.

"But you've never been there?"

He shook his head.

"My mistake, then; not *every* lowlife, apparently."

"Thanks a bunch," but he was smiling.

"The rest of us have all been there, though," Drake pointed out, "which probably proves your point."

Jen grinned and raised her beer to him.

Nate seemed to be settling in well, though Mosi had not had a great deal to do with him as yet, and there appeared to be some sort of friction between him and the captain that predated current events. Cornische wasn't making a big thing of it, but Mosi felt the newcomer had some way to go before the captain fully accepted him.

"A bit too full of himself, if you ask me," Naj supplied.

"I think that was just nerves," Mosi said, recalling Nate's overly bullish attitude when he first arrived. "He's calmed down a bit since then."

"We'll see."

"Besides, if he's going to be Ramrod a bit of attitude is no bad thing."

Conversation broke into clumps, with Mosi talking to Saavi, who sat immediately beside him.

"I don't think I've heard you talk about what you've been doing in the past ten years," he said. "How did you cope with the reverse aging thing?"

"Oh, very subtle," Naj said in his thoughts. "Nothing like hitting a nerve to start a conversation."

Saavi didn't seem to mind, though. "At first it was fine," she said. "I mean I didn't notice right off – it's not exactly something I was looking for. I got a job in strategy prediction with a big corporation."

"I'll bet you were outstanding at that."

"I did okay. I didn't have to work, not with the money I brought away after we broke up, but I wanted to feel useful, to still feel relevant, you know?"

Mosi did, all too well.

"After a couple of years, though, it was clear something was going on. People started commenting on how young I looked, people started noticing, so I went and got myself checked out, thoroughly."

"That's when you found out."

"Yeah. Hell of a shock, as you can imagine. Plus, it cost me a fortune to hush things up, to pay specialists to keep their mouths shut – the last thing I wanted was to become some sort of test subject. Still not convinced all of them did. I'd mastered the paintpad by then and had worked out how to use it to read potentials, up to a point. I saw that someone was hunting me and that, if they caught me, it wouldn't end well. At the time, I thought it was most likely to be the government, or maybe the media, but now I wonder if it mightn't have been Saflik. I didn't wait to find out. I went on the run. Leaving my job and the life I'd started to build proved a lot easier than I'd expected it to be, and after that I avoided putting down any sort of roots anywhere, just kept moving around.

"Realising that as time passed I was getting younger and smaller, which left me vulnerable, I sought out the T'kai and commissioned them to build Jai to my specifications. As soon as he was by my side, the potentials looked much brighter, and then one day I saw that – against all reason – the *Iron Raider* would be at a port in the city of la Gossa on a world called Babylon. I was nowhere near that sector of space and must have broken some sort of record to get there in time, but I made it."

"And before meeting up with Jen and Leesa again, you didn't have any trouble travelling around on your own, even as you got younger and younger?"

"Not really. Being able to predict the future – however vaguely – can be a real boon when it comes to accumulating wealth, and you'd be amazed at how frequently rules turn flexible or even irrelevant once you've thrown enough money at them."

"And you gave up all that freedom and wealth for this?" Mosi gestured around them.

She actually laughed, a girlish giggle which, Mosi realised, was the most relaxed expression he'd seen from her.

"I gave all that up for the cloud chamber," she corrected him.

"Is it really that special?"

"Don't push it," Naj whispered in his head, "or she might clam up. You're doing so well at getting her to relax, don't blow it."

"It's like nothing else," Saavi said. "The chamber is liberation, it's mind-expanding, it's like breathing freely after you've been shut away and stifled in a small hot room."

Mosi shook his head. "It's so difficult to grasp what that must be like. How do you actually do what you do?

"Careful," Naj warned again.

"It's complicated," Saavi said.

"I don't doubt that for a minute, but I'm genuinely curious. Could you try to give me some idea? Just pretend I'm an idiot, and I'll keep up as best I can."

For a moment he thought she was going to refuse, to retreat into her customary privacy, but after a further plaintive 'please' to prompt her, she said, "Okay, I'll try."

Saavi reached into a pocket in her overalls and produced what looked to be a folded square of dark-coloured cellophane. She placed it in the flattened palm of her hand. As soon as she let go, the square commenced to unfurl and open, stiffening to become a wafer thin paintpad.

Saavi touched one corner of the surface with a fingertip, and a red spot appeared, slowly spreading outwards as she kept the finger in place, as if blood were being drawn out of her through its tip. When she was satisfied, she moved her hand to the opposite corner, placing the tips of all four fingers and thumb on the screen in a cluster, slowly drawing them apart to create a far larger and less regular red stain.

She then lifted her hand slowly from the screen, spreading the fingers a little wider as she went. The red stain lifted in response, as if drawn upward by invisible threads, becoming a clump, a cloud, that hovered above the paintpad.

Saavi drew her hand rapidly away and the cloud stayed in place. "This is where we are now," she said, pointing to the original dot, "and this is where we're going to be in the future," and she indicated the hovering cloud.

"The question is: how do we get from there to here?"

The tip of her index finger moved rapidly, to create a series of thread-like red lines leading from the spot to the cloud, some straight but most curving outward and back, creating a tracery that resembled an elongated sphere, reminding Mosi of the cantaloupe melons that he and Najat had enjoyed so much as children.

All other conversation in the room had ceased, as everyone concentrated on Saavi's explanation. Mosi suspected that most if not all of them were hearing this for the first time.

"These threads represent the possible paths from now till then," she said. "What I try to do is explore each one to work out which is the best, but as I do, more possibilities spread out from each one, to create even more potentials, which I have to navigate and eliminate."

She sat back. "That's it in a nutshell, but it's a huge over-simplification, because there are many more than one possible tomorrows, so at any given moment our current state is connected by potential pathways to dozens of different clouds. Some are connected so tenuously that I can discount them because they are so unlikely. Unless, of course, one of them represents the only desirable outcome. In that situation, I have to look for the path that will heighten their likelihood and eliminate the more probable but less favourable outcomes. I try to advise accordingly."

"Gods," Mosi said, impressed and appalled in equal measure.

"Bet you're glad you got me rather than becoming Cloud," Naj said in his head.

"How do you stay sane?" Jen asked quietly.

Saavi laughed. "Some would argue that I lost that particular battle a long time ago. The truth is, I love it. This," and she held up the paintpad, "is a mere toy compared to the chamber. With this I can conjure lines and pick at potential futures, trying to persuade them to reveal their secrets. In there, I'm immersed in them. I can step between possible futures, taste them, feel them, reject the worst ones in seconds and promote the best once I've identified them, working out where we need to go to produce the most favourable outcome. It's..." She shook her head. "Sorry, I can't even begin to put the differences into words."

"Sounds like with you on our side, we can't lose," Nate said.

"If only it were that simple," Saavi said. "Right now there are so many possible outcomes, and so many of them are bad – *beyond* bad – that it's taking me an age to eliminate missteps and plot the best path. Even then, 'best' isn't always great, it's just the least worst option."

"If you need help..." Mosi blurted.

"*Really?*" Naj said in his head. "You want to go into that room of madness?"

He ignored her and ploughed on, "I mean, surely Raider could step in and eliminate some of the least promising options, if nothing else."

"Thanks for the thought, and I know you mean well, but it doesn't work like that," Saavi assured him. "So much of what I do is intuitive, and Raider is an AI, albeit one paired with an Elder aspect. The two don't mix, not at this level, trust me."

"Cloud is quite correct," Raider said.

"The potentials are unpredictable and increasingly volatile, to the extent that even the best options can be ambiguous. Sometimes I can see a detail clearly but at others it's all nebulous, because things might shift at any moment. It's as if I'm peering through thick fog or trying to tear away layers of gauze veils in order to glimpse what lies beneath them. That's why I can provide specifics one minute but can only offer broad guidelines the next. I'm doing my best, I really am, but I worry that it won't be good enough. Putting Barbary forward as our next destination, for example, that doesn't look to be entirely a good move, but *some* good is likely to come of it, and it represents the best way forward I can find."

"What do you mean 'doesn't look to be entirely a good move'?" Leesa asked sharply.

"I don't *know!* That's the frustration."

Mosi instinctively put an arm round her shoulders. She didn't resist, and seemed to draw a degree of comfort from the gesture.

"I can't *see* where the danger lurks at Barbary," Saavi continued, "but I know it's there, a dark shadow looming over our visit, and I know we'll all have to be on our toes... It's just that every other move we might have made looked to be far worse."

"Now there's a cheery summary," Naj whispered.

"It's okay, Saavi" Mosi said. "We all appreciate that you're doing everything possible, and no one means to put pressure on you."

"No one has to, believe me," she replied. "Even sitting here with you now, I feel guilty for not being in there, trying to make sense of it."

"Everyone needs a break, Saavi, even you."

"But events don't take a break when I do, Jen. Potentials keep evolving, and there's so little time left to stop what's coming. For all our sakes, I can't afford to stop for long. I just can't."

TWELVE

The next morning, Mosi found himself brooding over his chat with Saavi. He couldn't claim that it had kept him awake, but it was the last thing on his mind when he fell asleep and was still there, picking away at his conscience, when he awoke. It seemed to him that they were all guilty of taking Saavi for granted, happy to go along with her habit of not socialising without accepting any responsibility for it. He determined to make amends moving forward, starting immediately.

"Raider, is Saavi in the cloud chamber?" he asked.

"Indeed she is," the ship's AI replied, "and has been for the past two hours."

Really? And he'd only just woken up. "Thank you," he said, and headed towards the cargo bay, where Saavi's private domain was situated.

"You do know she had the hots for you, back in the day," Najat said as they walked.

"Don't be daft."

"I'm serious."

"And I'm ignoring you. Even if that were true, it's hardly relevant now, is it?"

"Oh, I realise that much, given her physiological age, but I thought I'd mention it."

"Plus that was a decade ago, and I've changed in the meantime as well," Mosi thought it worth adding. "I'm ten years older now."

"Don't put yourself down. You're still in pretty good shape... for an old man."

"Thanks, sis."

"You know you can always count on me."

The cargo bay was a cavernous area at the back of the ship,

accessed via the rear of the ship but extending beneath the living quarters. It was largely empty these days, though a good half its floor space had been given over to the gym and the two additional chambers.

"A trading vessel that doesn't trade," Naj said, following his thoughts. "Now there's a novelty."

Even in the old days, before they disbanded, trading in the traditional sense had become far less of a priority, particularly as their notoriety grew. This enabled them to convert large areas of the bay for other purposes – the artefact room, the gym and, of course, the cloud chamber.

The bay still had plenty of empty floor space, though, which was accessed via a metal gantry that led from the deck where the sleeping quarters were housed. As Mosi came down the metal steps that would bring him to the bay's floor, he realised that someone else was already there ahead of him.

"Morning, Mosi."

"Jen."

"Just thought I'd pop in and see how Saavi's doing. It's an age since I last saw inside the cloud chamber."

"I know what you mean."

"Of course that's the only reason she's here," Naj said in his head. "Great minds think alike."

They walked beside each other towards the oblong bloc of the cloud chamber.

"To be honest, some of what she said yesterday evening set me thinking," Jen admitted. "We've all got a lot going on right now, but perhaps, even so, we could put a bit more effort into making Saavi feel included, to show we understand what she's gone through, and what she puts herself through constantly for all our sakes."

Mosi found himself nodding. "Yeah, that's pretty much why I'm here too."

"Mind you, turning up mob-handed like this, she's going to think we planned it."

"Better that than she thinks we don't care."

"True."

They had arrived in front of the huge metal box which Cloud had made her own. It always put Mosi in mind of an oversized shipping container.

"What do we do now," Mosi wondered, "knock?"

"We *could* try that," Jen said. "Or we could do this instead: Raider, please tell Saavi she has visitors."

"Yeah, there is always that option," Mosi conceded, feeling like an idiot, but the comment earned him a grin from Jen.

"Cloud says for you to go straight in," Raider said almost immediately.

Jen looked at him, ruefully. "Well," she said, "here goes."

At which point Mosi realised that, although he had made the decision to be here for Saavi's sake, he wasn't looking forward to this at all.

The door to the cloud chamber slid open, and they stepped inside. Waiting for them was a surrealist's dream.

"Wow!" Mosi said, quietly. He was stunned. Astonished.

He couldn't make out the far side of the room. The air was filled with shades and rainbows. He hesitated to call them mists, or clouds, or *anything*. It was as if coloured powders swirled up and around, each carried on its own current of air. They blended at times to form new colours and tones but for the most part entwined around one other, touching and separating but remaining distinct.

"I've... I've been in here before but it was never like this," Jen murmured.

A little ahead of them, standing near the centre of the chamber with her back to them, stood Saavi. Her outstretched arms swept this way and that, her fingers weaving and gesturing as if she were performing some arcane ritual. She drew in strands of colour and created transient images that formed and dissipated before Mosi could be certain of what he was looking at.

She seemed even more diminutive, somehow, set against this

chaos of roiling colour and form, yet at the same time there was an authority to her movements, a deftness that suggested here was a master craftsman at work in their specialist medium, or perhaps a virtuoso creating an entirely new form of music.

"Jess, Mosi, just give me a sec and I'll be with you."

True to her word, after a further moment conducting her rainbow symphony, Saavi brought her arms together in front of her and then slowly dropped her hands to her side. The strands she had been moulding receded, and all around them the frenetic movement quieted. It didn't stop, continuing to swirl in brooding fashion, but there was no doubting the comparative calm.

"Sorry about that, you caught me right in the middle of something," Saavi said, turning around and smiling at them.

"Is this what you do all day?" Mosi asked.

"No, not exactly that at any rate. I just had to try a few things, to eliminate a batch of potentials in a hurry, and that's the quickest way of doing so. A lot of what I do is pretty serene compared to that. Come and sit down."

Mosi hadn't even seen the chairs until Saavi gestured towards them. They were against the wall to their left – two of them, powder blue and comfortable-looking. Jai stood beside them, configured as a sapphire lizard, a slightly darker shade of blue than the chairs.

"No one ever comes to see me in here," Saavi said, sounding delighted that they had. She insisted they took the chairs.

"Can I get you something to drink? Raider installed a drinks machine for me to save having to run up and down to the galley all the time."

She reminded Mosi of a teenager showing off her room to honoured visitors. He had never appreciated until that moment just how lonely Saavi might be in here.

The offer reminded him that he hadn't stopped for breakfast yet that morning. "I'll take a coffee, please," he said, "with milk but strong."

"And I'll go for the same," Jen added.

The two of them exchanged a glance, which convinced Mosi they were both now intending to stay here longer than either had originally planned.

Drake sat in ops, nursing a bulb of fresh coffee. Leesa occupied the other pilot's chair beside him, sipping a bright orange viscous-looking fruit juice. It was early morning and no one else had surfaced as yet.

"We need to decide how we're going to play this," Drake said.

"Coming into Barbary, you mean?"

He nodded. "We've already been caught out by the *Blue Angel* ident once."

"Yeah, and we both know how the Barbary authorities will react to any ship they catch trying to sneak in under a false ident."

The dubious nature of many of the vessels and crew that habitually docked at Barbary meant the authorities were warier than most and sensitive to any deception. The last thing they wanted was for a snatch team to infiltrate the place with a view to spiriting away some infamous scoundrel to face justice – a not unknown occurrence in Barbary's early days as a safe haven. For the sake of their reputation and credibility among the shadier elements that frequented the spaceways, those who ran and profited from Barbary's lucrative status took measures to protect it. These measures included a network of automated defence platforms, which now orbited the planet. If not exactly a fortress world, Barbary had become a place no one ventured to lightly.

"Shoot first and ask questions later," Drake agreed.

"On the other hand, if we go in openly as the *Ion Raider*…"

"Word will get out. Everyone on the planet will know who we are long before we touch down."

"Crowds to greet us," Leesa said, "either adulation or a lynch mob, depending on how many of the folk we've pissed off in the past are around. Maybe a mixture of both – competing mobs, all eager to claim a piece of us. After that, liggers, anyone still nurturing a perceived grudge and doubtless the authorities, all watching our every move. We won't be able to go anywhere, won't be able to *sneeze* without it being observed and reported."

Drake nodded. "And if there are any agents of Saflik hanging around on Barbary in hope of snaring a former Dark Angel or two, we'd make an irresistible target."

"Bearing all this in mind, is it such a good idea to go to Barbary at all?"

"Unfortunately, I reckon it is, despite the risks. We have to trust Cloud's judgement. Doing so has worked for us so far, and if she says this is the best place for us to be right now, I'm willing to back her up. We just need to figure out the best approach."

"Okay, so going in as ourselves beats going in as *Blue Angel* but is still far from ideal, which leaves…?"

"Option three."

"Which doubtless you're making up on the spot, but let's hear it anyway."

"Raider," Drake said, "what was the name of the ship we used as false ident when we needed to in the past?"

"The *Lion of Lincoln*," Raider supplied.

"That's the one."

"Not so sure option three was worth the wait after all. Our use of the *Lion of Lincoln* was featured in that ridiculous holodrama they made about the Dark Angels. People will know it's us."

"Good. I'm counting on it."

Leesa nodded, as she followed his reasoning. "You know, that might just work. No one could accuse us of trying to sneak in because it's public knowledge that we use that ident, but at the same time we're not shouting from the rooftops that the Dark Angels are back in town. Some people are going to work out it's us, no doubt, or at least suspect as much, but the reaction ought to be far more muted than if we went in brazenly."

"Precisely. Just to play safe, we'll contact Barbary Control on approach, making no bones about who we really are, and trust they don't hold it against us. They're not idiots, and their whole economy relies on sailing close to the wind, bending the rules when necessary. I'm counting on them having the nounce to recognise our actions for the ploy it is and realise why we're so keen to keep things low key."

"And hopefully they won't blow us to bits in the meantime."

"Hopefully not."

"What could possibly go wrong?"

In the final hours before they emerged from Rz, Drake excused himself from ops and headed down to the cargo hold. He and Leesa had run the plan past the rest of the crew, being entirely frank about the risks involved, and no one had any objections; nor did anyone have any better ideas. So by the time they emerged into Barbary's space, the *Ion Raider* would show up as the *Lion of Lincoln*.

For the plan to work there was one final piece Drake needed to put in place, and in order to do so he would have to visit the artefact room; not a prospect he relished.

He had been avoiding the coat and hat ever since returning to *Raider* and the Dark Angels, telling himself it wasn't necessary just yet, but the truth went deeper than that. Even though he'd assumed the responsibilities of being Cornische once again, he hadn't felt at home with the role, not completely, and donning the costume would have made it too real, too inevitable.

Now, though, there was no choice, not if they were going to pitch up in a disguise as thin as this and hope to convince the authorities on Barbary that they were the real deal. Otherwise, the Dark Angels return was likely to be a lot briefer than intended.

The door to the artefact room slid open and he stood on the threshold for a moment, contemplating the dramatically posed figure immediately inside – the first thing to greet anyone who entered. He felt certain he had never looked as dynamic as this in real life, nor so athletic, but he couldn't fault the figure's impact.

Seeing no reason to delay the inevitable, he stepped inside and crossed to the mannequin. The moment he slipped the grey coat off the figure and felt the familiar weight in his hand – which was not, in truth, as great as might be expected from the heavy-looking garment – memories stirred. He slipped first his right and then his left arm through the long sleeves and shrugged the coat into a more comfortable position, flexing his shoulders, feeling the material's give. Then he took the twin smartguns in their tough-weave holsters and strapped them around his waist. Finally he lifted the hat, a tired-looking wide-brimmed excuse for a cowboy hat, and placed it on his head. A few years back he had suffered a recurring dream about this moment, in which he put the hat on again after many years only to find that it no longer fitted, it was too small. Reality delivered no such dramas; the hat fitted snuggly, just as it always had.

Ironically, Cornische was unique among the Dark Angels in that his identity and abilities were not reliant on Elder technology. His smartguns had been developed entirely from human know-how, likewise the privacy screen which dropped down when required from the rim of his hat, to obscure his face and disguise his voice.

He was happy to leave the spectacular to others, reckoning the rest of the crew had more than enough Elder tech wizardry going on between them to go round.

Before leaving the artefact room, he placed his cane – such a hallmark of Drake – with the now naked mannequin, leaning it against the figure's alabaster legs. Purely a symbolic gesture, perhaps, but it felt the right thing to do. For the first time since Leesa had saved him from suffocation on a distant world, he no longer felt like Corbin Thadeus Drake, registered agent of First Solar Bank. Once again he was ready to be Francis Cornische, captain of the *Ion Raider*.

Jen was the first to see him as he returned to ops. She cheered and started to clap, with Mosi joining in a fraction later.

Leesa just regarded him with critical eye, as if assessing a new outfit on a friend. "The good news is that it still fits," she said at length. "A little tighter than it used to be, perhaps, but we'll just have to work with what we've got."

"Thank you so much for that confidence-boosting appraisal," Drake replied. "Not all of us have suits that adjust to our changing physique, you know. Some of us have to work at staying in shape."

"I hope you're not suggesting that Leesa doesn't, Captain," Jen said. "I mean, if you *were* looking to piss off one of the most dangerous people in the galaxy that would be a great way to start."

"He'd have to do better than that, Jen," Leesa assured her, "a lot better."

"All right. Now, if you've all had your fun?" Cornische said.

"For the moment, but don't get complacent."

"Raider, how long until we arrive at Barbary?" he said, ignoring Leesa.

"I'll be bringing the ship out of Rz in ten standard minutes, Captain. We should be in range of their scanning systems almost immediately. Our ident has been reconfigured to present as the *Lion of Lincoln*, as requested."

"Thank you, Raider. Ten minutes, everyone. Take up your positions as soon as we're out of Rz." He wanted to make certain that when he contacted Barbary Control he did so with a full complement of highly visible Angels behind him: Hel N, Shadow, Geminum and Ramrod, which ought to go some way to convincing the inevitable doubters at Control precisely who it was that had come a-calling. Or at least buy them enough time to convince said doubters,

Cornische timed the message carefully, wanting to give Barbary the chance to register this new arrival's supposed identity and realise it was a false one. Three minutes after they emerged from Rz, and Raider confirmed they had done so close enough to Barbary for Control to be aware of them, he sent the message: audio and image. He kept it simple.

"Barbary Control, this is the *Lion of Lincoln*, under the

command of Captain Francis Cornische, seeking permission to land at Worley Central."

The unavoidable delay proved as interminable as ever, but at last the response came through.

"Barbary Control to the *Lion of Lincoln*, if this is someone's idea of a joke there's going to be all hell to pay. Please confirm identity of both your ship and your captain."

"Control, we would prefer to keep our presence as low key as possible, so the *Lion of Lincoln* is all we're prepared to admit to, but please feel free to draw your own conclusions. As for confirming who *I* am, you know full well. We're communicating with you in audio and visual. You can analyse both aspects to your hearts' content and make comparisons with data that you must have on record. All of which will confirm that I am Captain Francis Hilary Cornische. This is no joke. The Dark Angels are back, but we'd rather our return did not become public knowledge just yet. We will be happy to explain further in person, once we've landed."

Again the lag, during which time he had the opportunity to review what he'd said in his mind and wish he'd said it better.

"Control to the *Lion of Lincoln*," the reply came at last, "please proceed to designated berth at Worley. We'll guide you in on approach. You will be met on landing. And… if you really are who you claim… welcome back."

Leesa snorted. "If we really are… Who else does he *think* we are? I mean, this would be one heck of an elaborate ruse."

"Can't blame them for being cautious," Cornische said. "It's been ten years, after all."

The welcoming committee was there as promised. A car, a bloated giant of its kind, with opaque tinted windows that could have hidden just about anything, up to and including a ship-busting energy cannon. Standing alongside the car and facing the *Ion Raider*'s berth were two burly men in crisp black business suits, with smartshades masking their eyes and hands clasped in

126

front of them.

"Glad to see the Barbarians – can we call them that? – aren't going in for any clichés," Leesa murmured.

"Maybe they feel intimidated," Jen suggested. "Perhaps they feel obliged to put on some sort of show given that we're all costumed up and what with us being living legends – just to prove to us that they're the ones in charge, sort of thing."

"Maybe," Cornische conceded. "Raider, any life signs from inside the car?"

"None. The vehicle is unoccupied."

"So, what are we thinking?" Leesa said. "We get in, and they either drive us somewhere, attempt to gas us, or…"

"… It's to be a virtual conference in an environment they feel in control of," Drake finished for her. "Raider, if needed, are you able to hack the car's controls?"

"I believe so. Would you like me to make the attempt now?"

"No," he said quickly. "There's no point in antagonising our hosts unless we have to. It's just good to know the option is there."

Having made sure his privacy screen was properly in place, Cornische headed for the airlock with Leesa, leaving Jen in charge of the bridge. She and Raider would monitor them throughout.

Outside, the two men in black – who were surely there more for show than because anyone thought they would be needed – stood aside and held a door to the car open, allowing the two Angels to enter.

The vehicle was more bus than car – Drake barely had to duck when climbing in. His hat stayed in place as it was designed to, without the need to be held, maintaining the privacy screen.

They sat beside each other on a long comfortably upholstered seat that could have readily sat three or four more. Opposite was an identical seat, facing theirs. Once they were in, security shut the door. Soft light suffused the cabin, filtering in through the tinted windows.

Abruptly, and perfectly synchronised, four figures appeared in the seat facing them. Two men, two women, with ages varying from a little younger than Cornische to a good deal older, or so he reckoned.

The man directly opposite him – who looked to be of similar age – had a prosthetic ear. That caught Cornische's attention, and he stared at the man's face more closely. It would have been a simple matter to blend a prosthetic like this into a person's face so that no one would ever guess it was there. It took a special kind of obstinate to wear such a thing openly, or someone with a point to prove. Now that he had that clue, Cornische could see it in the man's face: fuller, older, more worry lines and less hair than there used to be, but...

"Seb?"

Seb Watkins grinned and the laughter lines multiplied. "Okay," he said, "now we're getting somewhere. Yes, that looked like you in the contact message, and it *sounded* like you, but none of that was conclusive given all the scrambling you've got going on through that screen of yours. I wanted to see you face to face."

"Or projection to face, at any rate," Leesa said.

"Hello, Hel N. Ten years away haven't cured you of being a smart ass, I see."

"Amazing how quickly it came back to me."

"Are you going to introduce us, Watkins?" said the other man, who looked to be the oldest of the quartet. "Or did you just want us here to witness this touching reunion?"

Watkins favoured the man with a glare, then waved a hand in the direction of Cornische and Leesa. "Ruling Council of Barbary, meet the Dark Angels. Dark Angels, meet the Ruling Council."

"How would we ever have coped without you?" Leesa said.

"You're sure it's really them?" the younger woman asked, staring intently as if she hoped to penetrate their disguises with willpower alone.

"Pretty sure, yes," Watkins confirmed.

"If you'd like any further proof, I could always punch a hole through the roof of this snazzy car of yours," Leesa said.

"Actually, I'm not so sure you could," Watkins said. "This limo is deceptively well protected, armoured with the toughest alloy... Hey!" he shouted, holding out a restraining hand between Leesa and the ceiling. "That wasn't a challenge." He drew the hand back quickly, perhaps realising what an empty gesture it was, given that he wasn't physically there.

"Sounded like one to me," she said, lowering her fist all the same.

"Let's stop pussyfooting around and cut to the chase, shall we?" said the older woman. "So you're the Dark Angels. Why are you back, and why are you here on Barbary?"

Much more like it. They'd discussed in advance exactly how much to reveal – which amounted to very little – and Corniche launched straight into the spiel. "For the past few years, an organisation has been quietly hunting down and assassinating former Dark Angels," he said. "We haven't kept in touch, so it was a while before we caught on – Hel N caught on, to be precise. Once we realised what was happening, we decided to do something about it."

"So you're putting the band back together," Watkins said.

"In effect, yes. Individually, they've caught former Angels unawares. Let's see how they do against a whole ship full of us, ready for them and out for revenge."

"Does this organisation have a name?"

"Saflik."

It was clear from their expressions that the name meant something to them.

"That's quite an adversary you've taken on there."

"It's quite an adversary they've taken on as well."

"Granted." The older woman seemed to have adopted the role of spokesperson. "Let's be entirely clear about this, the decision to let you land here was not welcomed by all of us." Good to know. "The return of the Dark Angels is, of course, sensational news, but we're not in the business of sensational. We're in the business of governance, and 'sensational' is the last thing we need. Therefore, we're perfectly happy to co-operate in keeping your brief stay here as quiet as possible, though your choice of ship ident doesn't exactly help on that score."

"That was deliberate," Cornische said, "a calculated risk."

"Presumably chosen on the basis that any of your former shipmates who are on Barbary will recognise the *Lion of Lincoln* and realise the significance."

"Precisely."

"Is that why you're here, then, to find old crewmates and recruit them to your cause?"

"Yes."

"Is that the *only* reason you're here?"

"Yes."

"Well, that and replacing a few salvaged engine parts, if opportunity allows," Leesa added.

"That too," Cornische conceded. "But we've come to Barbary specifically because it strikes us as a likely place for former Angels to have settled. We don't know that for sure, but we're here to find out, preferably without attracting unwanted attention."

Cornische suspected that a hurried exchange of views was taking place off screen, for all that the four projected figures looked pensive and silent.

After a few seconds' pause, the woman spoke again. "Trouble used to follow the Dark Angels around, and I don't suppose that's changed. Added to which, you tell us that an interstellar criminal organisation is after you. It hardly makes you the most desirable of guests... We've no great love of Saflik, but at the same time we wouldn't want to antagonise them. Also, the longer you stay here, the more difficult it will be to keep your presence a secret. Word's bound to get out at some point. So, taking all of that into account, we'll give you three days.

"After that, we'll tell the whole world and its mother you're here, then sit back to watch you cope with the consequences."

Three days. It was better than nothing – better than they might have expected, in truth..

"Agreed," Drake said. "And thank you. I suppose it would be too much to ask that you leave us to our own devices unobserved?"

"It would. Meeting you has proven to be... interesting, Captain Cornische. I hope it's not a meeting we need to repeat. Three days."

With that, she winked out, followed by the other councillors. Watkins was the last to leave.

"A councillor, no less," said Leesa when it was just the three of them. "You've done well for yourself, Seb."

When they'd known him, Seb Watkins had been a local 'businessman', a facilitator with fingers in multiple pies. A useful contact, but not someone who had ever shown an interest in politics.

"A lot's happened in ten years, Hel N. Listen, I know you well enough to realise you're probably not telling us everything, but don't do anything stupid. Nobody gets to the top in a place like Barbary by being a fool – present company excepted. If you can conclude your business here in two days rather than three, don't hang around."

"Thanks for the advice, Seb. You take care."

He nodded, and with that was gone.

No sooner were they alone than the door opened and they were ushered out of the car by the men in black, who then climbed into the vehicle before it pulled away, with barely a purr from its engine.

"Three days," Leesa said. "Do you think that'll be long enough?"

"It's going to have to be."

"Have you seen that?" Leesa pointed to the wall on the far side of the space the car had occupied. Emblazoned across it in tall lettering was:

Richard Worley: Creator of the Jolly Roger.

"As fitting a person as any to name a town after, I suppose."

"Especially this town," Cornische agreed.

"I still don't get why you weren't more open with them," Almont said. The crew had gathered in ops to hear how the meeting had gone. "I mean, we've come here to look for allies, haven't we? Wouldn't it make more sense to mention the fabled riches of Lenbya as an incentive to recruiting folk?"

Cornische was shaking his head. "Given what we're about to face, I want allies we can trust, not those that we'd be afraid to let out of our sight."

"This is Barbary, Nate," Leesa added. "If you've done something to be ashamed of and there's nowhere to go, there'll always be Barbary. Walk into any bar in Worley and you'll find more chancers and lowlifes than anywhere else in the human worlds – people willing to risk everything if there's a big enough profit in it. You're right, one mention of Lenbya and overnight we could raise a fleet to lead into battle. But they'd spend the entire trip sizing up the competition and deciding on which of their fellows they need to take out first."

"And when the battle itself actually kicks off, one half of our 'allies' would open fire on the other half, and the few that choose not to take part in all of that squabbling would stay close behind us until the battle is won, at which point they'd merrily stab us in the back and claim all the Elder tech for themselves."

"And that," Cornische summarised, "is why we chose to be somewhat economical with the truth."

"Dear gods," Nate said. "And you've come to this place by choice?"

"Oh, it's not so bad," Leesa assured him. "You just have to bear in mind where you are and keep your wits about you."

"Saavi," Cornische said, "any progress on narrowing down why we need to be here?"

"No. Sorry."

"That's okay." He didn't say 'keep working on it', he didn't need to. "Okay, we've got three days. I think we can assume the Barbary authorities are going to keep tabs on our comings and goings, which might make it tricky for anyone concerned about maintaining their anonymity once this is over. Either we'll have to leave the ship as Dark Angels, and advertise our presence here, or we go into town in civvies knowing that Barbary will record and identify our faces as we disembark.

"We can do something about this but not necessarily enough. Their most likely methods of watching us," and he counted them off on his fingers. "Fixed cameras, spyflies, satellite observation – let's not forget how big they are on satellites around here – human agents, and tracking spores.

"Lees, Raider, can you identify any fixed cameras set to watch us and deal with those?"

"I can locate any that are within a given parameter," Raider confirmed.

"And we should be able to hack them to set up a looped image showing a view of the empty field if and when needed," Leesa added.

"I can clear the immediate area of any spyflies seconds before anyone leaves the ship, utilising focussed EMP bursts," Raider added. "And will disrupt any satellite observation by releasing a swarm of mirror flies at the same time. They'll be virtually invisible from the ground but will reflect the sky back to any aerial observer at whatever altitude."

"I'll rig a warning device to identify the presence of tracking spores should any of us walk through a cloud and collect them," Leesa said.

"And I can do a quick sweep in shadow form to spot any human observers," Jen added.

"Is everyone happy with that?" Cornische asked. "I don't pretend it'll safeguard against everything, and if Barbary decide we're worth more sophisticated methods there's little we can do,

but it should take care of most approaches."
   Nobody voiced any objections.
   "Right then, let's get to work."

THIRTEEN

"Are you coming out for a drink?" Leesa asked.

They'd spent the afternoon in research, getting up to speed with what had changed on Barbary in the past ten years, or rather, what hadn't; tracing old contacts, people they could approach without fear of their presence being broadcast, and looking for anything that might hint of a former colleague having settled in the vicinity. It was laborious and time consuming work, even with Raider's help, and unsurprisingly many of the people they'd known had moved on, retired, or were dead. The opportunity to relax a little and get off the ship to visit a local bar was welcomed by just about everyone.

"We're heading over to the Wayward Star," Leesa continued, "Carlton's old place – it's still there, can you believe that?"

"Good to know some things never change," Cornische said, remembering the bar fondly. "Thanks for the invitation, but I think I'll give it a miss."

"Are you sure? Raider's already preparing loops to feed the council's cameras and Shadow's doing a quick recce to make sure there are no human observers. This might be the last chance we get to kick back and let off some steam for a while."

"Tempting, but I'd like to keep an eye on things here."

"Oh? Something I should worry about?"

"No, just me being overly cautious. Saavi's insistence that there could be a downside to our visit here is niggling at me, and I can't shake the concern that if *we* think Barbary is a good place to look for former Angels…"

"…Saflik may have reached the same conclusion," Leesa finished for him. "I'll stay on board with you."

"No, as you say, chances to relax are going to be few and far between, so make the most of this one. Raider will call you back if anything happens, and odds are that nothing will."

She delayed a moment longer, clearly undecided.

"Go!" He shooed her away.

"Okay, I'm gone, but the Wayward Star isn't far away if you need us."

Nate found himself intrigued by Jen, much to his own surprise. The impression he'd gained of her from the holodrama and various accounts of the Dark Angels' exploits didn't do her justice. But then he supposed they'd been concerned purely with Shadow – the cold efficient warrior, capable of being brutal: the killer from the dark. They'd made no attempt to portray the woman behind that persona, presumably because they could discover little or nothing about her. The person he was slowly getting to know could not have been more different from the general perception. She was intelligent, compassionate, amusing, and when you added in her physical attributes – Jen was lithe, and moved with an elegance that saw every movement flowing into the next in a manner he'd never encountered before, like a dancer but not in a considered or deliberate way; it was all natural unstudied grace – the combination proved fascinating.

Saavi chose to stay in the cloud chamber, complaining that the potentials were especially obscure at the moment – as far as Nate could tell, that had been the constant state of things ever since he came aboard – while Drake had declined the invitation to join them. Not that Nate could pretend to be sorry about the latter. He and the captain had reached a sort of unspoken mutual acceptance, but he doubted they would ever be friends. That left Jen, Mosi, and Leesa to accompany him on the short walk to the Wayward Star, a bar which the others were familiar with from previous visits.

"So you've been to Barbary before?" he asked once they'd claimed a table and organised the first round of drinks.

"A few times, yes," Jen confirmed. "It was a semi-regular port of call back in the Dark Angels' heyday."

"A useful place to hang out when things got too intense," Leesa added. "Somewhere to lie low while we waited for things to cool down a bit and public attention to shift elsewhere."

"You'll have been to safer ports," Mosi added. "This isn't somewhere we stayed around for any longer than we needed to."

"Yeah, well, if you will open your doors to the sort of folk other ports don't invite in..." Leesa said. "Not everyone you'll meet here is an arsehole, but it's safer to assume they are until proven otherwise."

Nate glanced around at the bar's other clientele; spacers for the most part, hard-bitten men and women, no doubt, but they seemed no more menacing than those he'd encountered on a hundred other worlds.

A second round of drinks followed the first, and then a third. Mosi was describing to Leesa the mechanisms of a Falcon racer, which gave Nate the opportunity to lean in closer to Jen and ask, "Have you ever eaten at a place called the Blue Buccaneer?"

She regarded him warily, "No, can't say that I have. Why do you ask?"

Leesa evidently overheard the exchange – either she had the hearing of a Manqulin desert bat, or Mosi's explanation must have been less absorbing than Nate had hoped. "This isn't one of your infamous gastronomic 'finds' is it, Nate?" she said.

Jen looked back and forth between the two.

"Nate was renowned for this sort of thing back when we were on *Pelquin's Comet*," Leesa explained. "He'd find a restaurant off the beaten track and drag his friend Pelquin there to sample the local cuisine. I gather they had a few... interesting experiences."

"Most of the time we shared *fabulous* experiences," Nate said. "We discovered some really wonderful food that we'd never have eaten otherwise, but I'll admit that along the way there were... one or two that weren't to our taste; disappointments, even. That's to be expected, though, when you boldly go into the unknown."

"You were discovering restaurants," Leesa pointed out, "not

blazing a trail to new star systems."

"The point is, I've been recommended the Blue Buccaneer," Nate continued, determined to plough on despite Leesa's scepticism. "And since Pel isn't around, I wondered if you lot would care to try the place out with me." He couldn't see any way to not include Leesa and Mosi at this stage. "It should be fun."

"If you can call food poisoning 'fun'," said Leesa.

"None of them were ever that bad," Nate insisted. His reputation deserved *some* defence. "And the number of really good meals Pel and I enjoyed more than compensated for the occasional let down. So what do you say?"

Leesa shook her head. "Count me out."

Mosi had yet to comment, and Jen hesitated, clearly undecided.

"It's in walking distance," Nate said quickly, "and if we don't like the look of it we can simply turn around and head back to the ship."

"Okay," Jen said. "Why not?"

"Your funeral," Leesa said, pushing her chair back and getting to her feet.

Mosi followed suit. "I'll come back with you, Lees. Not sure I fancy adventures in gastronomy right now."

"We really can't tempt you?" Nate said.

"Not a chance. I need to have a word with the captain in any case," Leesa said. "We'll see you two back at the ship."

Nate worked hard at not smiling as they left.

The cool evening air held the promise of more rain, and the puddles that had gathered at the edges of the road were testament to some heavy downpours while they were in the bar, but no new ones assailed them as they made their way on foot to the restaurant.

"Normally I try out places like this first before taking anyone there," Nate said, "but I haven't had the chance to do so with this one, so I can't guarantee a thing."

"Well, we'll soon find out," Jen said. "You like your food, I take it."

"What gave it away? It just seems to me a shame that we visit a new world, a new culture, without trying the cuisine. I mean everywhere has something different to offer – new spices, new techniques, a revolutionary form of marinade, a unique species of fowl or fish, a breed of animal found nowhere else or legumes that aren't grown on any other world... Can you imagine being within a few metres of something truly spectacular and missing out on it completely, blithely walking away without ever knowing it was there?"

She laughed. "You really *do* like your food!"

"Sorry," he said, worried that he was coming across as obsessed.

"No, you've no need to apologise. It's refreshing to see a man so passionate about something."

His perminal was next to useless here, as he'd failed to synch it with the local web, but he had been given directions to the restaurant and so knew where to look, which was just as well. All that identified the Blue Buccaneer was a simple engraved sign – no gimmicks, no wooden schooner in 3D projection leaping out of the frontage to ensure you couldn't stroll past unheeding, just a brushed metal plaque affixed to the wall bearing the restaurant's name and a stylised fish of some sort beneath it. A small strip light protruded to shine on the sign from above, but that was all the flamboyance they allowed themselves. Nate had a good feeling about the place from the moment it first came into view. He would have been hard pressed to explain why – certainly it bucked the convention of eateries that were pristine and modern, with bright fascia and consciously sophisticated appeal. Instead, it looked lived in and warm, with timber-framed windows and tendrils of ivy – or a local equivalent – climbing the walls; an establishment assured in what it served and comfortable with its lot. Here was a place with no pretensions, no striving to be anything other than what it was.

"Looks... inviting," Jen said.

And that summed up his own response in a nutshell.

"Oh!" Jen said, staring at the name plaque.

"What?"

She pointed to the symbol beneath the lettering. "A fish with a unicorn's horn – Saavi asked us to keep an eye open for a sign like that. She called it a gnawed whale, I think, or something of the sort. Must remember to tell her about it when we get back to the ship."

The solid wooden door swung open at the lightest of touches to usher them inside. Beyond it, the comfortable vibe continued; the décor was simple and unpretentious, the service – human waiting staff rather than automated or virtual – charming and efficient. They were given a table by the window, through a dining room that was busy without being packed.

The only slight disappointment proved to be the food; not that there was anything wrong with it as such, consisting as it did of simple honest fare, well prepared and enjoyable to eat – Jen opted for a steak, medium rare, topped with a pat of herb butter, while he went with fish: a local variety of ray served in a citrus sauce with frond-like herbs and what appeared to be tiny pickled flower buds. The white flesh pulled away in curved strips that put him in mind of bleached ribs, but they were soft and succulent to eat and full of flavour.

In many ways, the food was fully in keeping with the surroundings. It was just that it lacked surprise; there was nothing here to make the experience stand out, no tang of spice he'd never encountered before, no sharp twist on the familiar. Nate felt he could have eaten a similar meal in any one of a hundred restaurants on a hundred different worlds, and suspected that in a year's time he wouldn't recall anything that he'd consumed.

The evening's two highlights were provided by the wine – a locally produced red made from a grape he'd never heard of: full bodied, a little dry but fruity, putting him in mind of a decent Merlot but more fragrant – and the company.

Jen proved a charming and interesting dining companion. She told him of life as a farmer, showing him calloused fingers to prove it hadn't all involved automated systems and there was still plenty of manual labour to be done. She shared with him her first disastrous attempt to bake her own bread and had him laughing appreciatively at an anecdote involving the escape of prize-winning livestock and the extraordinary lengths they resorted to in order to capture the final stubborn escapee without injuring it.

For his part, he regaled her with stories of life aboard *Pelquin's Comet*, of his friendship with Pel and some of the scrapes they'd found themselves in. Eking out a living on a trading ship, particularly one that employed a flexible approach to legal niceties, had resulted in a number of incidents that were a lot more amusing in hindsight than they had been to live through.

"What about Cornische," she wanted to know. "What was he like?"

"Honestly? He was a pain. The unwanted cousin you drag along to a party because your parents say you have to." Nate drew a deep breath. "In fairness, he was in an uncomfortable position from the off. We were a tight-knit crew who had worked together for years." He saw no reason to mention the period he'd spent estranged from Pel and the others following the argument over Julia. "Drake was forced upon us by the bank, whose backing we needed to finance the trip, but no one wanted him there. He must have been used to that, though – to being the outsider, I mean. It was his job, after all... And I have to admit he did have his uses." Nate recalled the incident on Brannan's World, the stand-off with port authorities when it looked certain the *Comet* was about to be impounded. Somehow, Drake had persuaded them to let the ship leave.

"But there was always something about him that got right up my nose," he continued. "Drake had this superior attitude that just made me want to punch him in the face, as if he knew things that the rest of us didn't. Of course, I had no idea then quite how true that was.

"I'm sorry," he said, realising that he'd been letting his mouth run away with him while talking about someone she knew well. "But you did ask."

She laughed. "No need to apologise. I can picture how irritating that whole situation must have been. The only thing I struggle with is the thought of the captain doing something like that... and for ten years."

"He was good at it as well, by all accounts," Nate felt obliged to concede.

In fairness, Drake seemed different now – less stiff and formal than Nate remembered. Had he been like this back on the *Comet*, maybe they would have got along a bit better. Then again, maybe not.

The meal ended soon afterwards, with Nate confident he would remember the conversation a lot longer than the food.

"Where did you hear about this place again?" Jen asked as they took their leave.

"From the barman at the Wayward Star," he admitted. "I'll know better next time."

"No, it was lovely," she insisted. "I can't remember the last time I had the chance to sit down and relax over good food in good company at a proper restaurant. Thank you."

She reached up, on tip toes, to kiss his cheek. He turned his head and their lips met. Suddenly, they were kissing in earnest, his arms closing around her, feeling the supple strength of her body.

After a few breathless seconds she pulled away, from both the kiss and his embrace.

"I... I can't do this. Sorry. I'm married, and I love my husband."

Married? Who gets married in this day and age? "Yeah, but we could all be dead tomorrow," was all he said. It sounded lame, even to his own ears.

They walked back to the ship in awkward silence for the most part, broken sporadically by stilted attempts to start conversation, forced words that withered away in the cool night air.

Shit! Shit! Shit! What had she been thinking? Jen relived that kiss over and over. She wanted to talk to Robin so badly, to hear his voice just for reassurance, but he was untold light years away – at least so she hoped – doubtless waiting patiently and faithfully for her to come back to him. And how did she repay him? By gallivanting round in fancy restaurants and snogging a man she'd only just met. *Shit!*

She went to bed early, in part to avoid Leesa, convinced that she had the word 'guilty' writ large across her face. The last thing she wanted was to field questions from a well-meaning but curious friend. Unfortunately, sleep was the furthest thing on her mind. After tossing and turning for what felt like an age but the clock insisted wasn't, she admitted defeat. What she really wanted was to punch something – herself, preferably – and the best place to do that without risk of starting a fight was the gym.

She got up, threw on some overalls and stormed along the gantry and down the stairs into the cargo hold. As she strode across the floor, Saavi emerged from the cloud chamber, presumably heading for her own bed.

"Are you all right, Jen?" she called.

"I'm fine," she assured her. "It's nothing a bout of controlled violence in the gym won't cure." Then, as an afterthought: "Oh, by the way, that fish with the horn on its nose you were asking about a while ago. I think I've seen it."

"Where?" Saavi asked, a little too sharply.

"On a sign outside a restaurant called the Blue Buccaneer, not far from here. Do you remember that bar we used to go to sometimes, the Wayward Star?"

"What, the place owned by that old spacer, Benny Carlton?"

"That's the one. Benny's not in charge any more but the bar's still there, and the Blue Buccaneer is a couple of minutes further on from there."

"Thanks, Jen!" Saavi turned back towards the cloud chamber, the door opening to admit her.

"If you need some muscle for whatever this leads to, you know where to find me," Jen called after her. "I'm in the mood for punching things."

"Will do."

A woman on a mission, Jen continued to the gym, determined to put the heaviest duty apparatus Raider could provide through its paces.

Saavi felt more excited, more confident, than she had in days. Lately, the potentials had been multiplying so rapidly that she risked losing control, but Jen had just provided her with the missing piece, the key that would enable her to reassert a semblance of order.

Of course it's here, she chastised herself, *not at the previous stopover where we picked up Nate Almont at all. Why didn't I see that?*

Because she was tired, over-extended, her attention fraying, and that made her liable to miss things, which would do none of them any good.

Simply fitting the presence of the narwhal here on Barbary into the models and patterns and data fields that surrounded her had an immediate impact. Suddenly everything began to make sense. Potentials evaporated, fading away like so much smoke on the wind, and the roiling confusion of colours and patterns that she had been battling to interpret for so long calmed to something approaching order, assuming a rhythm she could now move with and comprehend, coaxing out individual strands to be examined, their contribution to the overall melody understood at last.

She saw the stylised narwhal, saw the unimposing building it adorned. She saw a gang of youths setting about an older man: a ragged remnant of a man, a rough-sleeping vagrant at the limits of his strength; a man who couldn't possibly defend himself; a man who was about to die.

No! He couldn't be allowed to. If he did, they would fail. This was the *only* thread that offered salvation. If this man lost his life that night, none of them would survive what was to come, and with them the future of humanity perished. The butterfly effect; she could see the ripples of his demise spreading out through the timelines, erasing potentials and creating new ones – poor alternatives in every case. This unprepossessing man, this apparent nobody, was the key to all their tomorrows. Not the key, she corrected herself, but a link; a vital link in the chain of fragile consequences that represented humankind's slender hopes. If that link failed, it would all fall apart.

Saavi finally saw what had to be done.

"Oh," she said, blinking and staring. This wasn't what she had expected, and it certainly wasn't what she wanted, but since when had personal preferences mattered in the grand scheme of things?

Now that such a clear course of action had presented itself, she set about following the alternative paths, those eclipsed by the likely, eliminating potentials and narrowing down the possibilities to confirm that she hadn't missed anything. She worked with diligence and focus, taking the same professional approach she always had, to ensure there were no mistakes or oversights.

Finally, satisfied that all other avenues had been considered and rejected, she sat back and smiled. There could be no doubt; this was the *only* way to proceed that would preserve the glimmer of hope for a favourable outcome.

She glanced down to where Jai, ever faithful, ever vigilant, stood guard. Currently configured as a doll with braided blonde hair, the automaton met her gaze. Saavi had always resisted the temptation to anthropomorphise Jai, but at times she couldn't help but think of him as the only one who didn't judge her.

There followed a brief wait, which was necessary for the real world to catch up with her intentions, before she stood up and left the cloud chamber, Jai at her heels. It always impressed her how easily her T'kai guardian coped with stairs. It reached the top of the flight leading from the cargo bay scant seconds behind her, and the two walked the gantry and entered the ship's living quarters. Everything was quiet. This was now early morning, and everyone else would be asleep; apart from Leesa, perhaps. Saavvi wasn't convinced she ever really slept.

As they reached the airlock, she spoke softly: "Raider?"

"Yes, Cloud?" came the subdued response.

"Under no circumstances are you to inform the captain or any of the crew that I've left the ship. Is that clear?"

"Protocol requires me to…"

"Raider," a little more firmly this time, "we both know you are more than just an AI and can act beyond the parameters of your programming. It is essential for the future wellbeing of the crew that no one should follow me. I need to do this alone, without interference from any of the others. It is the only way to safeguard their future. Is that clear?"

"It is. Given your explanation, I shall comply."

"Thank you."

She took her leave, walking through the airlock and stepping out into the cool night air, unnoticed by anyone.

FOURTEEN

Cornische was woken by Raider. It was still dark, which meant night both internally and externally – they'd synched ship's hours to local time when it became clear they would likely be here for a few days.

"Captain, you're needed."

"What is it, Raider?" he asked, trying to kick start his brain even as he registered that it was a little past two in the morning.

"We have both a visitor and a tragedy to contend with."

That did the trick, fast-tracking him to a rough approximation of wakefulness.

He pulled on some clothes, saying, "Show me."

Raider summoned an image of outside, where a man stood, bathed in sensor lights from both the ship and a nearby port building. He looked unkempt, in mismatched shabby clothing, long hair and beard. Cradled in his arms was a slight form, unmoving.

"Is that... *Saavi*?" Cornische said, not wanting to accept the image.

"Yes."

Cornische was out of his quarters, hurrying towards the airlock. "I didn't even know she'd left the ship. Why wasn't I informed?"

"Cloud gave strict instructions that I shouldn't tell you."

"When this is over, you and I are going to have serious words regarding responsibility and the chain of command," he snapped.

Cornische reached the airlock, slamming the manual control without even stopping to ask Raider to open it for him. Then he was through the outer door and down the stairs before they'd fully extended.

He strode across the solid ground – hardened by the multiple

147

take offs and landings of countless ships over many years – to where the vagrant waited. The man was tottering, looking to be at the limits of his strength. He held Saavi's unmoving form out to Cornische.

"I'm sorry," the stranger said, and a corner of Cornische's numbed mind realised that the man was crying. "I… There was nothing I could do. She saved my life, but there was *nothing…*"

The streets were all but deserted, the few people abroad at this hour either in a hurry to be somewhere else or too drunk to concentrate on anything beyond getting home. Nobody paid her and Jai any attention, and Saavi found the Blue Buccaneer easily enough, despite its discrete signage.

She'd seen the restaurant in the timelines and she'd seen a violent assault, a beating that would turn murderous if no one intervened, but she hadn't seen how the two were connected. For a moment she simply stood in the street, listening, waiting. Then she heard it: the grunt of someone gasping in pain, the growl of someone venting their rage.

The building was detached. To its right a narrow alleyway led to a side entrance – for the kitchens or perhaps deliveries – and here she found them.

As she'd seen in the potential, the victim appeared to be a vagrant, a down-and-out, the sort that societies throughout history had done their best to ignore unless their collective conscience was stirred.

Three men and a woman stood around him in a loose circle, all much younger, all laughing and jeering as they pushed him from one to the other across the space between them. A further man stood slightly removed, lounging against some crates and swigging from a bottle.

This one was mouthing a stream of vitriol, encouraging the others to shove harder. "You fucking leach! You're worse than scum, shit we'd be disgusted to find on the soles of our shoes. The universe'll breathe a sigh of relief when you're gone. No one's gonna miss you. We're doing the world a favour, wiping you away."

It was inevitable that, made to stumble back and forth between the circling youths and propelled by ever rougher shoves, the man would lose his footing. He fell almost comically, trying desperately to stay upright, perhaps realising that once on the ground he might never get up again.

First one, then another boot went in, the youths taking run ups as if kicking a ball, sending their victim from his hands and knees to curl up in a foetal position, trying to protect his head.

Saavi had seen enough. None of them had noticed her as yet.

"Jai," she said quietly. "The five figures standing are all hostiles. When I give the word, go offensive."

"Hey! Leave him alone!" she yelled, stepping forward. "I've seen you. I've recorded your faces and I'll report you if you don't stop now."

They noticed her then, all right.

"Piss off, little girl," said the bottle swigger, evidently the gang's leader.

One of the others detached himself from the kicking ring and came towards her – a little unsteadily, clearly high on something. "Maybe the little girl wants to join the party," he said, leering.

"Jai, offensive."

The bodyguard stepped in front of her, its small hands peeling back to reveal gun barrels. The deceptively quiet pop of their discharge was almost lost against the ongoing sounds of the kicking the other three continued to administer with such dedication and evident glee.

The leering youth's expression changed into one of puzzlement, as he convulsed and went down.

"What the hell?"

The laughter and the jeering and the kicking stopped.

The leader, the one who stood apart, pointed to Saavi and Jai. "Get the doll," he shouted. "That's what's doing the shooting."

The other three might have broken and run, Saavi thought –

being shot at clearly hadn't been part of their plans for the night – but the leader's goading stopped them, his authority wouldn't let them. They hesitated for a moment, staring at their fallen friend, as if still struggling to process what had happened to him.

"Go on!" the leader yelled.

That tipped the balance, and the three charged, snarling, shouting, and drawing weapons as they came – one a knife, one a cudgel adorned with glowing red script, the other some sort of energy weapon, its muzzle crackling with blue light as he raised it.

Jai was quicker. Again the double popping sound and two of them stumbled and fell – the girl and the boy holding the energy weapon – but the third kept coming, voicing a wordless yell as he raised the cudgel over his head. There was no hope that he might stop and run, not any more; he was committed: do or die.

Jai decided it would be the latter.

The bodyguard's guns fired another round, and this final youth jerked and fell, the cudgel spinning from his hand. But he was in motion, and had closed the distance between them considerably, so that he was almost on top of Jai when the morph nailed him. He skidded forward, his momentum carrying him into Jai, bowling over the bodyguard as his body came to rest on top of it. The small morph disappeared beneath his outstretched arm and chest.

"Jai! No!"

A horrified Saavi rushed forward, to push and roll the youth's unresisting but heavy body off her companion.

Once uncovered, the mechanoid stirred and tried to stand, but seemed unable to operate its legs. She picked it up, lifting it away from the dead man.

"It's all right, Jai," she said. "We'll get you fixed once we're back at the ship."

She screamed as pain exploded through her left shoulder.

"Bitch!" a voice snarled.

Only then did she remember the fifth man, the one who had seemed to be the thugs' leader. She struggled to turn, to lift a hand in defence, catching the flash of a blade as he stabbed her again. Lower this time, just above the waist, agony lancing up through her back, her side.

Saavi tried to crawl away, dreading the next blow and remembering the frenzied kicking she had seen meted out mere seconds earlier. She knew she couldn't take any more of this, but felt helpless.

Then the whole world seemed to throb, to pull apart and congeal again, pulsating in jagged lurches of splintered reality.

At first she thought it was the pain, her injuries and the loss of blood loosening her grip on consciousness, but her attacker didn't press his assault. In fact he shuffled away, just a step or two, staggering as if disorientated and mouthing an inarticulate bellow, part rage and part fear, so perhaps it wasn't her at all.

Frame...

She heard again the unmistakeable pop of Jai's gun. The man above her grunted, having assumed no doubt that her bodyguard was disabled and no longer a factor. Big mistake. She saw him grimace and watched as he collapsed forwards, his face coming to rest on the ground close to where she now lay, his unfocussed eyes staring into her own.

Then the pain grew too great, welling up to sweep through her, swallowing any possibility of coherent thought and driving consciousness before it.

She came round to find a stranger cradling her head and staring at her, a bewhiskered face framed by a tangle of unkempt hair; nice eyes, she noted, kind eyes, though his breath could have done with some freshening.

"Miss, little girl... Please don't be dead. You can't be dead."

"I'm not yet," she tried to say, but the muscles in her face refused to obey and her mouth struggled to form the words; all that emerged was an unintelligible groan.

"Thank God!" He seemed on the verge of crying. "And thank you. For saving my life, I mean."

"Ship," she croaked. This one word took all of her

concentration and required more effort than any single word ought to, but her perseverance paid off.

"Ship? You're from a ship?" the vagrant said.

"Yss... Mst g' back..."

"Yes, of course. I'll take you back. What's it called, this ship of yours?"

She focussed and with the last of her fading strength gasped, "Line... a Linkin,"

No, that wasn't right, but it must have been close enough, because the man seemed to understand her. *"The Lion of Lincoln, really?"*

She barely heard that at all, his words floating away as darkness reached out to wrap her in an all-consuming embrace.

Cornische accepted Saavi from the vagrant, cradling her tenderly in his arms. Her eyes were closed – whether naturally or shut by the vagrant as a mark of respect, he couldn't say. She seemed even smaller now than she had in life: so light, so frail. He could tell immediately that she wasn't breathing.

"Saavi!"

The cry came from behind him. He looked round, to see Jen and Leesa rushing down the steps towards him. Of course they would have heard the commotion despite the hour, especially Leesa.

"I'll get the gurney," Jen called, turning halfway down the landing ramp to rush back into the ship.

Too late, he wanted to say but didn't. He wouldn't rob her of at least the attempt to help, however futile.

Leesa was there beside him, staring at his face as if searching for a reason to hope, but all he could do was shake his head.

"Saavi," she murmured, reaching out to stroke the girl's head.

"Saavi?" the vagrant said, as if the name meant something to him. "I didn't realise... didn't know her name."

"You said that she saved your life," Cornische said. "What happened?"

"I was taking a beating from a gang of youths high on goodness knows what... Five of them. They were really getting into it and weren't about to stop, not while I was still breathing at any rate. Then the girl turns up out of nowhere, demands they leave me alone. And she had this weird looking doll with her that *shot* one of the thugs. After that they turned on her and the doll, and..." He gestured to the lifeless form. "Why did she do it? Why did she risk her life for me?"

Why indeed? Cornische was missing something, he knew that. The only reason Cloud would sneak off the ship to help a stranger was if the man were important in some way. If that was the case, why didn't she *tell* somebody? Someone who could have gone with her and helped; someone who could have saved her.

Mosi and Jen arrived with the gurney, and he placed Saavi's small form down gently. She looked lost in its embrace.

As he did so, the vagrant staggered. They'd been so focussed on Saavi they'd forgotten the man who brought her back to them.

"You're hurt," Cornische said, and reached out instinctively to offer support.

"I'm all right," the man mumbled. "Beatings aren't exactly unknown when you live rough on Barbary."

"You could have broken ribs, internal bleeding, who knows? Come up into the ship and let's check you over, just to make sure."

"No!" The vagrant pulled away from Cornische's touch and looked up, almost pleading. For a moment there was something in his eyes... "No," he repeated. "I don't want to intrude on your grief. I'll be fine"

So saying, the man took a step back but wilted, and he had to grasp the gurney to avoid collapsing entirely.

"No intrusion," Leesa assured him. "You brought our friend back to us. Please don't belittle her sacrifice by refusing our help when you so clearly need it."

He could hardly say no after that, so the vagrant joined their sombre group, accepting Leesa's support as they made their way back into the ship, though Cornische still had the impression he did so with a degree of reluctance.

As they stepped aboard, Raider spoke up. "Greetings, Frame, welcome home."

Everyone stopped, and stared.

"Billy?" Jen whispered.

The vagrant was visibly sobbing now, his shoulders shaking with grief. "I'm sorry," he said. "I didn't even recognise her as Cloud until I brought her back here and you said 'Saavi', how could I? Why did she do that for *me*?"

His legs buckled completely, and he collapsed to his knees on the deck, Leesa letting him go gently. His head was bowed, tears falling freely.

"I'm nobody," he murmured. "Why would she do this?"

Before Cornische could react, Jen crouched down beside him. "You're not nobody," she insisted. "You're one of us, and that matters to everyone here. On top of which, Saavi wouldn't have sacrificed her life for a 'nobody'. You're important in what's to come. Somehow, in some way that none of us can begin to guess, you have a part to play. You're a Dark Angel, Billy."

"Some Angel. *Look* at me."

That was the reason he'd been so reluctant to accompany them on board, Cornische realised: pride; shame; he didn't want his former crewmates to recognise him, to see what had become of him. He didn't want their pity.

"You're the reason we're here, Billy," Cornische said. "We need you."

"Yeah, and we'll need you a whole lot more once you've had a dry shower and a change of clothes," Leesa added, gripping his arm and half helping, half hauling him back to his feet. "Come on."

As Leesa took Billy to sickbay, Cornische said to Jen, "Actually, I reckon Saavi would have put her life on the line for just about anybody."

"So do I, but it seemed the right thing to say at the time."

"Oh it was, it certainly was. You did well."

"Can you believe that's Billy?" Mosi said. "I mean I know it's been ten years, but I'd never have recognised him."

They placed Saavi in one of the cryochambers – a hangover from the pre-RzSpace days of space travel, but one which all ships with any sense subscribed to. The chambers were a last resort, a means of preserving life in the event of a ship suffering catastrophic damage far from help.

Cornische had never been convinced; if things were *that* bad and you were so far from anywhere, what were the chances you'd be able to reach the cryochambers on a failing ship before vacuum claimed you, or that anyone would ever find you if you did? A frozen corpsicle entombed in a high tech casket, forever suspended in the limbo between life and death – or at least until the systems failed.

However, psychologically it did the crew good to know the chambers were there; just in case.

The lights dimmed and the Dark Angels left their fallen friend in peace.

They gathered in the galley to raise a glass and bid Saavi farewell. Initially it was just Cornische, Jen, Mosi and Nate, with Leesa still off tending to Billy.

"Maybe we should stick to fruit juice," Mosi suggested, recalling the fact that Saavi didn't drink alcohol.

"Feel free to, if you like," said Jen, opening a beer.

"No," said Mosi, raising his own beer. "She never objected to our drinking while she was alive…" His words trailed off, as he realised where that was leading.

Leesa soon joined them. "He's sedated," she said. "Raider's checked him over."

"How badly hurt is he, Raider?" Cornische asked.

"Fractured ribs, damage to pancreas and liver, a herniated disc, considerable internal bruising, ligament damage to the right knee, a…"

"Okay, we get the picture," Leesa cut in. "We don't need a comprehensive list, thanks all the same."

"Are all his injuries readily treatable?" Cornische asked.

"Yes, he should recover fully, given sufficient time and the correct care."

"And what can be managed without sufficient time? Would you be able to get him up on his feet in a few days?"

"Theoretically, yes. I can accelerate treatment and take care of the more serious injuries, and provide painkillers if required, though I wouldn't necessarily recommend doing so from a medical perspective."

"Noted. That'll have to do, then."

"The longer he has to recuperate, the better," Raider added.

"Understood. We'll let him rest in sickbay for as long as we possibly can."

"First the captain, then Mosi, now Billy," Leesa said. "That bed's getting more use than any other on the ship."

"I need to talk to him," Cornische said, not relishing the prospect. "We can't pluck him away from whatever life he has here and drag him off to a war he knows nothing about. He needs to know what he's getting into and give some level of consent."

"And if he says 'no'?"

"Then we leave him here."

A moment's silence followed, as it sank in for all of them that leaving Billy behind would mean Saavi had died for nothing.

"Did he say any more about what might have happened to Jai?" Jen wondered, breaking the silence.

"No, he didn't say much more about anything."

"It's a good question, though," Cornische said. It was hardly surprising that Billy's attention had been focussed elsewhere, but the last thing any of them wanted was for some child to stumble across the T'kai killing machine and take a fancy to it, mistaking Jai for a genuine retro toy.

He glanced across to Jen, who met his gaze and gave a

resigned nod. "I'll go and check."

"We'll join you," Mosi said. "Naj will meet you there, if that's okay."

Cornische kept quiet. It seemed unlikely there was anything Jen and Najat could achieve together that Jen couldn't manage on her own, but he recognised Mosi's need to contribute.

While they did their thing, he went to see Billy.

The man Cornische found sleeping peacefully in sickbay was unrecognisable as the dishevelled figure that had come aboard such a short time ago. In repose, with beard and hair trimmed and face cleaned, he looked much younger, and Cornische could now see the hint of a resemblance to the person he recalled from a decade ago.

A few days back he'd been sitting in this same chair waiting for Mosi to come round, and he still felt the effects of his own ordeal every now and then. Sometimes it felt as if he was going into battle at the head of the Walking Wounded rather than the Dark Angels…

He waited as Raider brought the patient round. Lips opening and closing, a twitch around the eyes, and finally the eyes blinked open. The eyes flicked from side to side, taking in the surroundings. Finally they focussed on Cornische.

"Captain?"

"Billy, how are you feeling?"

"Terrible… Actually no, that's not true, it's more the memory of how I *was* feeling. Whatever meds Raider's feeding me are working wonders. I feel much more comfortable, thank you."

"Glad to hear it. Are you up to a brief chat? There are some things I need to explain."

"Yeah, I reckon so. Go ahead."

Cornische then summarised the situation and explained their mission to reunite the Dark Angels in order to thwart Mudball and Saflik. He finished with, "I can't pretend that what we're about to undertake will be easy, but it is necessary. Every additional Angel we're able to count on will make a difference, possibly *the* difference. Sorry to put you on the spot after all you've been through, but we have to leave shortly. Are you with us?"

He could only hope that Billy was able to think clearly enough to understand, despite the injuries and the sedation. His next words suggested that he might be.

"So… Cloud died trying to recruit me."

"That's a simplification, but in essence, yes."

Billy closed his eyes and for a moment Cornische feared that he might be drifting off again, but then he said, "For her sake, then, I don't see how I can say no."

"For all our sakes, I hope you don't, but no one wants to force you, and it will mean leaving your life here on Barbary behind."

Billy made a barking sound that might have been a laugh. "That won't be hard, Captain, I promise you. You've seen me, you can work out what's become of me in recent years. There's nothing much to leave."

"You're in, then?"

"Yes, I'm in."

He left Billy to Raider's tender ministrations and headed back to the galley, to discover that Jen and Najat had just returned, having recovered Jai from the alley. The T'kai mechanoid was damaged but still functioning.

"Raider reckons he might be able to repair it," Jen said.

"The T'kai technology appears to be entirely human in its derivation," Raider explained, "without any contamination from Elder tech, as far as I can tell. They have developed rather singular skills, and while it will be a challenge to restore the morph to its former elegant state, this is a challenge I would relish."

Cornische wasn't entirely certain why anyone would want to have the bodyguard rebuilt without Saavi being around, but he didn't object.

"What about the muggers?" he asked.

"Three bodies in the alley, all male," Jen reported, "which I left in situ."

"The other two must have slithered off to find a rock to hide beneath so they could lick their wounds," Mosi said.

"Was there anything to suggest this wasn't just a gang of local thugs high on drugs and bloodlust?"

"No," Jen confirmed, "but how would we tell if there *was* anything more to them?"

She was right; it had been a stupid question. He was seeing Saflik in every misfortune, which didn't mean they weren't there.

"Does anyone harbour any doubts that Billy is the reason we're here?" he asked.

"No, it fits the pattern," Leesa replied.

They all agreed.

"If only I hadn't told Saavi about seeing that stupid horned fish…"

"Don't beat yourself up over it, Jen. You couldn't anticipate she'd go off on her own like that, and, let's face it, if anyone knew what they were walking into, it was Saavi."

"I told her to come and get me if the information led to anything… Why didn't she just do that?"

"Saavi had her reasons," Cornische said. "We may never know what they were but she persuaded Raider to cover for her, so she must have believed that having company would affect the outcome, changing things for the worse going forward. I know that's difficult to get our heads around, given what's happened, but we have to trust her and believe that her death, her *sacrifice*, will benefit us in some manner we may never even recognise."

"That's a hard one to buy, Captain."

"I know, but it's the only way I can see to make sense of this."

They couldn't afford the luxury of taking time to mourn, and Cornische was concerned about the effect Saavi's death might have on morale. He had to keep them moving forward, to

159

maintain the momentum they'd built.

"All right, most of us have been off the ship in the last few hours without any thought of disguise – understandable, given what else has been going on – but it means we've no idea what intel, if any, Barbary may now hold on us.

"Given that we've found one former Angel in Frame, I propose we get the hell off Barbary immediately. Does anyone object?" He waited a silent second. "Good. We also have to accept that without Saavi here to guide us, the likelihood of our finding any more long lost crewmates is somewhere between slim and none.

"Fortunately, we now have a pretty strong roster of Dark Angels on board, and I reckon we're as ready as we'll ever be. While we *can* try to chase others down by more traditional methods, we have to remember Saavi's warnings that almost anything we do from here on in is more likely to hinder than help us.

"So, once we're clear of Barbary, I intend to head straight to Lenbya."

"Can't see any reason not to," Jen agreed.

"Raider?"

"Now would be a good time, Captain. The Elder composite and its allies are making progress in forcing a way through to the cache. Intervention will soon be required."

"That settles it," said Leesa. "Let's go save the universe."

FIFTEEN

Cornische was surprised when Seb Watkins answered his call.

"Have you any idea what time it is?" the bleary-eyed councillor asked.

"Yes, which is why I was expecting to speak to an automated answer service rather than an actual person."

"I've had you listed as a priority, so that any contact from you gets transferred to me wherever I am and whenever. It seemed like a good idea at the time."

"I'm flattered."

"And I'm shattered, so let's cut to the chase. Why the out of hours call?"

"Just wanted to let you know that we're leaving."

"What? You only just got here."

"I know – change of plans."

"You found what you came for, then. That was quick."

"Sort of," Cornische conceded. "We gained a crewmember and we lost one, so it's more of a quid pro quo."

"Enlighten me."

"There was an incident an hour or two ago, a mugging. You'll find three of the attackers dead in an alley beside a restaurant called the Blue Buccaneer, close to the port. Two others were shot but presumably survived, because they're not there now. I wouldn't want you to think we were running away because of this."

"For Elder's sake, you haven't even been here for a full day yet. Deyna was right. Trouble really does follow you lot around. How does any of this relate to you swapping out a crewmember?"

"We lost somebody, we gained somebody." Cornische did his best to keep his voice steady.

161

"That's all you're telling me? You and your stupid secrets… I won't lie, there are more than a few folk around here who'll be relieved to see you go. When will you be ready to lift off?"

"As soon as we get clearance."

"Okay, leave that with me. Control will be in touch shortly to give you the green light."

"Thanks, Seb."

"I wish I could say it's been a pleasure, but…"

"…You'll be glad when we're off world and become someone else's problem rather than yours."

"Pretty much. Take care, Cornische. Don't hurry back, but good luck with whatever it is the Dark Angels are up to."

"What exactly does Frame do?" Nate asked.

It was late the next morning. Leesa, Jen and Nate were having breakfast in the galley. Neither Mosi nor the captain had surfaced as yet, but given what they'd been through the previous night anyone could be excused an extended lie in, and Leesa knew that Cornische had stayed up later than the rest of them. She'd been with him long enough to see the *Ion Raider* lift off from Barbary and enter RzSpace, but had then left him to his own devices and headed for bed.

The mood in the galley was subdued, and none of them were attacking their food with any great relish, despite Raider's ability to synthesise just about anything they could think of. The lack of enthusiasm could be explained in part by the customary dampening of senses caused by travelling through Rz – including appetite and taste – but on this particular morning there was, of course, more to it than that. Saavi. No one had mentioned her but her absence weighed heavy and painful.

"His abilities, I mean," Nate added.

"He interferes with reality," Leesa said, glad of the distraction, glad to have something to think about that didn't include the empty cloud chamber sitting in the cargo hold.

"He staggers time," Jen added.

"What?"

"It's a little hard to explain unless you've seen him in action," Leesa admitted, "but he can... *pause* I suppose is the best word, the world, so that everything within the area he targets freezes, just for a second, and then snaps back into action an instant later, immediately catching up to where it would have been without the pause, only to freeze again – like a series of stop-start transitions from then to now, rather than the continuous flow of events we're used to. It's sort of how life might seem if viewed through the medium of a stroboscope."

"And in those transitions he can tweak things, take away a wall that's in the way, for example, but it comes back again when he stops," Jen added.

"That sounds outrageous."

"Wait till you see him actually do it. Outrageous is as good a word as any. In this crowd, Jen and I are the normal ones, trust me."

"Yeah, of course you are. Why 'Frame', though, where did the name come from?"

"That's down to Kyle – your predecessor as Ramrod," Jen explained. "First time he saw Billy do his tinkering, he said it was like watching a really ancient movie one frame at a time, with the continuity out of synch. The name stuck."

"Actually, Billy's a bit like Jen in one sense, in that the basic strobetech has melded with his body, so he can produce the effect to a limited extent even without his suit, but the suit amplifies things enormously. He's much more effective and in control when wearing it."

"If you call the technology 'strobetech', why isn't Billy called Strobe?"

Jen shrugged. "I guess he liked Frame better."

Mosi wandered into the galley, looking as if he could have done with another hour or two in bed. He grunted a 'good morning' and shuffled over to the autochef, coming across to join them a moment later carrying a mug of strong coffee and a small stack of crisped bacon atop a style of flatbread he favoured.

Leesa sipped at her citrus drink, which was cooling rapidly to the point where it no longer scalded her throat on the way down, and glanced at the plate in front of her, where a half-eaten slice of hi-fibre toast topped with smoked fish lay abandoned.

"We're still a good few days out from Lenbya," she said to Nate – Lenbya was situated in human space but at the fringe, where few people ventured unless they had good reason to. "That gives us the opportunity to complete your training."

"I thought I was doing okay," he replied, sounding overly defensive.

"You are, you're doing brilliantly," she said quickly. "At the moment you're one hell of a threat to your enemies and only a minor threat to us, but we'd like to downgrade that to 'negligible'."

"It's just a matter of honing your control," Jen joined in, giving Leesa a quick irritated glare before smiling encouragement at Nate. "The more you practice, the more natural it will all come to you. I can take this morning's session, if that's okay with everyone – it's not as if I've anything else to do."

Mosi held his hands up defensively. "Hey, don't look at me when it comes to training. You two are the fighters. Naj and I are more on the scouting side of things."

Leesa shrugged. "Sure, why not?" She wanted to give the engines a further once over in any case, just to make certain the parts salvaged from the Night Hammer ship were holding up. Not that there was much she could do about it at this juncture if they weren't, but she enjoyed the tinkering.

"Right, that's settled then," Jen said, standing up and slapping Nate on the back. "I'll see you in the gym in fifteen minutes."

Nate was feeling distinctly awkward as he waited for Jen to arrive at the gym. She had seemed perfectly okay with him at breakfast, but that was in company. How would she be with him when they were alone? On the other hand, she had volunteered to take the training session, so clearly she wasn't trying to avoid him. He didn't know whether to say anything or just ignore it and trust they could both move on.

He was still undecided when she showed up, a few moments later, which didn't prevent him from blurting out, "About last night...?"

"Saavi, you mean?"

"No! I mean the meal... after the meal."

"Nate, it happened. It was just a kiss. I hope we can both put that moment behind us and still work together, otherwise we've got a problem."

"No problem," he said quickly, relieved at how pragmatic she was being. "That's fine by me."

So why did he feel disappointed alongside the relief?

"Good. Let's crack on, then."

The morning session was all about focus. Nate had always assumed that Ramrod was like a human battering ram, that his suit gave him extraordinary strength and was robust enough to withstand deadly force of varying types – which was what most people thought. While that still stood as a summary, the truth proved to be a little more complex.

He had been surprised to discover that the 'suit' was nothing more than a skeletal frame and a helmet – which immediately scuppered the myth of it being woven from impenetrable material. In fact, the frame generated an energy field which surrounded the wearer and was activated by movement. The tighter that field remained to the wearer's body, the stronger it made them seem and the greater the protection it afforded. It all came down to a combination of momentum to generate the field and concentration to focus it. If he relaxed, the field would dissipate, spreading out and weakening. If he focussed on holding the field close to him, he could literally run through walls.

The part he struggled with was maintaining that level of concentration for any length of time. It had to be relentless; the moment he allowed himself to be distracted, the moment his focus turned elsewhere, the field would spread, leaving him correspondingly weaker and more vulnerable.

It was exhausting. "No one told me that being a Dark Angel would be this hard!" he complained.

Jen grinned. "Hey, you *chose* to be Ramrod."

"Is it too late to change my mind? Remind me again, what does that Quill character do?"

"Something lame, as I recall. Are you ready for the next one?"

"No, but that's not gonna stop you, is it?

"Not a chance."

He hated the next exercise. He was jogging down dimly lit streets. A series of targets presented themselves at random intervals from random directions – some emerging from the ground, some from walls, others seeming to materialise out of the very air, and he had to strike each one without stopping. That would have been tricky enough in itself, but, just to make things interesting, each target was surrounded by a ring of fragile discs, and he was expected to hit the target without shattering any of the discs. To stand any chance of doing that, especially with the smaller targets, he had to hit them dead centre while keeping Ramrod's energy field as tightly focussed as possible.

To start with, he was rubbish, shattering more of the peripheral discs than not, but he got better, and was pretty pleased with his progress, until it started to get worse again.

"Okay, that's enough for now," Jen said, mercifully. "And don't worry about the last part, that was just fatigue setting in."

"No kidding," Nate said, bent over with hands on his knees as he attempted to catch his breath.

Something had been bothering him, and Jen was his best bet of getting a straight answer. After they'd both taken a dry shower, he blurted out, "What exactly are the Dark Angels?"

In the face of her puzzled frown, he continued, "I've agreed to join up and am now in training... and it occurs to me that I know next to nothing about who you – who *we* – are. Not really."

"You've seen the holodrama," she said, grinning. "I thought

you were the expert."

"I'm serious."

"Okay, so what do you want to know?"

"How it all started, *why* it started."

"I wasn't part of the original crew who first discovered Lenbya," Jen said. "I joined later. If you want to hear about that, you'd be better off asking Leesa."

"You've been there, though, to Lenbya I mean?"

"Yes, just once, when I first became Shadow."

"Start with that, then, if you're willing."

"Not much to tell, to be honest. I hooked up with the Dark Angels by accident – in the right place at the right time, sort of thing – at least that's what I thought at the time. Having seen what Saavi can do since, I'm not so sure. She was different then – the 'adult' Saavi – to the version of her you've seen: more involved, more a part of things, less insular. Anyway, I used to be in the military but I wasn't any more, the Dark Angels were looking for a new recruit and I seemed a good fit, so they invited me to join. This was in the early days, but I'd heard rumour of the Dark Angels – the mystique had begun to form around them even then. I was at a loose end, looking for some excitement in my life, and they were offering to provide it, so I said 'yes'. And they took me to Lenbya."

"What was that like?"

"Nothing I'd experienced before. I'd never seen the inside of a cache chamber at that point, but it was a bit like stepping into one of those but neater, more organised. I got to visit a couple of cache chambers after that, and they were both cluttered, the organisation that might have been there once upon a time having become muddled over the centuries, but not here. Everything was neat and tidy and in its proper place. And the whole thing was huge. I only got to see one chamber but it was clear that there were others, lots of others."

"So Lenbya isn't a single chamber, but rather a whole bunch of them joined together?"

"Possibly, or maybe there's one huge central chamber and several satellite rooms and I was taken to one of those, I don't know."

"And the tech that enabled you to become Shadow was waiting for you in that chamber?"

"Essentially, but it wasn't as simple as that. There was this long counter, and I was invited to walk its length, to see what I reacted to. Arranged along it were these neat little packages of tech and clothing and... *things.*

"What sort of things?"

"All sorts. Weapons, oddments, jewels..."

"And each parcel represented a potential Angel?"

"Yes, but none of them really grabbed me. It was all a bit overwhelming to be honest. I felt the pressure of expectation, you know? The captain and Leesa had brought me there, but they then stood back, leaving me to browse, and I knew I was supposed to choose one of these parcels, but none of them stood out. I thought I'd end up having to just pick one at random, to keep everyone happy, but that didn't feel right. Not for something as big as this.

"I'd almost reached the end of the counter and had just about given up, when I saw it. A dish of deep ebony darkness, which looked like oil. That was it. No fancy suit, no exotic tech, nothing that resembled a gadget or a weapon, just a shallow dish of perfectly still liquid. When I gazed into it, I saw my own reflection, but in negative – don't ask me how. The simplicity of it fascinated me in a way that nothing else in the chamber had. Almost before I realised, I was reaching out to touch the dish, to dip my finger into the darkness.

"As soon as my fingertip touched the surface the liquid started to flow into me – not over me, I couldn't see it run up my hand or anything like that, but into me. I could feel it coursing through me veins, making my hand, my arm and then my whole body tingle. The sense of energy, the thrill of it, was almost erotic, but more intense than even that. One touch with a single finger was enough to draw the dish's contents entirely into me. Nothing remained on the dish, not a single drop."

"And you were Shadow."

"And I was Shadow," she confirmed.

He pondered that for a moment, then said, "One thing I still don't get. I've always discounted Lenbya as a myth, an old spacer's tale, but if the place is real, which clearly it must be, how has it stayed hidden for so long? I mean if the Dark Angels found it, how come no other ship has? It's not as if there haven't been folk looking."

"Ah, now therein lies Lenbya's greatest secret."

He waited for her to continue, but all she did was grin.

"Oh come on, you can't leave me hanging like that."

"After lunch we'll do a bit of work on the defensive side of things," she said. "If you do well enough at that, I'll tell you."

"Really?" Nate couldn't help wondering if she was punishing him for that kiss after all.

"Yes, really."

They dropped out of Rz late afternoon, still days short of their destination but deep within a planetary system, as close to its sun as Raider dared take them. They stayed just long enough to bury Saavi, sending her body on a trajectory that would bring her swiftly into the star's fiery embrace.

Nate was still mulling over what Jen had told him regarding Lenbya – evidently he'd acquitted himself well enough in the day's final training session to merit the promised information. *A pocket universe...* He hadn't even known such a thing was possible. It was hardly surprising that no other ship had stumbled upon the place; it didn't exist – not in this reality at any rate – and could only be accessed via a specific gateway that linked it to the larger universe. Quite how the *Iron Raider* had ended up there was another question entirely, and one that Jen claimed she couldn't answer. "I wasn't there then, remember," she told him.

The brief ceremony in Saavi's honour brought back memories

of the last time he'd taken part in something like this. That had been for Anna, pilot and longstanding crewmember on *Pelquin's Comet*. Drake and Leesa had been present then, too – Anna had lost her life during their successful cache raid, at the periphery of Xter space. The recollection was particularly uncomfortable for Nate, because it reminded him of just how ill he had felt throughout – poisoned, it later emerged, by the ship's treacherous doctor.

Poisoning aside, the difference between then and now was that he had known Anna, whereas Saavi he'd barely met. For most of his brief time on board she'd been closeted away in the Cloud Chamber. While he could sympathise with the grief displayed by the others, he couldn't match it, standing mute while each Dark Angel took it in turn to say a brief sentence or two. He felt like an imposter for being there at all.

Sleeping arrangements on the *Ion Raider* were much the same as on any other ship of the class, including *Pelquin's Comet*, so the accommodation had hardly come as a surprise to Nate: a recessed alcove just deep enough and long enough to contain a bed and a compact cabinet for clothing and personal effects, with a small lip providing minimal personal space and a privacy screen that could be activated if wanted.

He'd stayed in far worse.

Nate lay in bed, his mind too restless to sleep. He still didn't feel at home aboard the *Raider*. They all knew each other and he didn't – not in this context, not even Leesa. The loss of Saavi was terrible, of course, but her funeral had only brought home just how distant he felt from the rest of the crew. It was one more thing that set him apart, and left him trying to figure out where he fitted in here. On the *Comet* he'd been Pelquin's confidante. They'd shared plans and plotted the next move together. Not something that was ever going to happen with this captain.

He'd also been the fixer. Nate would often slip off the ship as soon as they docked to organise supplies, parts, cargo, or to negotiate the more sensitive transactions and arrangements. He had contacts on many worlds and an eye for a profit, but none of that was of much use to the crew of the *Ion Raider*. No, they wanted him to fight, and he still wasn't entirely sure how to feel about that.

Pelquin would have said that he was living the dream, shipping with the Dark Angels, but for Nate the dream had begun to lose much of its sparkle. The holodrama had never been like this.

Eventually, sleep sidled up and mugged him, but not for long. He came awake in a rush, convinced that he'd barely closed his eyes and sensing immediately that he wasn't alone.

A figure loomed over him. He went to move, to struggle, but stopped when he realised it was Jen.

"Wh...?" he started to ask.

"Shhh..." Her shush was soft, quiet; a finger lifted to her lips, then slowly lowered to his lips, before its tip gently traced a line down his chin to caress his neck.

"I thought..." He was on the verge of saying something about her husband, but stopped himself, reckoning that was the last thing he wanted her thinking about just then.

"As you pointed out, we could all be dead tomorrow," she said, and leant forward to kiss him.

Her lips were warm against his, her tongue small and darting. Too soon for his liking, she pulled away, but only in order to slip out of her clothes.

For a moment, all he could do was stare. She looked stunning. Slender, toned, with narrow waist, small breasts: just perfect. She moved her arms to cover herself, in a self-conscious way that made him smile.

He lifted the duvet, inviting her in.

She climbed on top, straddling his waist, gazing down into his eyes a little anxiously.

"I just hope I can remember what to do," she whispered. "It's been a while."

He reached up to run his hands down the sides of her body, feeling the contours of each rib, marvelling at the supple strength of her, the absence of any surplus. She felt vital, alive, wonderful.

"For you and me both," he assured her, as he sat up to kiss first one nipple then the other, loving the way she trembled slightly as he did so.

As it turned out, both of them remembered a good deal more than they'd feared.

They made love twice, the second time especially slow and tender. Afterwards, limbs entwined in a post-coital tangle, she asked, "Are you all right?"

He smiled, hoping he could express just *how* all right he was.

"Yeah," he assured her. "More than all right – I'm living the dream."

Sixteen

The next morning, Cornische called a meeting first thing. Nate wasn't normally a fan of meetings, but he welcomed this one, if only because it gave him a break from training. The crew gathered in ops, which was one area where the *Ion Raider* definitely won out over his old ship, the *Comet*. Pelquin's vessel followed the standard pattern for the class, with a small cockpit area for the pilots which was barely large enough to accommodate the two chairs and their occupants. Comets were built as trading ships and designed to be functional, with most everything reduced to a bare minimum, sacrificed to allow for as large a cargo bay as possible.

The *Ion Raider* demonstrated different priorities. The ship had been extensively modified to provide a higher degree of comfort in a number of areas, which included the cockpit being expanded to produce a sizeable ops room, with enough space for all of them to sit.

Nate sat down next to Jen, without being overly familiar. He wasn't sure how public their liaison was supposed to be, and reckoned it was up to her to decide such things.

As he took his seat, he made some quip about being glad the day's training was delayed, which prompted her to say, "You'll thank us for all of it when the actual fighting starts."

Somehow, he doubted it.

Mind you, on the plus side, he now felt fitter than he'd been at any time since his teens.

"As most of you know, Billy's making good progress," the captain began. "Raider's keeping him sedated for now but the accelerated healing is doing its job and he's on schedule to be up and about before we reach Lenbya. When he is, let's all try to make him feel welcome, okay? He's obviously had a tough time of it on Barbary."

Nate had slept rough a couple of times himself, but only for a night or two when seeking to stay under the radar at some port or other, and never because he had nowhere else to go. He didn't envy anyone who found themselves there.

Cornische was speaking again. "Most of you have visited Lenbya at least once before, so you're aware that it exists in its own separate fold of reality, adjacent to the universe we know but not quite a part of it. The only access is via a gateway under the control of the Lenbya Entity, of which Raider is an aspect. The composite Elder has been trying to force the gateway, to allow Saflik access. After months of striving, it is on the verge of succeeding, so the clock is well and truly ticking.

"I called this meeting because I wanted to pool our knowledge on the Night Hammers, to give us some clue as to what we might be facing. Jen, you were in the military before they went rogue, weren't you? What can you tell us about them?"

Jen felt the blood in her veins turn to ice, having been put well and truly on the spot. She knew the captain hadn't deliberately set out to ambush her with this, it just felt that way.

"Yes," she confirmed, finding her voice. "They were still viewed as an elite unit during my time, the pride of the service – highly respected and admired, even feared to some extent. Their commander, General Haaland, had a reputation as a bad-ass."

"They're vicious bastards," Leesa said. "They spearheaded many of the engagements during the Auganics Wars – the government used them as shock troops. Even we were wary of them, *hated* them for the brutality they showed. They were responsible for the deaths of many of my sisters and brothers."

"Combat drugs," Jen said quietly.

"What?"

"It was an open secret that the Hammers were dosed up with drugs before being deployed, giving them artificially sustained levels of adrenaline, quicker reactions, reduced lactic acid build up, increased levels of aggression, and raised pain threshold, among other things. The aftereffects are said to have been a bitch, but it meant they had a real edge in battle."

"Sounds a bit like you when you've got those blades in your hands," Leesa quipped with a grin. Jen didn't trust herself to respond.

"Do you think they still have access to these drugs or can synthesise their own equivalents?" Cornische asked.

"No idea. Those we encountered on *Darkness Mourning* didn't demonstrate any heightened reactions, but to be fair I didn't give them much chance to demonstrate anything."

"How many of them can we expect to be facing?"

Jen shook her head. "There's no way of knowing. A 'regiment' is a moveable feast, not a specific head count. At the time they went rogue there were around six or seven hundred of them, with four ships. We know what became of *Darkness Mourning*. Unless she was able to get a call for help through immediately and was then repaired in record time, she's out the picture. *Night's Bride* was destroyed with all hands in an engagement off Caster III when the Hammers first went awol. Assuming their forces were split evenly between the four vessels, that means they were then down to four or five hundred, not allowing for other losses. Attrition over the years will inevitably have reduced this, even if they have been keeping a low profile."

"Presumably, though, they could have recruited to replace those they've lost," Cornische said.

"Yes, no doubt they'll have looked at that, but I'm not convinced they'll have done so, at least not in any great numbers. Haaland was always proud of their 'elite' status. Given the regiment's reduced circumstances, there won't be a large pool of potential recruits for them to pick and choose from like they had in the army, and most of those that are available won't be of the calibre they're used to – not having benefited from the sort of initial training that's standard in the military, apart from anything else.

"What about ex-military?" the captain asked. "There must be plenty of former soldiers knocking around."

"It wouldn't surprise me if that's the route Haaland has tried, but given the Night Hammers' disgrace, there'll be a limit to how many veterans would consider signing up with him."

"So, all in all, there are still likely to be as many as three or four hundred of them," Cornische said.

"At most. My best guess would be the lower end of that or fewer. Some must have deserted when the regiment went rogue. Haaland is a charismatic figure, but I can't see seven hundred men blindly following him into disgrace and obscurity, and I'm sure more will have gone since. The years of exile must have been dispiriting. Then there was the skeleton crew we found aboard *Darkness Mourning* – the ship's complement was clearly needed elsewhere, which suggests they're stretched."

"That still leaves us facing a few hundred elite troops, though," Leesa pointed out. "And we've no idea how many bodies Saflik can put into the field."

"Let's just hope your friends on New Sparta send in the cavalry, Captain," Mosi said.

"Nice thought, but hardly something we can count on," Cornische said. "In our favour, Lenbya is strongly defended – far more robustly than your average Elder cache. Raider can coordinate those defences, so once we hit the ground we can expect support from that quarter."

"First, though, we have to get there," Jen said, "and presumably that will mean getting past the two remaining Night Hammer warships – the *Mark of Mímir* and the *Scourge of Samael* – assuming they avoided being decommissioned as effectively as *Darkness Mourning* did when the regiment was cornered and supposedly disbanded."

"Dear gods, where do they get the names of their ships from?"

"That's down to Haaland, he fancies himself a classicist," Jen supplied.

Leesa gave her an odd look.

Mosi was less circumspect. "You seem to know a great deal about them," he said.

She shrugged. "It's surprising what you pick up along the way." That wasn't enough, and she knew it. "To be honest, when I served in the military, the Night Hammers were held up as heroes, the ideal we should all aspire to. I was gutted when they turned bad. Some of the atrocities ascribed to them during the Auganics Wars were... unacceptable." She risked a quick glance towards Leesa, whose expression remained neutral. "I've kept tabs of their fall from grace with a sort of morbid curiosity."

That seemed to satisfy them, but not her. She still felt ashamed on one front, and determined to clear the air once the meeting broke up, seeking out Leesa.

She recalled Leesa telling her once that the best thing about being Hel N was not having to hide any more. Being Auganic meant that she was faster, stronger, much quicker to react than 'normal' folk, able to metabolise and negate toxins and drugs, even able to mesh with automated systems given the right circumstances. Yes, the suit enhanced her strength and protected her from all but the deadliest inimical force. Yes, it heightened her senses and granted her preternatural energy, but it was still only part of the story. As soon as she put that silver suit on, though, people assumed that everything she did was down to Elder tech and never looked beyond that. As Hel N, there was no need to disguise her auganic nature, no more underperforming to avoid standing out.

In a sense, Jen was guilty of something similar. It was easy to assume that everything *she* did was due to the shadowtech melded to her body, and she'd done nothing to discourage that belief, even with those closest to her.

She was drawn from her reveries by an odd look in Leesa's eye. Her friend then confounded her by asking, "Did you sleep okay?"

On the surface, this was an innocent enough question, but it wasn't one that Jen could recall Leesa ever asking her before. Much to her annoyance, she felt her cheeks redden.

"Fine thanks," she said, as nonchalantly as she could manage. "You?"

"Oh, you know me. I'm a light sleeper at the best of times, and the augmented part of me never fully switches off, despite my organic aspect's need to."

Jen said nothing, not taking the bait, refusing to ask if her friend had seen or heard anything. After all, assuming she had, it was up to her raise the subject, if she wanted to.

"That's the problem with these ships," Leesa said. "There's so little chance of privacy."

"As I'm starting to realise."

Leesa burst out laughing; a rarity, especially these days. It made the conversation Jen was determined to have with her all the more difficult.

"Lees, look… There's something I have to tell you. Do you fancy a coffee?"

To Jen's considerable relief, the galley was empty. She was dreading this. She knew how vehemently Leesa hated the Night Hammers. The regiment had spearheaded the government assault on Tyson Five, the engagement that finally decided the Auganics Wars. Victory was ensured via the deployment of a new weapon, a device that scythed through the minds of the auganic army, wiping them out; all bar one, leaving Leesa forever alone in the universe. But if Jen were ever going to speak up, it had to be now: none of them knew if they would survive what lay ahead, and she didn't want to carry this deception to her grave.

"Well," Leesa said. "I'm all ears."

Taking a deep breath, Jen tightened the flexor muscle in her right arm and the image of Mjölnir appeared above it.

Leesa stared at the projection, then at Jen, then back to the hovering image of the hammer.

"I know, Jen," she said quietly. "I know."

"What…? How could you possibly know?"

"Well, strongly suspected at any rate. It's the way you've always reacted when the Night Hammers are mentioned, the way you tense and try to hide the fact. Even without the shadowtech you're one hell of a fighter. If you were in the military, it made sense you'd be in an elite unit of some sort." She shrugged. "It just all adds up."

"Why didn't you *say* something? Have you any idea of the tortures I've gone through, wanting to tell you but not daring to in case I lost you as a friend?"

"Not my place to say anything. It was your secret to keep or not. I figured you'd tell me, when and if you chose to."

Jen couldn't believe it. "Elders! If only one of us had said *something*."

"One of us did, eventually. Look, Jen, we all have a past. I've done things I'm not proud of, believe me. When I first figured this out I was livid, but I managed not to say anything, and as time went on I realised that you'd made the decision to walk away from them. When the poison set in, you refused to be a part of it."

"So we're okay?" Jen reached out to her friend, who took her hand and squeezed it, gently.

"Of course we're okay. Now, tell me about last night…"

Nate came away from the meeting stunned. If that had been Cornische's idea of a pep-talk, the man was in the wrong job. Those odds were ridiculous. Even if the injured vagrant in sickbay recovered in time, that still meant there were only six of them. He had sat there listening to Jen speak, watching the others take it all in and contribute their own thoughts as if the proposed action were the most reasonable thing in the world. At no point did anyone stand up and say, "What the hell are we doing?" Was he the only one on board who recognised this as a suicide mission?

"Are you okay?"

It was Mosi who spoke to him. Nate wasn't entirely sure

179

where Jen and Leesa had vanished off to, but Mosi had evidently spotted his dazed expression.

"Not really," he admitted. "Not after hearing that."

"Yeah, it was all a bit doom and gloom, wasn't it?" Mosi agreed.

"Then how can everyone be so… *cheerful?*" he said. "We're going up against a frigging army and you're all reacting as if you've just heard it might be a bit chilly outside."

"You can't have come into this blind, Nate. You must have been told the situation when the captain first recruited you."

"Yeah, but then it all sounded so exciting – join the Dark Angels, be a hero. Yay! Now, put as plainly as that, what we're doing sounds *insane.*"

Mosi regarded him for a moment, as if struggling to find the right words – or perhaps he was conversing internally with his sister.

"Look," he said at last, "you're new to this, so it's hardly surprising if it's all a bit overwhelming. I'm not gonna pat you on the back and say anything as glib as 'trust in the captain and Raider', because you would just think I was deluded, but that's exactly what the rest of us are doing. We've seen what those two are capable of. You haven't.

"Naj and I have been in situations where, logically, we should have died a dozen times over – a ship plummeting towards the heart of a star with refugee families on board, settlements whose populace had been reduced to slavery under martial law, a planet where entire populations were dying from synthesised plague, outposts under siege by rogue military factions… Each and every time we've come through it, beaten the odds, and along the way saved lives which would otherwise have been doomed."

"You make it all sound so noble. The Dark Angels couldn't really have been that altruistic, surely."

"No, never. That's only in the stories. There was always an angle, always an advantage to be gained, but somehow we ended up doing good more often than not, and this whole 'hero of the people' thing sprung up. The point is that with the captain and Raider by my side, and Leesa and Jen out front – not to mention Ramrod – I wouldn't bet against us in any situation. And this time we're going to be operating on Raider's home turf, which gives us more of an edge than Saflik and their allies can possibly imagine. Yes, the odds may still be stacked against us, but we see those odds as a challenge rather than a threat."

"So what you're saying is, 'trust in the captain and Raider'."

Mosi grinned. "It sounds so much more reasonable when you say it."

Nate tried hard to buckle down to training that morning, but his heart wasn't in it. He was distracted, and it showed in his performance. He made silly errors and took more bruises than at any time since his first sessions.

"What in Elders' name is wrong with you today?" Jen asked. "Did I really sap your energy that much last night?"

"No, no it's not that." And he told her about his reaction to the meeting and his chat with Mosi afterwards.

"Raider, kill the simulation," she said. The street scene they had been training in vanished. "I know," she said to him. "Shit just got real."

"We're not gonna survive this, are we?"

"Honestly? I've no idea."

She sat down on a piece of gym equipment revealed now that the simulation had shut off. Following her lead, he perched beside her.

"Look, Nate, friends of mine have died – picked off by Saflik without ever knowing they were in the firing line. If I were just a smidgeon less paranoid I'd be among them: burned to a crisp in the wreckage of my own home. Then there's Saavi, who sacrificed herself – in full knowledge of the consequences, I've no doubt – so that we could find Frame. *She* saw a way forward, one that would bring a positive result, and gave her life to ensure that was the future we followed. We have to believe in her vision and in our ability to see it through. For the sake of all that's happened, these bastards have to be stopped."

"Yeah, I get that, but do we have to be the ones to do it?"

"Who else? Do you really think government could mobilise in time, even if they stopped bickering and debating long enough to take the threat seriously?"

"There must be –"

"There isn't," she cut him off. "It's us or nothing, and humanity loses. What Mosi said to you is right. We're a lot more formidable than you realise, far more dangerous than Saflik and their allies can possibly imagine. Trust me, the outcome here is by no means a foregone conclusion, despite the numerical odds.

"Now, let's take a break from training until this afternoon, but please use that time to pull yourself together. So far today your defence has been lousy. We're approaching the endgame and if you're not fully focused, you won't survive. Simple as that."

"Okay. I'll do my best."

He was committed, had been since he agreed to become Ramrod. There was no backing out now, and despite his reluctance he knew that all of Jen and Leesa's efforts were intended to give him the best possible chance of coming through this. He'd be an idiot not to give it everything.

"Good. And, Nate, let's be clear about one thing: none of us are doing this because we want to. We're doing it because we *have* to."

Seventeen

There was a palpable sense of excitement as the *Ion Raider* came out of Rz.

Two things had happened in the hours leading up to their arrival that acted to lift the crew's spirits. The first involved Billy, who emerged from his induced coma in considerably better condition than he entered it.

"All bruising and minor injuries have been treated," Raider reported. "The fragment of disc nucleus has been repositioned in his spine and the rupture in the annulus repaired, while anti-inflammatories have successfully eased the pain and swelling. Affected organ tissue has been replaced as appropriate and the torn ligaments in the right knee successfully restored. In addition to damage caused by the beating, the liver was also showing longer term issues typical of alcohol abuse. These too have been dealt with. Essentially, Frame is healed, although in ideal circumstances I would recommend a further period of rest and recuperation."

"In ideal circumstances I'd be happy to grant it," Cornische assured the AI. "However…"

He was there when Raider roused Billy, welcoming him back to consciousness, and sat with him while he sipped at a vitamin-laced drink, before accompanying him to the artefact room to reclaim Frame's very basic costume. Billy had paused before stepping inside, though not, it seemed to Cornische, due to any apparent misgivings, but rather to stare at the other vast metal box that sat beside the artefact room in cargo: Saavi's cloud chamber; empty now, it's mists dormant.

Neither of them spoke. After a moment's contemplation, Billy went into the white room in which so many ghosts resided. He did so without any hint of nerves or excitement, but more an air of resignation. He donned the simple brown smock as if this was something he did every day, clipping in place the twin metal wristbands that focussed and intensified Frame's abilities as if they too were just another part of his routine.

Frame's costume came without any sort of mask, so they had designed one to be worn with it, but this Billy spurned, leaving it in place on the blank-featured white head.

"I don't really see the point, do you?" he said.

There was a sense of the ineffable about Billy, an almost spiritual calmness the like of which Cornische had rarely seen before, and one that was certainly at odds with the man he remembered.

"Sorry to throw you in at the deep end," he said as they headed towards ops where the others waited. "But we'll be emerging from Rz shortly, close to Lenbya and, no doubt, straight into battle."

"I'm ready to play my part, Captain," Billy assured him.

Billy appeared almost sheepish when they entered ops, as if the prospect of others making a fuss of him wasn't something he relished. The other Angels didn't disappoint; Jen hugged him, Mosi gave him a brief embrace and even Leesa treated him to a quick peck on the cheek. He accepted the attention stoically.

Jen introduced him to Nate, explaining, "He's joined us as the new Ramrod."

"The whiskers actually suit you," Leesa commented, "now that they've had a trim and been tidied up a bit."

Cornische stood back and observed all this: the calm before the storm. *Are we enough?* he couldn't help but wonder. They would have to be.

The second encouraging development was brought to them by Raider, shortly after Frame had made his appearance and as they were about to return to normal space.

"There is conflict in the immediate vicinity of the entrance to Lenbya," the AI announced.

"Conflict? Who's involved?" Cornische wanted to know. "Is this a falling out between allies or is there a new factor?"

"A number of ships have emerged from Rz to contest the space around the entrance with the Saflik and Night Hammer vessels already stationed there. The allegiance of the new arrivals is unclear at this stage."

"Could it be New Sparta, do you think?" Leesa asked.

"Maybe."

"I never thought I'd be glad to see the banks meddle in anything."

"It doesn't really matter who they are," Cornische said. "If they can keep the Saflik ships occupied, it might give us a chance to slip past them to reach Lenbya."

The last time the *Ion Raider* exited Rz in the midst of a battle she had done so blind; this time the crew were better informed, thanks to Raider's link with Lenbya's Elder entity.

No one shot at them, deliberately or inadvertently, though Leesa was soon conjuring screens that showed the ongoing engagement.

As with any such situation, a degree of confusion reigned, but between them Raider and Leesa were able to form a pretty good impression of what was going on.

"The two Night Hammer warships hold the key," Leesa explained. "One, the *Mark of Mimir*, is sitting deep, held back from the engagement, presumably to block access to Lenbya should any of the attackers slip past the rest of the siege fleet. The other, the *Scourge of Samael*, is the focal point of the whole battle." She pointed to the relevant positions of the two ships on her arrays.

"Have we any clue yet as to who the attackers are?"

"The majority of their ships show no ident at all," Raider reported, "but a number appear to be of similar design to the vessel previously encountered that identified as *Sabre 1*."

"So it *is* New Sparta," Jen said.

"Looks like it."

"There is a need for increased urgency, Captain," Raider said. "The composite and its allies have now broken through to Lenbya and have succeeded in establishing a beachhead. They are currently engaging my defences on the ground."

"Will those defences hold?"

"For now, yes, but they will not do so indefinitely."

"Lees, can you plot a course that will take us to the gate without our becoming target practice for every ship out there?"

"Already on it. There are no guarantees, mind – it's an ever-changing situation ..."

"Appreciated. Best option will have to do. As soon as you can, take us in. Maintain a steady speed – we don't want to dawdle but let's not draw attention by darting flat-out towards the gate."

"Understood. Okay, here we go."

The next few moments were intense. The battle around them unfolded on the displays. Ships died, crews perished in the dispassionate winking of a light, with no accompanying sound or even vibration disturbing those gathered in the *Ion Raider*'s ops room. They might almost have been viewing the whole battle from a distance, rather than attempting to tiptoe around its fringes without getting directly involved.

Their luck held long enough for Cornische to think they might get away with it, but not long enough for them to actually do so.

"Ident's showing as the *Silver Spear*," Leesa reported, as a blip detached itself from the ongoing hostilities and moved to intercept them. "An old military cruiser, Apex class."

"How heavily armed is it?"

"There's no telling how its weaponry might have been upgraded, but, even with the original specs, a lot more heavily than us. Can't be certain of its allegiance, either, but, given the sophistication of the ships that we *know* to be New Spartan, I'm guessing she won't be one of theirs."

"I agree. More likely Saflik."

"The point's moot in any case. She's firing at us. Hang on!"

Leesa threw the ship into a tight curve, giving Cornische reason to be glad of his seat's padding. The display showed a straight line of light lancing past them: energy weapon.

"Respond with missiles," Cornische instructed. "I'd rather hold Dead Leg back if we can. We may need it to get past the picket ship that's stationed across the gateway."

The *Ion Raider's* limited arsenal made it a titan in terms of trading vessels, but still a lightweight in this sort of scenario; she carried enough weapons to hold her own against a single enemy, but not in a full blown battle. Among the five missiles the *Raider* was equipped with were a grand total of two hunter seekers, for use against another vessel. Both were launched now, just as Leesa and Raider took the ship into a further sharp manoeuvre to avoid another pulse of energy from the cruiser.

They all watched anxiously as a thin line charted the missiles' progress on the display. The *Silver Spear* countered with missiles of her own, and their two birds were destroyed, short of their target.

It wasn't that big a surprise, but Cornische still felt a slump of disappointment.

For a third time they were forced to hold on tightly as the cruiser fired at them. This time, they weren't quite quick enough; whether through luck or learning, the *Silver Spear's* targeting had improved, and the deck bucked violently beneath the Angels.

Leesa swore.

"Not your fault," Jen said. "They were going to nail us at some point."

"Raider, damage report!" Cornische barked.

"A glancing blow only. There is damage to a number of systems, which I'm still correlating, but nothing immediately vital. Hull integrity remains sound, though that will not continue if we take another such hit. There is significant weakening in the vicinity of the cargo hold."

They had no choice. "All right, Raider, hit the *Silver Spear* with both beams."

On the displays a line of light arrowed from the *Ion Raider* towards the cruiser.

"Dammit!" Leesa yelled.

"Captain, the Dead Leg is not responding," Raider reported at the same instant. "Only the tight beam has fired."

"Cause?"

"The Elder tech is evidently one of the systems affected by the cruiser's successful strike on us. Damage is not significant but I will need to recalibrate."

Mosi was already out of his seat. "If you need hands, I can help," he said.

"Unnecessary," Raider responded. "The correction is not physical."

Mosi looked across at Cornische, who waved him back to his chair, saying, "Looks as if we'll have to leave this one to Raider."

"Will the tight beam on its own be enough?" Nate wondered.

"No," Jen replied. "It's a powerful, highly focused weapon and will undoubtedly do *some* damage, but we'd need the luck of the gods on our side to hit something vital and cripple a ship of that size."

As if to emphasise the point, the *Silver Spear* fired on them again, prompting more evasions from Leesa.

"How much longer, Raider?"

"Five minutes, thirty-nine seconds by my estimation."

"They can take a lot of pot shots at us in five and a half minutes," Jen noted.

Cornische knew it; and if they got lucky with just one of them... He didn't want to flee, to take the *Ion Raider* away from the battle while Raider brought Dead Leg back on line, but better that than dead.

Reluctantly, he was about to give the order, when a cry from Leesa stopped him.

"Captain, look!"

He followed Leesa's pointing fingers and saw that two other

ships had broken away from the main battle and were closing in on the cruiser.

"Raider, can you identify?"

Even as he spoke, the two new arrivals opened up on the cruiser with energy weapons.

"Not specifically, Captain, though both are of the same class as *Sabre 1* and... There is an incoming message from the closer of the two."

"Drake, is that you aboard the Comet that now shows as the *Lion of Lincoln*?"

"Thapa! Yes, who else were you expecting?"

"Get on with what you're up to, then. Leave the *Silver Spear* to us."

"Thank you." He nodded towards Leesa. "You heard the man."

They moved swiftly, leaving the cruiser and the stealth ships behind and successfully skirting the battle which still raged without drawing any further attention. Closing in on the gateway to Lenbya and the Night Hammer ship that guarded it. Unfortunately, the minutes required to bring Dead Leg back into service appeared to be counting down in slow motion, and they would be within the *Mark of Mimir*'s range before the weapon was ready.

Leesa didn't need to be told to slow the ship down, she was already doing so.

"They must be aware of us," Leesa muttered.

"Yes, and the longer we sit here the more chance there is of a Saflik ally breaking away from the engagement and coming at us again," Jen said.

"We've no choice but to ride our luck and wait on Dead Leg," Cornische said. "Unless anyone has a better idea?"

Heads shaken all round. Then...

"Captain," Raider said, "there is another ship emerging from Rz close to the *Mark of Mimir*."

"A big one too, by the look of it," Jen said. "And that's some shit-hot navigation to emerge from Rz right there."

"I see it," said Leesa, totally immersed in her monitors. "Not sure I believe *what* I'm seeing, mind you... That's an Xter ship."

"Xters? What the hell are they doing here?"

"Are you sure?"

"I'm sure" Leesa replied. "I grew up on an Xter colony world, remember."

"Bollocks!" said Jen. "As if Saflik, a resurrected patchwork Elder and the Night Hammers weren't enough to contend with, now we've got Xters too? What have we done to the universe to deserve all this?"

"It's not just any Xter ship, either," said Leesa. "You don't see this design too often."

"I thought there *was* only one design," Cornische said. "Cone shaped prow at the front, with three to five interchangeable cylinders clustered behind, linking the command section to the engines at the rear. Isn't that the whole idea, a uniformity of design that allows for easy repair and the swapping in and out of sections that are damaged or no longer required?"

"Yes, you're right – that's the type of ship we're used to seeing, and just about all Xter ships are of that general design, but there is a second far less common class – again, based on modular construction – in which the tubes are replaced by a series of spheres, lined up like beads on a thread. The ship that's just arrived is one of these."

She summoned up an image to float in the air beside the one charting the battle.

"I've only ever seen one example of this type before," Leesa continued. "I'd assumed it was a research vessel of some sort, a space going lab, because that's the context I saw it in."

"So why bring a science lab to a battle?"

As they watched, the Xter ship broke apart.

"What the... Has it been hit by something?"

"No. I don't think so. Look at the way the spheres are separating – it's too smooth, too co-ordinated."

"You're right. And they're not simply careering off along a straight vector, as debris would if there had been an explosion, they're changing course... Each spherical section must be independently mobile."

"Raider," Cornische said, "are you able to analyse what they're attempting by extrapolating their current manoeuvres?"

"They're assuming an attack formation," Leesa said before the AI could respond, her voice conveying a lack of conviction at her own conclusion.

"Hel N is quite right," Raider confirmed. "The Xter spheres would appear to be converging on the Night Hammer ship the *Mark of Mímir*."

"You mean the Xters are on our side?"

"Looks that way, yes."

"Just when I thought the universe couldn't get any weirder."

"Or maybe on their own side which just happens to coincide with ours for now," Jen suggested.

"That, I could probably buy," Leesa acknowledged.

Raider continued to update the image Leesa had summoned, to depict events as they happened in real time. The tableau had expanded to take in the *Mark of Mímir*, with their perspective receding, as the spheres advanced on the warship in a co-ordinated approach from three directions. They were dwarfed by its bulk.

"That's the disadvantage of standing guard," Jen commented. "It robs the Night Hammers of any wriggle room."

"Do you think the spheres are manned – or Xterred – or are they drones slaved to the command module?"

"No idea. Drones would make more sense, though."

"Or even autonomous AIs working in synch..."

Speculation quieted when the image lit up, as *Mark of Mímir* defended itself against the attack with missiles and energy weapons – Raider rendering the path of the beams in the visible spectrum for the watching Dark Angels' benefit.

The missiles detonated short of their targets and the beams

spent themselves against the spheres' shields without inflicting any damage, while the spheres responded with energy weapons of their own.

"Well, we wanted a distraction…" Cornische said. "Raider, can you plot a route that will take us around the *Mark of Mímir* using those spheres as a shield where possible and offering minimum exposure to the Night Hammers' weapons?"

"Already working on it, Captain. Sending recommended course to Hel N's systems now, allowing for the attack vectors the Xter spheres are currently pursuing."

Leesa didn't look up but said, "Got it."

"Everyone strap yourselves in, *now!*" Cornische said. "Lees, go for it and don't hold back."

"When does she ever?" Jen quipped, just as acceleration kicked in.

Even though he knew what to expect, Cornische felt the wind knocked out of him, as an invisible hand pressed him back into the pilot's chair, crushing his chest, while the chair's purpose-built padding struggled in vain to keep him comfortable.

The projection of the ongoing engagement remained but had now receded, moving away from Leesa's line of sight as she concentrated on taking them past the battle and on to Lenbya.

The pressure on his chest eased as they approached optimum speed and acceleration let up, but the relief was short-lived as the whole ship bucked and shook around him.

"Have we been hit?" someone called out – Almont, by the sound of it.

"No, not directly," Cornische was able to reassure him after a glance up at the projection. "One of the Xter spheres has, though, the nearest to us."

"It's gone off like a bomb," Jen added. "We were caught in the blast wave, but we're not showing any resultant damage."

Leesa kept quiet, Cornische noted, concentrating on her piloting, knowing that the more distance they could put between themselves and the picket ship the better. She must have realised, as he did, that the blast wave was the least of their worries. With the sphere destroyed, the buffer between the *Iron Raider* and the *Mark of Mímir* had been removed, leaving them vulnerable to the warship's heavy armaments. Their only ally now was the distraction caused by the remaining two spheres. Cornische just hoped that would prove enough.

Seconds later, his worst fears were realised. A red warning light winked into life, demanding his attention.

He cursed silently. "Don't relax just yet, folks," he said aloud. "We've got incoming fire from the warship."

"I see it," Leesa confirmed from the other pilot's chair. "Three missiles."

Despite the acceleration they'd endured, the missiles were significantly quicker.

"Is there any chance we can catch two of them in a single blast by detonating one of them close to the other?" Cornische knew they only carried two anti-missile missiles in their limited arsenal.

"Highly unlikely."

Of course not. "Fire countermeasures."

"Missiles away."

Tense minutes passed as they watched their two 'birds' – an archaic term that still prevailed – on the projection. Both flew true and two of the Night Hammer missiles died in a suitably dramatic flowering of flame – the detonations too distant to be felt by those on board the *Raider.*

The third kept coming.

"Let's just hope it's not a hunter seeker," Mosi murmured.

What else would it be? Cornische thought but didn't say, reckoning it was the last thing Leesa needed to hear, as she concentrated all her skills on evasion, taking the ship into a corkscrew loop that had them pressed back into their seats again.

The missile adjusted its course to follow them and it was closing far too rapidly. *So much for hope.* They had seconds left.

"Captain, I may be able to help."

"Billy? Can you reach that far?" *And are you up to it?* The second question he kept to himself. For all their sakes, Billy had to be.

"I think so, yes."

"Don't wait for an invitation, then, just do it!"

The world lurched, as if the whole of existence stuttered – it was one of the most bizarre feelings Cornische had ever experienced, making the worst crossing into RzSpace seem like a smooth transition in comparison. Nor was this a one-time thing. Just as he thought his 'self' was coalescing into some semblance of mental and physical equilibrium, he felt his body wrenched apart again, and then a third time.

"Dear gods," he heard Jen gasp as fragmented thoughts aligned and reason started to reassert itself. "Don't ever let me go through that again."

Somehow, impossibly, the missile was now in front of them rather than behind.

Leesa had clearly coped with the aftermath of Frame's reality tampering far better than the rest of them, because Cornische knew that he would have been incapable of any coherent action for at least a few more precious seconds while his brain unscrambled, but not her.

The Night Hammer missile came about in a long arc. He stared at it, convinced the image should hold great significance for him, but not quite able to fathom what that might be.

Where he could only watch, Leesa acted.

Before the hunter could complete its turn and arrow in on the *Ion Raider* again, she triggered the ship's tight beam energy weapon, doing so while the missile still showed its broadside to them and so offered a larger target. Cornische would never know if the accuracy of the strike was all down to her or if Raider had surreptitiously helped, nor did he care. All that mattered was that the beam lanced straight and true, triggering the missile's deadly payload at too great a distance to damage them.

A ragged cheer went up from those around him. Cornische

merely caught Leesa's gaze and puffed his cheeks out in relief.

"Frame, good job," he then said.

"Any more where those three came from?" Mosi asked.

"I shouldn't think so," Cornische replied, his composure recovered. "We've been moving away from the *Mark of Mímir*'s position at quite a lick throughout, thanks to the gs Leesa poured on to begin with. We're now beyond effective missile range. Even if they try their luck and chance sending more missiles after us we'll be at the jump gate before they could possibly catch up – and that's assuming the Night Hammers can spare enough attention to make the attempt, with the Xter spheres still harassing them."

"And where the hell did those spheres come from? Do you think the banks have reached out to the Xters, bringing them into this?

"Maybe." It was as good a hypothesis as any Cornische had been able to come up with. After all, he had seen delegations of the aliens at First Solar's offices from time to time, but he wasn't convinced – he'd heard nothing that would suggest any of the banks worked that closely with the aliens.

"Billy!"

Jen's shout brought his attention back to the man who had just saved them all. He was slumped in his seat, head lolling forward. Jen was already out of her own chair and across to him.

"I'm... I'm all right," Billy said, lifting his head, but slowly, as if it weighed a ton. "Just been a long time since I attempted anything that big, if I *ever* have before. Even with the wristbands, that was tough."

"I can confirm that Frame is uninjured, but depleted," Raider reported.

"Billy, go and get some energy supplements from the galley, but don't hang around. We'll be at the gate in a few moments."

"I'll go," said Nate. "I'll be quicker."

"Okay," Cornische said, glad to see that Nate was willing to contribute. Perhaps he was going to work out after all. Not that there was much they could do about it if not.

"You all right, Lees?" Jen asked, coming to stand by her friend in the brief respite before they reached the gateway.

"I'm fine. I was just thinking about Saavi. Do you reckon she knew?"

"What, that Billy would save us?"

"Yeah. Without him being here to do his reality fiddling thing, I'd never have targeted the tight beam in time and taken out that missile."

"You can't know that for sure."

"Yes I can. Without Billy here, we'd all have died, trust me."

"To answer your question, yes, I think Saavi knew. She must have seen it among the potentials she was grappling so hard to understand. What I don't get is why she went off to find him on her own. If you or I had been there, she would still be with us, I'm sure of it."

"Yes, but would Billy?"

"How do you mean?"

"Well, did you recognise him when you first laid eyes on him?" Leesa asked.

"No, not at all, not looking like that."

"And we all saw how reluctant he was to come on board. I reckon the only reason he came to the ship at all was to deliver Saavi's body, because he felt he owed her that much; and he hung around afterwards due to that same sense of obligation, because the debt of Saavi's sacrifice hadn't been repaid. If you or I had been there in that alleyway, Cloud would most likely have lived, and we would have returned to the ship without ever realising the identity of the scruffy vagrant whose life we'd just saved. Saavi's death is what binds him to us. It's the reason Billy was here when we needed him."

"That's deep," Jen said.

"That's Saavi for you."

"I'm not sure I could have done that – gone to that alley, knowing what was to come... She's the real hero in all of this."

"Always."

Eighteen

Cornische recalled his extreme discomfort when first taking the 'elevator' to the pocket universe where the cache on Enduril II had lain hidden. The sensation had caught him by surprise, his memories of crossings to Lenbya supressed at that point. This time, with his memories restored, he knew what to expect, which didn't make the sensation any more pleasant.

It was not so much the actual pain, though there was some of that, but rather a sense of intense pressure, as if his insides were being squeezed together in a vice. Just as the feeling threatened to become unbearable, it was gone, and he was able to breathe again.

"For Elders' sake!" The exclamation came from Nate, who sat doubled over in his seat, retching as if he might be sick. "First whatever Frame did, and then this... What is it with you people?"

"Welcome to the Dark Angels," Leesa said.

"Raider, what's waiting for us?"

"You'll find a breathable atmosphere and Earth-standard gravity. A number of transports occupy the landing stage. The composite and the majority of personnel have moved inward, pursuing their campaign to seize control of Lenbya, but a contingent has remained with the ships."

"Our welcoming committee, no doubt," Jen said.

"They have also deployed defensive weaponry to ward off any further ships attempting to land. Before we begin final approach, I will neutralise these, but the soldiers will remain."

"Glad to hear you're leaving something for us to do."

"You will find plenty to do once you have disembarked, Hel N."

"I'll bet."

Cornische took control of the ship, bringing it in to land, Jen and Leesa having vacated the bridge to take up positions by the airlock. As Raider had promised, nothing fired at them on approach.

"All systems in the area have been neutralised," Raider reported. "This includes any energy weapons carried by the Saflik forces in situ."

As soon as the ship touched down they were out, Leesa heading left, Jen to the right. Cornische unbuckled from the pilot's chair and hurried to join them; Geminum, Ramrod and Frame were with him. The sporadic sounds of gunfire and an occasional scream came to them from ahead via the open airlock doors, but by the time they reached the foot of the landing ramp, the sounds had ceased.

Mosi, who had slipped into his zombie-like trance state, snapped out of it just as Jen stepped from shadow to join them.

"The landing area is secure," Mosi reported. "All hostiles are down."

"I could have told you that," said a silver figure as she sauntered towards them.

They moved inward without ceremony, entering a broad high-ceilinged corridor that led towards Lenbya's centre, and passing the first bodies almost immediately – two of them, in Night Hammer uniforms. The signs of conflict came thick and fast after that: jagged holes in the wall with charred edges and melted equipment, smoke curling up from one of them; wrecked vehicles that might have been automated mobile guns at some point; a luminous pink goo that dripped from the ceiling above an archway – beneath it in a pink puddle lay a twisted *something* that could once have been human – and many more bodies, some Night Hammers and others in plain black uniforms.

"Saflik."

At first they moved in eerie silence, as if tiptoeing through the aftermath of battle that had flared and burned out, rather than reeling in step by step a conflict that still raged somewhere ahead of them.

Then they heard the distant rumble of an explosion and, as if that were a catalyst, the sounds of battle multiplied from there: the chatter of small arms fire, the whine of more sophisticated munitions, the pop pop sound of small detonations.

By unspoken consent, the Angels broke into a jog, conscious that they were catching up with the fighting.

The way Cornische envisaged this going, the Angels would slow down once they were closer to the battle and attack the enemy from the rear in a co-ordinated manner, catching them by surprise while their attention was focussed on Lenbya's defences.

Things didn't quite work out like that.

They came to a junction, with the way ahead splitting. It was difficult to be certain if the sounds of conflict came from one branch or the other or both.

"Mosi, you and Naj check the right hand fork," Cornische said. "Don't materialise, no matter what you encounter, just..."

He was interrupted by an explosion; more concussion than fire and shrapnel, but Cornische felt as if he'd been punched by a giant fist. It was enough to fling them all from their feet, even Hel N and Ramrod.

He came up against a wall, momentarily winded, but there was no time to recover as gunfire peppered them. Bullets thudded into the wall beside him and one struck his arm with bruising force, though the stibre in his coat prevented it from penetrating. He scrambled into a crouch, drawing one of his own guns – not trusting his left arm just yet, numbed as it was by the bullet's impact – and looked for a target.

Figures, advancing towards them through the smoke of the explosion that filled the corridor on the right, targeting lasers seeking out the Dark Angels. Abruptly those figures warped, strobing in and out of view as Billy let loose.

Having so recently experienced the effect of Frame's ability himself, Cornische would prefer to take a concussion blast any day. The Dark Angels opened up, picking off targets before they could regain their equilibrium. As the smoke cleared, none of the figures remained standing.

"Where's Shadow?" Leesa said.

Until that moment, no one had even realised she was missing.

Jen hadn't meant to desert the others, at least not for long. When the concussion round hit she had automatically slipped into shadow, with the intention of doing her bit against the advancing soldiers, but she hesitated when Frame struck. Seeing that the Angels then had the situation under control, she decided to go on ahead and do a bit of scouting.

This was Geminum's speciality, of course, but Jen had her own methods and there were things she needed to confirm that she couldn't share with Mosi. Just a quick look, just to see, then she would return to her crewmates.

It soon became apparent that things were more complex than she'd realised. The corridors divided several more times in a manner that didn't match her recollection of Lenbya, causing her to wonder if Raider's parent entity had deliberately added to the construction in the knowledge that an attack was imminent, building a labyrinthine approach to hamper the invaders.

She passed several squads of soldiers – Night Hammer mainly but also others – jogging in orderly fashion but not hanging around. It seemed the battle for Lenbya was no longer being fought on a single front but several, which she suspected was another deliberate tactic. Judging by the number of bodies they had passed on the way in, the Saflik advance had been costly. Forcing them to divide their forces this way must mean that they were spread pretty thin, hence the troop movements she'd seen – redistribution of resources as required.

Then she got lucky: a face she recognised. Not a full squad this time, just three of them: senior officer flanked by two soldiers. The fact that command was on the move like this made her wonder if the guardian entity had somehow compromised their communications. She crossed back from shadow around a corner, out of sight of the three, and pulled her mask back so that her head and face were exposed. She wanted the bastard to know who was about to kill him.

Knives drawn, she waited, back pressed against the wall, listening as the rhythmic slap of their feet drew closer. When she judged the moment to be right, with the three almost upon her, she stepped out, blades first, and plunged both into the nearest Night Hammer. Stibre polymer armour: lightweight and tough enough to deflect most calibre of bullet and just about any blade. Not hers. They plunged straight through, to puncture the uncomprehending trooper's chest.

The bulky gun the man carried clattered to the floor. His body was already following suit as she dragged the blades out and passed behind the officer to engage the woman on his far side.

She felt almost disappointed: this was a combat situation. They should have been alert, but her attack had evidently caught them by surprise. Both were reacting, but too slowly, almost as if they had been lulled a little by the rhythm of their own jogging – three together: safety in numbers.

The woman was trying to bring her gun to bear – trust a Night Hammer to bring a gun to a knife fight – but Jen was already upon her. She brought her right arm up sharply beneath the woman's left elbow, knocking her arm and the weapon it held upward, taking both out of the equation. She then drove the blade in her left hand deep into the woman's exposed armpit, a blow that may well have been fatal in itself, but to remove any doubt Jen stabbed her in the neck with her other knife.

Breathing hard but evenly, Jen stepped away from the corpse, a bloodied blade held loosely in each hand, to face the last of the three still standing. He looked much the same; older, of course, but still fit and hard-bodied, his eyes that same ice blue.

"Hello, Haaland," she said, and smiled. "Long time no see."

He was staring at her, incredulous. "*Mia...?* How...? I mean, it *can't* be you. You're supposed to be dead."

"So are the Night Hammers."

"Oh they tried. Believe me, they tried. But..." He shrugged.

"You struck a deal."

It wasn't a question. *Politicians!* Jen could well imagine the reasoning. The cost in terms of men and munitions required to take down the Night Hammers for good would have been considerable; far simpler to reach an agreement that saw them simply go away and then claim victory to the public and the media.

"Something like that."

"Which, true to form, you're now dishonouring."

"What can I say? Circumstances change, the balance of power shifts, and options have to be reassessed."

"And you saw an opportunity – you always did like a gamble."

"You know me too well."

Without further preamble, Haaland struck.

From nowhere, he produced a dagger – the standard Night Hammer combat knife, or so it appeared to be, but she soon discovered there was nothing standard about this version. As the blade thrust towards her, a flash of silver light lashed out from beside the fixed metal blade.

Energy blade she realised, hidden within the handle of the knife. The length was governed but it still extended a good way beyond its fixed counterpart, more than doubling the weapon's reach.

Jen had leapt back instinctively as he attacked, but not quite far enough to avoid this unexpected addition. Pain exploded in her left side as the energy blade bit home.

She staggered backwards, continuing her retreat, but he pressed his advantage as a good soldier should, following, not allowing her any respite. He struck again, arm extending to thrust the knife at her midriff.

Pride had made her want to do this without relying on shadowtech, to fight her former commander on a level playing field: soldier to soldier, blade to blade, may the best warrior win, but screw pride; he'd been the one to break the rules of fair play, after all.

She stepped into shadow.

The shock on his face was reward in itself. Clearly, he hadn't worked out who she was – things must have happened too rapidly for him to appreciate the significance of her all-black outfit. He *must* have realised that she was allied with the New Spartan banks and the forces they raised to oppose Saflik's ambitions, but not until now that she was the Dark Angel known as Shadow.

"Well I'll be a..."

He got no further, as Jen leapt at him, crossing from shadow to solid form as she did so. She'd moved quickly, striking from a different position and giving him minimal time to react. He didn't see her coming – from his side and slightly behind – until the very last instant, enabling her to thrust both her blades deep into his exposed side. She didn't overthink it, didn't attempt to target specific organs or maximise the damage to tissues, she just channelled all the rage and frustration that had accumulated over many years; her hatred for this man, her horror at what this once proud regiment had been reduced to under his command and her shame at ever being associated with it. All of this she put into the twin strikes, which had to be among the strongest she had ever delivered.

He screamed. General Haaland, feared commander of the Night Hammers, the iron fist that shaped and wielded the most feared of all military units, let rip an unbridled admission of raw pain. It was a reaction he would have ridiculed and punished if it had issued from the throat of any of his men.

Haaland crumpled in on himself, knees threatening to give way, and Jen thought for a moment he was about to sink to the ground, but somehow he kept his feet. She hesitated, holding back the blood lust that battered against her resolve and urged her to step forward to stab him again and again and again. It was important that she should keep control. To lose it now, to savage him as the primal part of her wanted to do so badly, would be to sink to his level, and she refused to do that.

"Come on then, bitch," he half snarled, half panted. "Finish me off, if you're up to it."

He clutched at his side, she thought to stem the loss of blood, but then his right wrist twisted and his hand opened. She had a split second to see the two flattened silver pearls he tossed down before they hit the ground and erupted.

Flare stones! There was just time to start turning her head away and begin to close her eyes, but not sufficient to do either fully, and some of the searing flash still got through to dazzle her and leave her temporarily blind.

Cursing, Jen fell back into shadow, not wanting to leave herself vulnerable to any retribution Haaland might have in mind. At the same moment, a claxon blared to life: piercingly shrill, deafening. *Cleverly done.* This had to be deliberate, the timing was too convenient otherwise. Having robbed her of sight, he then removed her ability to hear as well, which meant she couldn't tell which direction he might take should he choose to run – and what else could he do? – and wouldn't be able to keep pace with him in shadow until her eyes started to recover.

To be this prepared... Did he know who I was after all? Then she remembered the energy weapon that had reached into shadow to hurt her in Sketch's basement soon after this all began. They'd done their homework, Saflik and the Night Hammers, so perhaps it wasn't surprising that their commanders routinely carried countermeasures. All she could do for now was wait. There was no point in heading off in some random direction – that way she stood as much chance of going away from her enemy rather than towards him. In her head, to pass the time, she ran through all the things she intended to do to Haaland once her vision cleared and she was able to track him down again.

Leesa didn't have time to worry about Jen. She had more pressing concerns. They were being met with increasing resistance, and the fighting was ferocious. The tactic of using Frame's reality shifting to soften the enemy up had worked the next couple of times but then Billy had been wounded. How badly, it was difficult to say. They'd stopped the bleeding, but he had barely been able to muster a flicker of warping since, and she feared for him.

That left her and Ramrod as the shock troops, with Shadow still missing. Her reservations about Nate had proven unfounded, so far. He fought well and seemed to be getting a taste for the action. It still felt odd, fighting beside Ramrod again and knowing this wasn't Kyle, but she was able to put that to one side. Nate's technique was a little bit too much by the numbers for her liking, but he was still new to the harness and that would change with experience.

The captain remained as proficient as ever with his smartguns, providing covering fire that swapped between bullets and energy and microbombs as he deemed appropriate, with Mosi laying down his own fire in support.

It worked, and they made good progress, until they came to the door.

This was no flimsy divider of the sort found in a home, but rather a heavy armoured plug more suited to an airlock or even a high security vault. It stood at the end of a long straight corridor which they had fought their way along, and presumably had been installed as part of the defences. Half a dozen Salik lay dead in front of it, but the rest had managed to flee through the door and slam it shut before the Angels could reach them.

For a moment they stood panting, frustrated. Behind them stretched the corridor, unbroken by any other doors or passages. They could go back until they found another route and try to work around the door, but that would mean losing ground and momentum. They could try going through the walls, which were likely to be weaker than this bloody door, but, the chances were, not by much: why build a door like that and then surround it with flimsy walls?

Billy clearly wasn't up to anything this big, which left…

"Geminum," Cornische said, having evidently reached the same conclusion.

"On our way, Captain."

There was a sense of panic on the far side of the door. These were Saflik rather than Night Hammers, and they *feared* the Dark Angels.

"Good. So they should," was Naj's reaction.

The soldiers were trying to organise a defence in anticipation of the door failing, and arguing about how best to do so.

Naj and Mosi studied the door. Presumably its mechanism couldn't be fully automated, or Raider would never have allowed the Saflik to close it on the advancing Angels. There had to be a manual override.

"That big red button, do you reckon?"Naj said.

It was built into the frame of the door at around chest height.

"Either that or we're about to blow the entire area to smithereens," Mosi replied. "Shall we?"

"Bro, I'm scared."

This wasn't an admission he ever expected to hear from Naj. "What, of the device they used against us on *Darkness Mourning?*"

"Yes. If they trap us again, there'll be no Jen or Leesa dashing to our rescue, not this time."

"Listen to me. That device was installed. It was already there, waiting for us, and it relied on an officer with augmentation. They're on the move here, in hostile territory. They won't have something like that with them, and even if they do they won't have had time to set it up yet."

"I know... I know. You're right. It's just that I was asleep for so long, away from you, and now that we're together again, I don't want to lose you, not so soon."

"You won't. We'll materialise, activate the door, and phase out again before anyone can react. We have to do this. The others are counting on us."

"I know. Sorry. I'm okay now."

He knew she wasn't. "Never thought I would be the one giving *you* a pep talk," he said.

"I guess at times we're more alike than we realise." He sensed her smile. "Let's get this over with."

They phased into solid state with Najat's hand already hovering over the manual control. By the time one of the soldiers saw them and shouted a warning, the button had already been pressed and the door was swinging open. By the time anyone thought to raise a weapon, they had already faded and were snapping back into Mosi's physical form.

Jen's ears were still ringing but she was no longer completely deafened and she could see again. A trail of blood spots on the floor gave her something to follow. Not constant, not in an unbroken line, just occasional bloody red breadcrumbs drawing her on.

There: a smear on a corridor corner where a blood-stained hand had reached for support. More spots on the ground, and then, abruptly, they stopped.

Haaland had found allies, someone to stem the bleeding and effect temporary repairs, no doubt patching the wounds with nuskin. Not to worry. He couldn't be far ahead. This merely delayed the inevitable, it wouldn't save him.

All thoughts of rejoining Cornische, Leesa and the others had been put on hold. Before she could do that, Jen had someone to kill.

Cornische was growing increasingly concerned about Billy. He'd taken a hit in his side. They'd stemmed the bleeding and patched the wound with nuskin, but that was just a temporary fix. He couldn't keep up unaided and they were taking it in turns to help him. Cornische was loath to leave him behind, with the fighting being so fragmented – goodness only knew who might stumble across him – but he was slowing them down. They had to find somewhere secure to hide him against later retrieval, but as yet nowhere had presented itself.

The sounds of conflict ahead were growing closer, which

meant they might have to leave Billy temporarily, to free up hands and weapons.

Abruptly the corridor turned a corner and opened up into a cavernous room, which might once have been an artefact chamber but not any more. It had been cleared of Elder treasures and was now the setting for a pitched battle.

Arrayed in front of him was by far the largest concentration of Night Hammer and Saflik troops they had yet encountered, and they were fighting in a more disciplined fashion. Facing them were an odd assortment of mechanisms and *things* – he wasn't sure how else to think of them. Vaporous clouds that crackled with energy but faded rapidly, gelatinous blobs that were proving to be anything but fireproof – one going up in a violent flare of heat and light as he watched – tentacle-like vines that wrapped around an enemy and constricted, flying, darting things – bird-sized but evidently packing a disabling sting… and more.

There was an air of desperation about these bizarre defenders, as if this was their last stand and the battle would be won or lost here, in this chamber.

Then Cornische spotted a presence he had been expecting but not entirely looking forward to seeing. A bloated body reared up above the combatants: prominent dark eyes and a wide lipless mouth fronted a face that projected from the greenish body without the delineation of a neck. The whole was supported by a mass of tentacles, two of which shot forward to grip one of the flat-bodied robotic defenders, pulling the machine apart as if it were formed of cardboard.

Somehow, despite being preoccupied and facing in a different direction, this bloated caricature of the small fluffy alien that had sat on his shoulder for so many years sensed him.

Drake! said an all-too-familiar voice in his head. *I'm so glad you survived. I felt cheated by your abrupt disappearance from the Enduril cache chamber. You'll have to tell me where that artefact sent you, by the way. Not that you'll have any choice* but *to tell me.*

Mudball. The alien's presence in his mind, which had once felt so reassuring, now made his spine crawl.

Come, come, that's no way to react to an old friend, is it? Think of all the fun times we had together, and they're not over! Once I've fully cleansed your mind and taken control of your body, you can help me finish off these little friends you've brought along for me to play with.

The alien's presence seemed to expand, exerting a mental pressure unlike anything he had experienced before. But it wasn't enough. *Mudball,* he thought calmly, clearly, *allow me to introduce another old friend of mine. Raider, meet Mudball.*

Hello, Composite. I've been looking forward to this. You've been avoiding me, but we knew you wouldn't be able to resist taking advantage of your old link to infiltrate the captain's thoughts when the opportunity presented itself, so I've been waiting here for you...

No!

Drake couldn't recall ever having sensed fear in Mudball's thoughts before.

Finally they had caught up with the main body of invaders. Leesa had begun to think they were destined to fritter away their time in skirmishes with outlying units, but this could only be the main event. Ahead of them was, by her reckoning, a deployment of around two hundred enemy troops, locked in battle with a motley of truly surreal defenders.

Somebody must have noticed their arrival – a squad of Night Hammers had peeled away from the main formation and were coming towards them. Leesa studied their approach – relaxed and confident – and was preparing to kick their asses, when a voice said: "Hel N, guard the captain at all costs." Raider, speaking in her ear. "He is likely to be distracted for a brief while, but what happens to him in the next few minutes may well decide the fate of everything."

Distracted? They were in the middle of a full blown battle for Elders' sake, how could anyone be distracted?

Yet he clearly was, lowering his guns and gazing in unfocused fashion at goodness only knew what.

Cornische made a tempting target like this, and clearly Leesa wasn't alone in reaching that conclusion. Even as she grabbed him and started to pull him down into at least a sitting position, something struck her shoulder. Judging by the heat generated by the impact, it was most likely a plasma bolt, though her suit did its job, deflecting and absorbing the blast.

Nate stared at her, clearly having seen the direct hit and its lack of effect. "Are you invulnerable inside that suit of yours?"

"No, but I'm damned hard to kill. Now, go take care of those bastards, will you? I have to cover the captain."

"With pleasure."

Jen, where the hell are you? She grabbed one of the captain's guns from his unresisting fingers, and set about laying down some covering fire. Mosi crouched down and did the same, as Ramrod charged.

Inevitably, the Night Hammers' fire centred on Nate, who offered the most immediate threat, but the momentum he built up while running meant that Ramrod's defensive field was at maximum strength. Bullets and energy beams simply bounced off him.

At the same time, Leesa and Mosi were free to choose their targets, largely untroubled by return fire.

Four of the Night Hammer squad were still standing when Nate reached them. To their credit, they hadn't turned and run but continued to rain fire on him until the last.

One he struck full on, with a force that Leesa knew would crush bones and rupture organs; a second caught a glancing blow but was unlikely to fare much better. A third came at him with a knife – which took a special kind of stupid after bullets and energy weapons had failed to make a scratch. Nate punched him, a blow that sent the unfortunate sailing through the air to crash to the ground many metres away, where he lay unmoving.

Only then did the survivor apparently conclude that a tactical retreat might be in order. Nate made no attempt to stop him as he sprinted to join the mass of his comrades.

Nate looked back at Leesa and Mosi and grinned. For a

moment she feared he was about to give them a thumbs up, but thankfully he stopped short of doing so.

Too late she saw the sniper. Too late she saw him fire.

"Nate, your defence! Keep moving!" she yelled, but again too late.

The bullet, an explosive charge, had enough momentum to break through the fading shields generated by Ramrod's earlier charge. It struck Nate in the back and detonated, ripping his torso apart.

Leesa targeted the sniper, a woman, and fired. Again and again and again.

The sniper went down. But too late.

Cornische was a bystander. No, that wasn't right. A bystander would be able to observe what was going on, to evaluate the ebb and flow of fortunes within a struggle. Here, his consciousness had merely been shoved rudely to one side, incidental to all that transpired. He had no sense of progress, no sense of loss or gain, nothing by which to understand the methods employed as the two Elder aspects strove to establish dominance over each other.

He wasn't an observer here; he was merely the conduit, the battlefield in which titans contested.

Raider had made it sound so simple when outlining the plan back on the ship. "The composite is avoiding me," it explained. "By posing as your chirpy companion Mudball, it was able to infiltrate a series of Elder caches, overwhelming the guardian entities and subsuming the essence of their psyches. In this way it grew stronger, until it felt complete upon absorbing the Enduril entity."

"At which point it no longer needed me," Cornische had interjected.

"Precisely. Now, however, it fears taking on my psyche in a similar fashion. Although we are of comparable strength, it is a patchwork creature, forged from components melded together, whereas I am a unified whole. If I can grapple with the composite psychically, I plan to unstitch those essences one by one, weakening it at every turn. It knows this, so will not confront me.

"We will use your long association with the creature to draw it out, to bring its psyche into the open. If you're willing."

Bait. The prospect didn't exactly thrill him, but Cornische was forever conscious of the part he'd played in enabling Mudball's ambitions. "Consider yourself invited," he'd said.

"Thank you. The experience is unlikely to be a pleasant one."

Nor had Raider been wrong. Sensations of nausea, of hot and cold, of vertigo, of pressure, pain and discomfort now swept through Cornische in waves, one after the other in random order. He lost all awareness of the outside world, his attention turned inward with none to spare for anything other than his own internal torment, and no means by which to interpret even that.

He had a sense of something tearing, of something being shredded. Indescribable pain shot through him and someone screamed. But not him. This issued from one of the gods contesting within his mind, and he had no reference, no means of telling which it might be.

The human psyche wasn't built for such misuse. Despite his determination not to succumb, Cornische felt consciousness slipping away, darkness reaching out to claim him.

No, he screamed at the stygian wall that rose up before him. *I won't let it end like this!*

Jen could hear the sounds of battle ahead. Not some incidental little scuffle, this promised to be the real thing. She had quartered and quartered after losing the blood trail, moving far more swiftly in shadow than she could in physical form, but had seen no sign of Haaland.

Frustration now gave way to hope: of course he would have sought the main body of his forces – safety in numbers.

She sped along the corridor, emerging into a vast chamber where the most surreal battle she had ever seen was unfolding. At another time she might have stopped and stared, but she had more important things on her mind this day.

There! At the back and at some remove from the conflict: Haaland, in a hoverchair that had to be some sort of mobile medical unit. With him were a smattering of guards and a handful of others, presumably advisors and Saflik higher ups. She didn't spare them a second glance, her attention focussed on Haaland, the bastard whose unwanted advances had driven her out of the Night Hammers and ended her military career, the man who had led the proudest regiment in the army into exile and disgrace.

There were shadows aplenty to mask her approach, racing along the floor and merging with those of Haaland and his party. She stepped out into the physical world directly in front of him.

No mistake this time. She relished the recognition in his eyes, the burgeoning look of horror on his face, as she cut his throat.

There followed a dance that had become second nature to her, flickering in and out of shadow, stabbing, cutting, ducking, spinning, kicking, as one by one the hapless guards fell to her blades.

There was always a frissant of risk, a chance that one of them would get lucky with an unexpected thrust or swing of a blade, but not this time. Five guards, all down. Three men not in uniform scampering for escape, fleeing away from the battle.

She might have let them go, but then she recognised one of them and pursued in shadow, to emerge in front of them, knives drawn.

The way they came stumbling to a halt, crashing into each other, was almost comical.

"Hello, Donal," she said to the foremost of the three. "Leaving so soon?

"It's Martin these days," he said. "No one's called me Donal in a long while."

"I can understand why you'd want to distance yourself. Hunting down and assassinating your former crewmates, your *friends*, must do that to a person." She smiled at the former Angel. "You know what comes next."

"Look, this doesn't have to end in violence," said one of Donal's companions – a slightly rotund individual who was panting for breath after having had to run. "I'm wealthy beyond your imagining. We can all leave here together and live out our days in luxury."

"You must be Ungar," Jen said coldly. "The captain's mentioned you. The head of Saflik, he believes."

"Quite so. Saflik is gone, finished after this endeavour, but the wealth…"

He got no further. One of Jen's blades flicked out, leaving a red line across his throat. "That's for Saavi," she said, "and for Gabriel, Spirit, and the others."

Ungar's eyes bulged. He started to lift a hand but to no avail, as blood pumped from the gaping wound and he died. His body dropped to the ground like a marionette set free.

"Jen, you have to understand…" Donal began.

She stabbed him in the heart. It was a quicker death than he deserved, but the blood lust had exhausted itself long before, leaving her tired of the killing. It was all about efficiency now.

That just left the last man. "Archer, I presume," she said. The corrupt First Solar agent.

He didn't reply, but held a gun levelled at her. Almost disappointed, she stepped into shadow as he fired. And she screamed as pain lanced through her. The shock of it was as disabling as the pain. This reminded her of the weapon Saflik agents had used against her when she first encountered them in Sketch's basement back in Opal. The one that could reach even into shadow.

Jen sought refuge, trying to hide in Archer's own shadow, but he anticipated the move and pointed the gun downwards to fire again. She fled behind him, narrowly avoiding being hit for a second time but feeling the backwash of the blast even so.

She emerged into the physical world, seeing no point in staying where she couldn't hurt him but he could her.

"I never thought I would get this pleasure," he said, turning to face her. "I've supervised the assassination of many of your kind, but to have the honour of killing one of you in person… Thank you." He fired again.

Jen threw herself out of the way, landing shoulder first, rolling and coming out in a crouch. As she did so, she threw one of her knives. They weren't really intended as throwing blades, but she had no qualms about improvising. Her aim was true, the blade striking him just below the left shoulder, causing him to stagger back and the gun to waver.

She followed up by charging. A couple of strides and she was on him, but he fired again, catching her at close range.

This time the pain was beyond anything she'd experienced before, and she knew she couldn't stay conscious for long. As oblivion swept over her, she stabbed and stabbed and stabbed.

Movement off to her left caught Leesa's attention. She looked across and finally learned where Jen was: flickering in and out of shadow, meting out death at every turn.

Three figures broke away from the mêlée, running. More fool them. Jen was on them in a trice, blocking their way. Leesa was too far away to hear what was said but watched as events unfurled, wishing Jen would hurry up and do what she obviously intended to; then perhaps they could finally regroup. Leesa would feel a lot better with Shadow at her side once more. Then, to her horror, she saw Jen shot by the last of the three, watched as they grappled and both went down.

"Jen!" She felt torn: stay with Mosi and the captain or head across to help Jen?

Mosi, *of course*. She didn't know if he'd even spotted Jen as yet, but Geminum could cover the distance and check on her wellbeing far more swiftly than she could.

Before she could ask him, a sound unlike anything she had heard before tore through her being. A scream of pain, of frustration, of complete despair. A scream that reached her not only via her ears but directly into her mind, her soul.

215

Wiping away tears, Leesa searched for the source, and saw that it emanated from the bloated effigy of Mudball that had led the Saflik assault. The creature was coming apart. Literally. There was no blood, no chunks of flesh dropping off to spin away from its body, but sections of that vast bulk were disappearing, as if consumed by some invisible attacker. This was not a coordinated winnowing in which the Elder manifestation simply shrank, keeping its proportions, but rather a random process where its form twisted and transformed with each lost element.

Beside her, the captain uttered a groan and simply wilted to the ground. He slumped beside Billy, who by this point was unconscious or worse. She instinctively reached for him but stopped as bullets ripped into the wall behind them.

Her attention switched back to the battle, but it wasn't a battle any more, it had become a rout. Saflik and even Night Hammer forces were in full retreat, leaving the thrashing, shrinking form of the god they had followed behind.

Most of them were charging straight towards her and Geminum: the last two Dark Angels, who stood between those fleeing and the main exit.

Leesa glanced at Mosi, seeing fear in his eyes, and resignation. "Mosi, Naj, if this is the end, it's been a pleasure knowing you."

"You too, Lees."

They took aim and started firing.

This 'last stand' had barely begun when something struck Leesa from behind.

Not an energy beam or a bullet, something much broader than that, like the slap of a giant open-palmed hand. At first she assumed it was a concussion round, but the effect was not as severe and it kept coming – a continuous push. With it there was sound: a bass howling as of wind channelled through a long fat tube.

Mosi had been knocked over but seemed otherwise unhurt. The same could not be said of the Saflik troops who had been rushing towards them. The effect on them was devastating; the charge broken, the retreat stalled. A wide channel carved through their ragged ranks, with individuals bowled over or flung far and wide. Leesa realised that whatever she had felt was no more than the edge of what had just hit the soldiers. She and Mosi were not the intended targets, just collateral damage. She looked behind her. From the corridor by which she and the other Dark Angels had entered the chamber, appeared…

"Xters." Mosi whispered the word in astonishment.

Leesa could understand why. Xters were the only other extant sentient species mankind had ever encountered, but the two races were anathema to one another and rarely mingled. To humans, Xters smelled appalling and their manner of movement was deeply unsettling at a primordial level. By all accounts, Xters had a similar reaction to humans, so the two civilisations co-existed by ignoring one another as much as possible, despite being neighbours.

Leesa had been raised on Dinares IV, an Xter colony world on the edge of human space, where a small scientific community had been established in the hope of greater understanding and furthering relations between the two species. This was where she had received her first augmentations, adjustments that allowed her to breathe an atmosphere which was ideal for Xters but not quite for humans.

Despite this upbringing, Leesa had rarely been close to an Xter, and her instinctive response to the aliens was much the same as anyone else's. She was, perhaps, just a little better at hiding it.

Seven, no eight of the aliens now emerged from the corridor, their darting scuttling movements as disconcerting as ever, their segmented bodies low to the ground. For the most part these individuals utilised a four-legged gait rather than the more natural six, because their forelimbs were raised and occupied with holding several outlandish items – weapons and devices which could only be Elder tech.

"They are on our side," Raider said in her ear."

"Xters... *seriously*? Who the hell are they?"

"They are termed the Demon's Breath, and are the Xter equivalent of the Dark Angels," Raider explained, as if it were the most natural thing in the world. "My champions in waiting should the need arise."

She had no idea what to say to that.

"You may leave the fighting to them at this point," Raider assured her. "Go to Shadow. She still lives but is gravely injured."

"What about the captain?"

"He is beyond your help, as is Frame, but Shadow can be saved, if she receives treatment quickly. Even now, human forces are sweeping through the corridors in the Xters' wake and will arrive here shortly. Leave the remaining Saflik forces to them and the Xters."

Leesa felt strangely undecided, unsure of what to feel or what to do. She felt betrayed. If Jen hadn't deserted them at the start of the fighting, would the captain be dead? Would Nate or Billy? On the other hand, Jen hadn't run away as such but had instead chosen her own route to reach here, to make a difference.

At the end of the day, Jen was her friend, and she had precious few of those.

Mosi had clambered back to his feet, and was looking to her for guidance. Leesa gave a rueful glance towards the captain, not wanting to leave him like this. He deserved better.

"I will take care of the captain," Raider assured her. "You take care of the still living."

She felt tired, drained, incapable of mounting even a token argument. "Come on, Mosi," she said. "Raider says Jen's still alive. Let's go get her."

As they trudged across the edge of the chamber to where Jen had fallen, Mosi asked, "Is it really over?"

"Yes, it's over," she assured him, relaying information Raider whispered in her ear. "Saflik is broken, the Night Hammers are finally disbanded for good, and Mudball's composite monster has been dismantled and destroyed. Humankind can rest easy at night, and we can go home."

"Wherever the hell that is," he said.

"Yeah, I'm still working on that part myself."

EPILOGUE

Mosi:

"Where to now, bro?"

"I have absolutely no idea," Mosi admitted.

They were on a transport, being ferried back to New Sparta at First Solar's expense. Not that they couldn't afford to pay passage themselves; Raider had been more than generous, making sure the surviving Angels were financially secure. Most importantly, no one had attempted to take Najat away from him.

"A casino," Naj suggested. "Somewhere they play poker for the highest of stakes."

"What?"

"Can you imagine it: me sneaking out to look at each player's hand without them ever realising? We'd make a fortune!"

"You reckon? With me slipping into a mini trance every time you did so? They might not know *how* we were cheating, but they'd be pretty sure we were. I was tortured on the last world I settled. I don't fancy being subjected to anything like that again, thanks all the same."

"Where's your sense of adventure?"

"More than sated after all we've been through of late, as should yours be."

"Well, let's go for somewhere they need mechanics, then. You've always been good with your hands…"

"That didn't work out so well for me last time, either."

"But you were on your own then," Najat said. "You've got me this time, and you'll never be alone again."

"That much does sound good." He couldn't help but smile. "You know what? I couldn't give a blind Hiolean Gilmat where

220

we end up, as long as we're together."

"Nor could I, bro, nor could I."

Drake:

"So as far as anyone else is concerned, I'm dead."

"Yes, as you requested," Raider confirmed.

The relief was immense. No more having to be Drake, no more Cornische; no more living up to the expectations of First Solar, of Leesa and the other Dark Angels, of a public that seemed desperate for him to be a hero.

A clean slate, beholden to no one.

"There is a small ship at your disposal and sufficient funds to establish a new identity in whatever capacity you choose," Raider continued.

This wasn't Raider, he knew that, or not *just* Raider. This was the Lenbya entity he'd first encountered when the Dark Angels were born, but it presented as Raider, and he felt comfortable thinking of it in those terms.

"What will happen," he asked, "now that Lenbya's location is known?"

"That will not be a problem. I have provided all parties who assisted us – essentially the banks on First Solar – with enough cache treasures to keep them happy. Next I will quietly move the location of the gateway. Lenbya will remain exactly where it is but, once again, no one will be able to find it."

The man who had been Drake nodded and smiled. It seemed a fitting solution. He didn't ask whether Jen, Leesa and Mosi would be looked after; he knew that already.

"You promised me some answers, too, and there are a couple of things I'd like to understand, now that I'm walking away from all this for good."

"Go on."

"The caches, this afterthought of the Elder civilisation, Lenbya and the cache guardians… What is your purpose, really? Why are you here at all?

"Ah... the caches. Very well.

"My people, whom you term the Elders, were an ancient race. Our individual longevity extended across thousands of years and we had established dominion over myriad star systems, a civilisation that lasted for aeons. However, we reached the limits of our potential within this physical reality and came to realise that we must find a way to evolve or stagnate and wither away.

"By this point, we had learned that existence offers infinite possibilities. We chose to explore them.

"However, there were a few individuals who did not wish to move on from the physical forms they were accustomed to, who chose to stay behind. Our society relied on tolerance, so the choice was theirs to make.

"Each such individual was provided with every amenity, with the concentrated knowledge of our race and any devices they chose. We knew that some of our work would survive long after we had gone, so across the myriad worlds we gathered the best of our achievements together and left them in the keeping of the stay-behinds. I should stress that these individuals represented a vanishingly small percentage of our populace, and it was rare for more than one to remain on any given world.

"I am one such, though I am atypical and have certain advantages over my fellows.

"Initially, despite not being as instinctively social as your species, many of us stayed in contact, using the long-established communications networks of our people. But as the centuries passed we grew further apart, more insular and reclusive. Slowly, we lost touch. My people are long-lived but not immortal. Over time, my fellows' essences faded, their homes shrunk as things fell into disrepair, were forgotten and failed. These increasingly inward-looking individuals would gather the remaining 'treasures' more closely to them, until only the hardiest of technology survived in far smaller surrounds, overseen by mere fragments of the beings who had once lived there.

"The caches," Drake said.

"Indeed. Each cache is a lingering remnant of a vast city, a culture, the concentrated echo of my people. They are the fossils of my race, surviving long after our bones have turned to dust."

"So the caches were never a benevolent legacy from a long vanished race bequeathed to help their distant successors, which is what many of my own people have always argued."

"No, not at all. They were for the comfort of our own stay-behinds, at least primarily. At the same time, we knew that these stay-behinds would age and eventually die, while many of our achievements were likely to outlast them. We also foresaw that the stay-behinds' fading would offer an opportunity for a particular threat to arise. Among those who chose to remain were a number of individuals who were psychologically... *unusual* for my people. It came to our attention that one or two extreme individuals were attempting to 'play the system' by maintaining a greater degree of integrity over a longer period. Were they to succeed, there was a possibility one of them might come to dominate their fellow remainers and form a composite intelligence, thereby posing a threat to emerging sentient civilisations.

"This was by no means a likely scenario and there was only so much that could be done to counter such a threat – we were making provisions for a far distant future long after the Elder exodus – but we put in place what measures we could, against the day they were needed."

"Lenbya and the Dark Angels."

"Indeed. *If* a composite built from the psyches of several cache guardians were ever going to appear, it could only do so now, as the stay-behinds aged and failed, leaving them vulnerable. It would also be dependent on a specific set of circumstances, requiring an emergent race to be seeking out and exploiting the cache sites, in the process providing the necessary cross pollination of the scattered guardian entities."

"And by taking Mudball with me on my missions for First Solar, I was the vector of that process," Drake murmured, faced with the full implications of his actions.

"If not you, it would have been somebody else. The responsibility is not yours but ours, and we could not allow such an act to be our final legacy. Unleashing ancient tyranny on a young sentient species would be a contradiction of all that we believed in. Therefore we created Lenbya, a concentration of our technology and achievements that dwarfed any other cache. The scale was necessary in order to support and sustain an entity that would represent a far more complete and enduring echo of my people. Me.

"To safeguard the treasures stored here, we then removed Lenbya from known space, to be hidden within its own pocket of reality, a fold in the fabric of the universe that could never be discovered by accident."

"How were we able to find it, then?"

"You were allowed to. In order for a composite being to form in the first place, and then to present a genuine threat once it had, this hypothetical monster would need allies among the emergent race. To combat that, Lenbya's guardian would need allies of its own – contemporary sentients with certain advantages over the standard technology of their race, beings who could employ with a degree of skill and understanding aspects of our surviving technology, to defend Lenbya when needed."

"So you deliberately created the Dark Angels to protect the legacy of your race from misappropriation," Drake said.

"Yes, and to safeguard the development of your own race as a consequence. Unfortunately, my timing, though accurate in a cosmic sense, was sufficiently out that it proved necessary to pause the process. The Dark Angels were equipped and primed a decade ago but no adversary had shown itself. In such a situation, with all the advantages Lenbya's technology afforded you, the Dark Angels could themselves have become a threat to the stability of your people."

"So you manipulated us into disbanding."

"Yes. It was necessary."

Drake found he couldn't resent the alien for that.

"Tell me, did the other team – our Xter counterparts – know all of this?

"No more than you did. I am having a similar conversation with the captain of the Demon's Breath at this precise moment. Our civilisation was vast and its residue, the cache sites, is spread widely over an area that encompasses both human and Xter space and beyond. Your two races are at comparable stages of development. That alone is an extremely unlikely occurrence, given how rare the evolution of sentient life is, but inherent within the concept of 'unlikely' is the acknowledgement that it remains possible.

"What couldn't be foreseen was in which region of space the composite being would arise, should it ever do so. Because of this, I deemed it prudent to recruit and equip teams of potential allies among both races."

Drake could appreciate the logic in that. "And, as things turned out, it's just as well you did."

"Indeed. It was unfortunate that the Mudball composite managed to ally itself with such a well-established and effective organisation as Saflik. All our resources were needed to thwart its ambitions."

"Why me?" Drake wanted to know. "Why did you choose to reveal Lenbya to us, to my ship and crew, out of all those who must have come looking for it?"

"It would be simple to say that you were in the right place at the right time, but there was a great deal more to the decision than that. You are quite correct. A number of vessels came here in response to the carefully seeded rumours, clues and legends of Lenbya that have been spread throughout your culture."

"So you deliberately cultivated the myth," Drake said. He'd always wondered. In order for tales of the ultimate Elder cache to have become so embedded in spacer lore, somebody must have been here before, or had contact of some sort with the place.

"Yes. That seemed to be the most effective method of

attracting and sustaining interest without revealing irrefutable proof of Lenbya's existence."

"Interest from the greedy and the gullible, perhaps," Drake said.

"It brought you to me, didn't it? As you doubtless appreciate, my race perfected technologies which are far in advance of your current level. What is preserved here represents a fragment of what we were, but it includes sufficient resources for me to infiltrate ships' systems without alerting the crew, and examine the records pertaining to previous actions."

Drake recalled how adept Mudball had been at doing much the same thing, which had proven invaluable on more than one occasion over the years.

"This enabled me to examine and reject several vessels and their crew as unsuitable candidates, prior to your arrival."

"Really? What had we done to merit your faith, then?"

"I found in your ship's data systems details of an incident that occurred in the Saeka 7 system, involving a ship called the *Belmont Star.*"

"Oh, that."

"Yes, that. You sacrificed potential profit – a significant profit at that – in order to aid a stricken vessel. You saved lives at the cost of your own self-interest."

"It wasn't really that altruistic," Drake insisted. "The owners of the *Belmont Star* compensated us generously for our losses."

Their cargo had been time-sensitive, the delay caused by the need to get injured crew from the damaged ship to the nearest medical facility ensuring that the goods perished before delivery.

"But there was no guarantee that they would," Raider said. "You acted as you did because it was the right thing to do."

"Anyone would have done the same."

"I can assure you that is far from the case and that not all would have done."

"And you selected us to become the Dark Angels because of that single well-intentioned act? Despite other examples you must have come across which would have cast us in a decidedly less favourable light?"

"All very true, but the *Belmont Star* incident showed you to be capable of compassion, of thinking and acting contrary to your own advantage if need be, which set you apart from the other crews I'd evaluated."

Drake wasn't sure what to say. It had never occurred to him that stopping to rescue the *Belmont Star* – an event he had all but forgotten about – was directly responsible for so much of what had followed, both in his own life and the lives of his crew.

Who was it that said no good deed ever went unpunished? Apparently, some did.

Jen:

The electric bike purred to a stop as Jen pulled up outside a sleepy taverna just off the beach. Azure sea, golden sands, and sunshine: a combination that was hard to better. Especially for someone whose horizons had been limited to a ship's bulkhead in recent times. As she stepped off the bike and stretched her cramped limbs and back, a soft breeze blew in off the water, taking the edge off the late summer's heat.

A man stood up from a table on the taverna's terrace and strode across to meet her. He wore faded shorts and a white cotton shirt, and looked a little broader about the waist than she remembered. They embraced, and kissed.

"You look as if you've lost weight," he said as they separated.

"Yeah, well, I've been getting a lot of exercise. You, on the other hand, look as if you've put a bit of weight on." She patted his stomach.

"Yeah, well, when it comes to exercise…" and he gestured towards a mostly-consumed platter of seafood on the table he'd just vacated. "I haven't."

"I don't know, take the farmer away from the farm, and he goes to seed."

"Guilty as charged."

They strolled across the sand towards the ocean, his arm draped around her shoulders, hers around his waist, stopping at the boundary so that the bolder waves just reached far enough to lap at their toes. They didn't say much — they didn't need to — stories and explanations could wait until later. For now, it was enough that they were together again. Jen had forgotten how calming Robin's presence could be, how right it felt to be with him. How he made her safe.

After a few minutes spent in contented silence, they headed back to the taverna, holding hands. They arrived just as another bike drew up alongside Jen's.

As the rider dismounted, Jen let go of Robin's hand and ran across to the other woman, embracing her, laughing. Jen then brought her across to where he waited.

"Lees, this is Robin, my husband. Robin, this is Leesa, my dearest friend. We lost touch for a long while, but that's not going to happen again."

Leesa shook his hand in a strangely formal way, saying, "So you're the man Jen considers worth committing her life to." Her broad smile smoothed away any edges from her words. "Pleasure to meet you."

"Likewise," he replied. "And no, I've no idea what she sees in me either."

The two women took seats at the table on the terrace — the plate of shellfish debris having been spirited away during the stroll down to the water's edge — while Robin went inside to organise some drinks.

"He's got a really good feel about him," Leesa said.

"Is that your way of saying you like him?"

Leesa grinned. "Probably." She gazed back and forth along the beach. "So, this is where you've made a home, then."

"Pretty much. Our farm was further inland, away from the coast, but the vibe here is much the same."

Leesa nodded, staring out to sea. "I envy you. I've never really settled down, never just kicked back and relaxed, not even in the decade in between…" Her words trailed off, and Jen guessed she was thinking of the captain; as she did, frequently. "There was always something to do," Leesa continued, "something to achieve, something to chase."

"You should try it some time," Jen said. "Just let go."

"I'm not sure I'd know how to."

"Hang around here with us for a while and we'll show you how it's done. You never know, you might surprise yourself."

Leesa didn't say anything for a while. The two women sat in comfortable silence, contemplating the ocean. Laughter drifted to them from inside the tavern. Jen recognised Robin's voice and suspected they might have to be patient where the drinks were concerned.

At length, Leesa said, "Do you mean it?"

"Of course I do."

"You know, I might just take you up on that."

About the Author

Ian Whates lives in a quiet cul-de-sac in an idyllic Cambridgeshire village, with his partner, Helen, and a bonkers cocker spaniel called Bundle. He writes science fiction, fantasy, and occasionally horror, and has been known to edit the same. *Dark Angels Rising* is his eighth published novel, tenth if you include two that were co-authored. In addition to novels, his novella *The Smallest of Things* appeared from PS Publishing in 2018 and he has seen some seventy of his short stories published in a variety of venues. Many of these have been collected into four volumes, most recently 2019's *Wourism and Other Stories* (Luna Press).

Ian has edited more than thirty anthologies, and his work has been shortlisted for the Philip K. Dick Award and on three occasions for BSFA Awards. In 2019, he was honoured with the Karl Edward Wagner Award from the British Fantasy Society and was also shortlisted for the SFW Author Award. His novel *Pelquin's Comet*, first of the Dark Angels trilogy, was an Amazon UK #1 best seller, and his work has been translated into Spanish, German, Hungarian, Czech and Greek.

In 2006 Ian founded award-winning independent publisher NewCon Press by accident, and has now published over 130 titles via the imprint; a fact that continues to bemuse him.

www.newconpress.co.uk
https://ianwhates.co.uk/

THE DARK ANGELS TRILOGY

Pelquin's Comet: In an age of exploration, the crew of the freetrader Pelquin's Comet — a rag-tag group of misfits, ex-soldiers and adventurers — set out to find a cache of alien technology, intent on making their fortunes; but they are not the only interested party and find themselves in a deadly race against corporate agents and hunted by the authorities. Forced to combat enemies without and within, they strive to overcome the odds under the watchful eye of an unwelcome guest: Drake, agent of the bank funding their expedition, who is far more than he seems and may represent the greatest threat of all.

The Ion Raider: As Corbin Drake receives his most unusual assignment for First Solar yet — one which he suspects is a trap but knows he can't refuse — his former crew, the notorious brigands known as the Dark Angels, are being hunted down one by one and murdered. Determined to find those responsible before they find her, Leesa teams up with Jen, another former Dark Angel, and together they set out to thwart the mysterious organization known as Saflik, little dreaming where that path will lead them.

"A good, unashamed, rip-roaring piece of space opera that hits the spot..." — *The Financial Times*

"A natural story-teller, Whates works his material with verve, obvious enjoyment, and an effortlessly breezy prose style." — *The Guardian*

More New Titles from NewCon Press

Simon Morden – Bright Morning Star

A ground-breaking take on first contact from scientist and novelist Simon Morden. Sent to Earth to explore, survey, collect samples and report back to its makers, an alien probe arrives in the middle of a warzone. Witnessing both the best and worst of humanity, the AI probe faces situations that go far beyond the parameters of its programming, and is forced to improvise, making decisions that may well reshape the future of a world.

Kim Lakin-Smith – Rise

Denounced by her own father and charged with crimes against the state, Kali Titian – pilot, soldier, and engineer – is sentenced to Erbärmlich prison camp, where she must survive among her fellow inmates the Vary, a race she has been raised to consider sub-human; a race facing genocide; a race who until recently she was routinely murdering to order. A potent tale of courage against the odds and the power of hope in the face of racial intolerance.

Liz Williams – Comet Weather

Practical Magic meets *The Witches of Eastwick*. A tale of four fey sisters set in contemporary London, rural Somerset, and beyond. The Fallow sisters: scattered like the four winds but now drawn back together, united in their desire to find their mother, Alys, who disappeared a year ago. They have help, of course, from the star spirits and the no-longer-living, but such advice tends to be cryptic and is hardly the most dependable of guides.

Nick Wood – Water Must Fall

In 2048, climate change has brought catastrophe and water companies play god with the lives of millions. In Africa, Graham Mason struggles to save his marriage to Lizette, who is torn between loyalty to their relationship and to her people. In California, Arthur Green battles to find ways of rooting out corruption, even when his family are threatened by those he seeks to expose. As the planet continues to thirst and slowly perish, will water ever fall?

Lightning Source UK Ltd.
Milton Keynes UK
UKHW011442270520
363925UK00010B/3069